Where The Rainbow Falls

The Rivers Series
Book 2

A Novel by
JOEY JONES

ISBN: 978-1-948978-16-3 (PAPERBACK)

ISBN: 978-1-948978-17-0 (EPUB)

ISBN: 978-1-948978-18-7 (MOBI)

For the teachers who inspired me:
Donna Matthews, Diane Tyndall, Mitch Fortescue, and others.
They have believed in me, loved me,
and continue to support and encourage me.

Also by Joey Jones

WHEN THE RIVERS RISE
(The Rivers Series, Book 1)

"A threatening hurricane is on the horizon and love is on the line . . . this captivating story of love and loss will keep you turning the pages and wishing for more. This is Joey Jones delivering what his fans have come to expect!" —Riley Costello, Author of *Waiting at Hayden's,* a shopfiction™ novel

THE DATE NIGHT JAR

"A beautiful love story, capturing the poignancy of both new affection and the power of deep, lasting devotion. Readers of Nicholas Sparks, Debbie Macomber, and Nicholas Evans should add THE DATE NIGHT JAR to their reading list." —Jeff Gunhus, *USA TODAY* Bestselling Author

A FIELD OF FIREFLIES

"This is a tale of tragedy, romance, heartbreak and, ultimately, redemption. With lyrical writing and strong character development, Joey Jones effortlessly pulls readers in." —Kristy Woodson Harvey, *NEW YORK TIMES* Bestselling Author

LOSING LONDON

"I read the entire book in one day... I could not put it down!
WOW!! LOSING LONDON was incredible; I laughed, I cried,
and I'm still in shock." —Erica Latrice, TV Host, Be Inspired

A BRIDGE APART

"Filled with romance, suspense, heartbreak, and a tense plot line,
Joey Jones' first novel is a must-read. It is the kind of book you
can lend to your mom and best friend." —Suzanne Lucey, Page
158 Books

Acknowledgments

I have now written half a dozen novels and can't imagine making it here without the people who have stood behind me, beside me, and led me through every step of this journey. Until halfway through writing *When the Rivers Rise (Book 1)*, I never imagined writing a sequel. Now, I have with *Where the Rainbow Falls (Book 2)*, and even though it was a new challenge, I enjoyed it. There is an abundance of amazing people who helped make this book a reality. First and foremost, I would like to thank God for giving me the ability to write and planting that passion within my soul. Branden, my oldest son, is now an adult, and it makes my heart happy to watch him forge his own path. Parker, my little guy, is the best sidekick for whom a dad could ask. I love spending every moment possible with him and making memories that will live forever.

I would also like to thank my wonderful family. My parents Joe and Patsy Jones taught me about the essential aspects of life, and I hope to leave a legacy that makes them proud. My dad now lives in Heaven, and I miss him dearly. My mom, who is my breakfast partner and one of my best friends, is the most humble person I know. My brothers and sisters, DeAnn, Judy, Lee, Penny, and Richard, are some of my closest friends. In many ways, their support is my foundation.

My editors Donna Matthews and Erin Haywood are incredibly talented at polishing my writing. My graphics designer Meredith Walsh did a fantastic job with each of my novel covers and supporting pieces. Amy Smith took my author photos, and our beach photoshoot was perfect. Polgarus Studio made the intricate process of formatting the interior of this novel a breeze. Once again, Deborah Dove worked her magic creating the book blurb.

Lastly, I would like to thank some people who have been influential throughout my life: some for a season but each for a reason. Thank you to Amy Smith, Andrew Haywood, BJ Horne, Billy Nobles, Bob Peele, Cathy Errick, Diane Tyndall, Jan Raynor, Jeanette Towne, Jim McConnell, Josh Haywood, Josh Towne, Kenny Ford, Kim Jones, Mitch Fortescue, Nicholas Sparks, Ray White, Rebekah Jones, Richard Banks, Steve Cobb, Steven Harrell, and Steve Haywood. It is a privilege to call each of you my friend.

Where The Rainbow Falls

1

The sudden fear that he might not ever see his five-year-old son again hit Niles North in the face like a brick slung through a window by a vicious tornado. Sitting impatiently in the passenger seat of the police Humvee being driven by his new friend Reese Kirby, his whole body was literally trembling as his fingers dug into his chin-length dirty blonde hair. Back in New Bern, North Carolina, from where he evacuated without his little guy who was currently there with his ex-wife, the outer bands of Hurricane Florence were beginning to roll into town. Yesterday morning when Niles left, this storm, which at that point was threatening to become a category five, was predicted to deliver a surge of water up to thirteen feet in parts of the Neuse River. Now, live reports on the radio confirmed tropical storm-force winds were already pelting the coastline this afternoon.

One moment Niles felt cold, the next hot. However, the vents on the dashboard weren't blowing any air whatsoever as his aqua green eyes stared aimlessly into the open slats. He was trying to control the foreign convulsions his body was experiencing, but Riley was all he could think about. He was mad at himself for not bending the law, possibly breaking it by bringing his son with him to Hickory where he and Reese met last night—where he still was although wishing to be closer to home.

As Reese maneuvered the vehicle with urgency, she explained to Niles why she wouldn't break the law by flipping on the blue lights or siren. Unfortunately, she was out of her jurisdiction.

"Try to relax your breathing," she recommended, her petite figure paling in comparison to the large SUV yet she drove it with authority as her short black hair swished every time they turned a corner. "Like you did after being sprayed with the pepper spray last night."

As painful as it was to be doused with that substance, Niles knew the feeling bubbling inside him was much more terrifying. He wished he had listened to his gut when it said to evacuate Riley. The opportunity had been there, and he passed it up. *I should have known not to depend on Eden to make the best decision*, he thought for what seemed like the hundredth time as his thumb grated against his ring finger. What made him even sicker to his stomach was that his ex didn't have the nerve to call and tell him about the change in plans. She and *their* son were hunkering down in New Bern, and Niles had to learn this news from Grandyma, Eden's mother.

"I am trying," Niles revealed. "But I am four and a half hours away from my son, and I feel absolutely helpless right now."

Meteorologists predicted the storm would make landfall between Jacksonville and Wilmington—just south of where his little guy was—around eight o'clock tomorrow morning. However, what many people who weren't familiar with hurricanes didn't understand was that this terminology related to the eye of the storm. The rain and winds would continue to pick up today as the outer bands slammed the coast. Flooding, which had already begun due to winds out in the ocean pushing the water inland, would increase throughout the day and overnight. The hurricane was much closer than it sounded; in fact, it was basically beating on the door like an unwelcome intruder.

As Reese guided the vehicle toward the motel where she and Niles spent last night in separate rooms, she could see him out of the corner of her eye pressing buttons on his phone. She felt terrible for him because nothing seemed to be going his way. He had attempted to call his ex-wife half a dozen times, but each went straight to voicemail. Sitting only a few feet away, Reese couldn't help but overhear the messages he left, and although his tone wasn't cordial, it was calmer than expected under the circumstances. Niles had also been trying to get ahold of Mickey who made the trip to Hickory with him, but his best friend wasn't answering calls or responding to text messages. Most likely, he was with the cute blonde from the bar who spent the night with him.

"Mickey better be at the motel when we get there," Niles exclaimed. "I have to get my car right away so that I can head back to New Bern."

Reese licked her lips but couldn't bite her tongue. "Are you sure that racing home to get your son is what's best?"

Niles breathed in deeply then exhaled. "Yes," he answered confidently. In his mind, there was no other option.

Reese didn't have children, so it was difficult for her to fathom what she might do in his shoes, but she had a feeling she might make the same choice. "Have you thought about calling someone who could help?" she suggested, knowing her mind was thinking more clearly than his at the present time.

"Who is going to help?" he cried without tears. "I don't have any family in the area, and it's not like I can send a friend over to my ex's house to snatch up my son. Then I'd probably be in more trouble than if I'd taken him myself. Plus that person would get arrested."

Sending a friend or family member to snatch Riley wasn't what Reese meant, but at least she now knew that Niles was thinking with a few ounces of logic. She rephrased: "Do you have a lawyer?"

"Yes," Niles answered excitedly. His mind had been traveling at warp speed and he completely forgot about the conversation when George Billings mentioned having ground to stand on if Eden didn't leave the area with Riley under a mandatory evacuation.

Niles scrolled through his phone without speaking another word and located the number for his attorney's office. He made the call, but of course, no one picked up. He knew from prior experiences with hurricanes that by now nearly every office and store in town had closed to wait out the storm. Earlier in the week, many hired him and Mickey to board up their windows and most of the shop owners in downtown asked for help moving merchandise and other items off the floor in case their buildings flooded. Placed in front of exterior doors, the countless sandbags, each about the size of a bag of concrete, would only keep out a foot or two of water. Niles left a detailed message for his lawyer but doubted he would hear back this evening. Everyone from the office was probably somewhere safe and work was the last thing on their minds.

"Do you have a mobile phone number or email address for your attorney?" Reese asked after realizing the first line of communication didn't pan out. "If you do, you could try one or both of those options."

Niles's closed eyes popped open. "I don't have a cell number but I do have an email address," he remembered.

He quickly pulled up his email on his phone, searched for the address, then sent a message basically saying the same thing he explained in the voicemail.

While he was busy with these tasks, Reese turned curves as sharply as possible without risking the search and rescue boat toppling over. She hurried through yellow lights, made rolling halts at stop signs, and pushed the maximum speed allowed. Needless to say, the tires squealed during several maneuvers. Being an officer herself, she knew local law enforcement most likely wouldn't pull over a police vehicle from another town unless the driver was completely irresponsible.

"Do you think I should call the police?" Niles asked Reese, figuring she should know the answer since she was the police.

Reese wiggled her lips as she contemplated the best way to answer. "I'm not sure there is anything they could do to help," she relayed honestly. "They would need an emergency order from a judge to remove your son from the custody of his mother," she explained. "Even if that were to happen, there is a meager chance the authorities would be able to evacuate him to a place other than one of the shelters where a social worker would most likely look after him." Reese hesitated to give her opinion but quickly decided she should. "I do not know Eden, but based on what you have shared about her, I can't imagine that you would rather your son be at a shelter with people he does not know than at home with his mom."

Niles shrugged his shoulders but didn't say anything for a few moments, and Reese could sense the steam rising from his body as he absentmindedly peered out the passenger window. The voice escaping through the speakers on the dash was still talking about the hurricane, mentioning how those planning to leave from coastal areas should have already done so by now.

"I will be back in New Bern before the worst part of the storm; I can evacuate him myself," Niles explained.

"Like I said, the police would need an order from a judge, who would first need to receive a complaint from your lawyer. A lot has to happen between now and when you could possibly make it to your hometown for the police to get involved."

As the Humvee screeched into the bumpy motel parking lot, Niles felt like it had taken an hour to get back to the place they departed from this morning when smiles lined their faces. He took note of how aggressively Reese drove to get them here, and he thanked her for doing so then felt like he'd been punched in the stomach again upon realizing the parking space where he left his car was as empty as his luck. His eyes quickly began to survey the rest of the lot; Reese did the same, and at the exact moment they came to a unanimous conclusion: Niles's car was gone. He left the keys with Mickey before leaving for breakfast, which meant his buddy and the blonde were who knows where with his vehicle, adding another problem to the rapidly growing dilemma.

"How can this day get any worse?" Niles wondered aloud.

The motorcycle gang could show up right now. For some odd reason this thought hit Reese's mind like a slap across the face but she didn't dare speak it out loud. She watched her newfound friend double over in his seat, and for a moment she wondered if he was going to puke on her floorboard. Thank God it was made of heavy duty rubber. He buried his hands in his long golden hair and she could hear frustration fuming from his mouth or nostrils sounding like a bull about to charge someone.

"Let's head up to your room and see if Mickey left a note saying where he was going," Reese suggested.

Even though Niles knew the chance of Mickey taking the time to write a message or even think about it was highly unlikely, both he and Reese scaled three flights of stairs in about five seconds. It wasn't until reaching the door that Niles remembered where he left the room key—on his keyring. At the mention of this information, he watched Reese pull her keys from her shoulder bag, and at first, he thought she was going to try her room's bronze key in this door.

"You didn't see me do this," she announced with a wry smile while wedging a thin silver pick tool into the keyhole. Within a matter of seconds, the doorknob willingly twisted open.

Niles smirked. "So, you can't turn on the blue lights but you can pick a lock?" he quizzed, stumbling into the first laugh he'd been able to muster since leaving the park after receiving the grim news from Grandyma. He hadn't told his son's grandmother that his instincts were telling him to rescue her grandson.

Reese grinned. "Technically, picking a lock isn't illegal if you are accessing something you are legally allowed to access," she revealed. "Since this is your room and you are with me, it's a gray area at worst," she added with a wink.

"Either way," Niles announced, "your secret is safe with me."

They hurriedly scoured the room for a note, but, as expected, there wasn't one. Then, as if in temporary defeat, Niles fell backward onto the mattress facing the speckled ceiling and wanting to punch a hole through the yellow stains. Instead, he grabbed Banana and squeezed the worn stuffed animal as tightly as ever.

"I'm so sorry," Reese pleaded. She sat on the edge of the bed and felt a sudden sense of deja vu. The scene from last night when the two of them were in her room flashed through her mind. "I can take you to look for Mickey," she offered willingly.

"He could be anywhere," Niles proclaimed, glancing at the phone he dropped onto the dated comforter. "Hopefully, he will respond to my messages soon."

Reese let her left hand fall onto Niles's knee. "I think I have bad news," she uttered, motioning to the nightstand with the pointer finger at the end of her other arm.

Niles rolled his head in that direction and saw what Detective Reese Kirby spotted within moments of being in the room. Next to the antique-looking lamp overlooking the bed where last night Mickey slept with his long legs dangling over the edge while the headboard tickled his puffy black hair, a cell phone lay in nearly the exact spot where Niles left the keys this morning. Hoping it belonged to the blonde and not Mickey, Niles quickly popped his head off the pillow and reached for the device.

No such luck. "That's Mickey's phone," he confirmed with a frown.

"I figured; it's too worn out to be the blonde's phone."

With an arm still wrapped around Banana, Niles sat up

bringing his face within a foot of Reese's as he stared into her mesmerizing evergreen eyes. "Do you remember last night when you said you owed me for helping you fight those biker dudes?"

Reese tilted her head slightly and clenched her brow. "Yes," she responded hesitantly. Seeing him on the bed grasping the monkey, she saw a completely different side of Niles North than when he helped her kick those guys' butts. Of course, she put two and two together that the stuffed animal must belong to his son; otherwise, it would be a serious red flag.

"Will you drive me to New Bern?" he pleaded.

2

$\mathcal{E}$arlier this morning once Eden determined she and Riley were not evacuating, she shut off her phone to avoid the inevitable calls and messages from her mother. The little boy from the Amber Alert case had been found, and Eden doubted her boss would need assistance with anything else during the next day or two. He was on the other side of the country with his wife, and the office and courthouse were both closed.

The conversation Eden had with her mom this morning about the decision to ride out the hurricane was mainly one-sided. While twirling her curly brown hair which fell just below the bra strap beneath her comfy t-shirt, Eden explained her point of view and then her mother went on and on about how she was disappointed and feared something terrible could happen. Eden figured she would turn the phone on again later in the day to share the promised hurricane updates with her mom although she knew her mother's eyes would be glued to one of the weather channels on the television in Aunt Becky's living room in Kentucky. Hopefully, Niles wouldn't find out she and Riley were still in New Bern until Florence blew over. She knew better than to post this bit of information on social media or tell friends who might relay the news to Niles whether purposefully or accidentally.

Kirk came over first thing this morning to help her prepare for the storm which, as he predicted, had been downgraded. Eden had stuck with her initial plan regarding the strength of the hurricane. If it was a category four or five, she was leaving. Heavy flooding was still expected, but as the storm weakened, she knew the wind damage would be minimal compared to what it could have been.

"What contents last occupied this cooler?" Kirk investigated after pulling it down off one of the shelves in her garage, his long hair dangling in a ponytail reaching toward his tight jeans. "The stench resembles rotten fish," he announced with a facial gesture matching the smell.

"My dad and his buddies probably used it on a fishing trip," Eden guessed. She meant to pull it down yesterday and wash it out, but like so many other things, she put it off while busy helping with the little boy who went missing. Speaking of little guys, she was thankful Riley seemed to be taking to Kirk quite well.

Riley stuck his head halfway into the cooler upon Kirk offering it to him as though it was a new candle scent deserving a sniff. "Yuck," he proclaimed, yanking himself out of the box as fast as a snapping turtle's bite.

"Why did you stick your face in there?" Eden quizzed with her left eye squinted, the hazel color catching Kirk's attention as though it was a wink at him.

Riley shrugged his shoulders.

"It's a guy thing," Kirk explained on the little fellow's behalf. "Courtesy sniffs are a duty and tradition."

Riley giggled. "Yeah, Mom," he agreed with sudden enthusiasm.

"We sniff each other's socks and—"

Eden cut off Kirk. "Don't teach my son that," she remarked laughing as she spoke.

"Uncle Mickey already taught me about courtesy sniffs," Riley revealed with a grin.

"That's gross," Eden exclaimed.

Kirk glanced in Eden's direction. "Is Uncle Mickey your brother?"

For a moment Eden's eyes danced between Riley and Kirk then Riley spoke up before she could figure out how to best explain Mickey. "Uncle Mickey is my dad's best friend. He lives with us in the treehouse," he announced.

Kirk furrowed his brow. "Your father resides in a treehouse?"

As Kirk sprayed the cooler with the water from the hose behind the house, droplets splattered everywhere in the vicinity, and Riley spent the next five minutes explaining every little detail about the treehouse as Kirk scrubbed the fish smell with a soapy old rag Eden retrieved from the bathroom.

Eventually, Riley ran off to play on his swing set even though the clouds overhead were spitting rain, and Eden used the opportunity to share her two cents about Uncle Mickey. "So, Mickey isn't really Riley's uncle, and yes, my ex lives in a grown-up playhouse in the trees."

"Sounds unusually groovy," Kirk assessed.

"You would think so," Eden clamored, using the response as a motive to swat Kirk with the smelly washcloth.

He jumped back then squirted the hose at her bare feet. "If you make me smell like fish, you are going to have to take another shower with me," he encouraged.

Eden glanced at Riley as he floated back and forth on one of the swings as if it was a trapeze at the circus. "I can't take a shower with you while Riley is around," she whispered, moving in to playfully steal the water hose.

Kirk halfway conceded the nozzle and the two began to soak one another as they wrestled to control the weapon. A moment later, Riley jumped from the swing, joined in, and within a few minutes all three were as wet as an umbrella top on a rainy day.

"That was so much fun," Riley announced with a chirp in his

voice when the water war came to an end, his light brown hair dripping like a rooftop after a thunderstorm.

Eden was relieved she hadn't worn the white top she first draped over her head this morning in the closet while Kirk was on his way to the house. The navy blue one concealed her breasts much better now that they were soaking wet along with the rest of her body. The idea of her son being a spectator at an impromptu wet t-shirt contest was a view she didn't want to imagine especially with his mother being the victim. When she shook her mind of the thought, Eden couldn't help but replay the shower with Kirk two nights ago and the friction between their bodies as they somewhat gracefully made out on the floor of the tub—at least that is where they ended up while the showerhead bounced water off their steamy bodies.

As Eden's mind fell back into that moment, she decided not to allow herself to get too wrapped up in these thoughts while Riley was standing in the grass between her and Kirk. Nonetheless, she felt the urge to kiss the handsome drummer with the long wet hair but opted not to this time around. She was also glad about finding the mental strength to fight the temptation of letting him take off her clothes when they stepped out of the shower at his place. There was something pure about knowing Niles North was the only man she had ever made love with although she knew at some point she would make a choice to have sex with another person. Divorce kind of meant you had to move on from both the physical and emotional attachment. However, a manual for things like this didn't exist. Some of her friends encouraged her to have a one-night stand the moment the divorce was official while others advised her to wait until she married again. Of course, most people stood somewhere in between those two camps of thought. Personally, she didn't know if she would wait until she dated a man for a month, six months, a year, or if a timetable even made sense. What she did know was something was satisfying about harnessing the willpower to ward off the temptation of one of the most pleasurable feelings the human body could experience. So far, she hadn't been on more than a handful of dates with any man and the prospects never turned into a relationship. She hung out with guy friends from time to time and enjoyed the freedom of not being tied down to one person.

"Mom!" Riley called out. "Did you hear me?"

Eden jolted herself out of the trance. "What, Riley?"

"When is the hurricane coming?" he asked for the second time as a steady breeze rustled the leaves in the nearby trees.

"The scattered rain we've been dodging today is from the storm and so is this wind," she explained, noticing that it seemed to be picking up a bit. "We will start feeling stronger effects this evening, but Florence is not supposed to hit land until early tomorrow morning."

Eden knew that the hurricane would be here well before the eye of the storm, but she didn't want to worry Riley and she hoped he would sleep through the worst of it. In fact, she planned to put him to bed early this evening. So far, he didn't seem bothered by the random gusts of wind traveling through the small trees in the backyard and the rainfall hadn't phased him one bit. Apparently, he and his dad often ran around in the rain. He shared that bit of information with Kirk during their water war, which for some reason reminded Eden of the time when she and Niles danced naked beneath a downpour in the middle of a grassy field near the river. That was a story she hadn't thought of in quite some time until that very moment. The heaviest downpour she let Riley experience today was the water falling from the water hose rather than the sky. Each time the rain picked up, they all scurried into the garage which was filled with outdoor items such as lawn chairs and every piece from Riley's swing set except the one swing he talked her into leaving up until the wind got too heavy for him to play safely. Thankfully, Niles cemented the steel frame into the ground the day they bought it.

3

"If we can't track down Mickey, I think it might be best if you rent a vehicle," Reese suggested knowing that deviating from the assignment passed down from the captain wouldn't sit well with the powers that be.

Sprawled out on the motel bed, Niles grimaced. "What are the chances that we will find Mickey?" he pondered into the stale air above his weary face.

Slim, Reese knew, but as a detective, tracking down people was a significant part of her job. "The finding him part is not what concerns me," she uttered. "I am just not sure we can locate Mickey before it's too late for you to make it back to New Bern for your son."

"Exactly," Niles clarified, "I don't have time to drive all over Hickory on a wild goose chase."

"I will be happy to take you to one of the car rental places."

Niles closed his eyelids for a moment then let them open back up slowly. "I can't rent a vehicle."

"Why not?"

"I'm not twenty-five."

"Some of the rental companies will let a person rent at age twenty-one although there might be a young driver's fee," she revealed. For the first time since meeting Niles, Reese wondered how old he was while figuring she initially assumed he was closer to her age. "How old are you?"

"How old do you think I am?" Niles quizzed even though he didn't really want to waste time on guessing games.

Reese's mind began to process the information she had gathered on Niles North in two short days. Given the fact that he said he couldn't rent a car, she presumed he must be under the age of twenty-five. However, there could be another reason, possibly related to a criminal history, but she already pulled the report last night and knew he was as clean as a whistle. Although, to be honest, she had been somewhat surprised to discover that the mouse named Mickey hadn't dragged him into at least one arrest for something juvenile. The military incident didn't show up on his civilian report.

"Twenty-three," she guessed as she considered that maybe he didn't have the money to rent a vehicle. It was quite possible the only greenery a landscaper who recently started his own business had to roll around in was grass.

Niles shook his head. "I am twenty," he revealed. "No one will let me rent a car."

If Mickey were in the room, Niles knew his best friend would argue: You can serve our country and raise a child but can't even rent a vehicle?

Reese didn't hide her surprise. "Really?" she questioned. "You're a baby," she asserted.

Niles gave off a look of discontent. "How old are you?" he barked even though his dad told him never to ask a woman her age.

"Twenty-five," she announced.

"You're five years older than me," he snarled. "It's not like that makes you old enough to be my mom or something." When he first met Reese at the bar last night, he thought she was closer to his age, but once she told him she was a detective, he figured she must be a bit older. At one point in his life, he thought about becoming a police officer, and he discovered through research that you had to serve a few years on the force before becoming eligible for the detective's exam.

Reese glared at him. "That was a snarky comment for someone who is trying to talk me into breaking protocol to drive him somewhere I am not supposed to be."

Niles exhaled. "I'm sorry," he apologized. "I am on edge; that's all." He waited a moment but Reese didn't respond. She simply sat there with her arms folded while staring into his eyes. "If you take me to New Bern this evening, you will be closer to Wilmington when you need to head that way," he pointed out. "It's less than a two-hour drive from where I live."

"The department hasn't already paid for me to have a hotel in New Bern," she pointed out.

"If you get me to my son, I will pay for you to stay at any hotel you want," he begged. "You can pick the most expensive one in town if you'd like."

Reese let her arms fall to her side. "I wouldn't let you do that—the expensive part," she confirmed. "However, I will let you pay for a normal hotel room which has to be nicer than this dump," she insisted, glancing up at the ceiling, around at the dated furniture, and finally down by her feet where the worn out carpet attacked her shoes.

Niles sprung off the mattress as quickly as if he just fell prostrate onto a trampoline. "So, you'll take me?" he checked for clarification's sake although pretty sure Reese Kirby just agreed to drive him to New Bern.

"Sure," she smiled. "But if I get fired for this you have to help me find a new job."

Niles's feet hit the floor, and as he hurriedly threw his belongings back into his suitcase, he responded to Reese. "How do you feel about mowing grass?"

Reese chuckled. "I could mow circles around a twenty-year-old," she teased.

Niles couldn't help but laugh. "I've been known to teach my elders a lesson or two," he joked back.

"Oh, yeah?" she responded. "I will keep that in mind."

Within three minutes they were out of Niles's room and hurrying down the rusty metal staircase toward Reese's door. She packed her bags faster than any woman he had ever known. When they climbed into the Hummer, nearly out of breath, he knew she was even more special than he initially imagined.

"What is your address?" she asked, reaching toward the GPS.

Niles suddenly wore a confused expression on his face. "We are going to Eden's house, not mine," he clarified.

"I know, but in case you do something stupid, I am not going to have her address in my GPS," Reese explained. "I am pretty sure you can show me how to get to her place once we make it to New Bern."

Reese's quick thinking impressed Niles, but at the same time he almost became irritated that she thought he might do something that would get her into trouble. He blurted out the address that would lead to the treehouse then said, "What makes you think I would do something stupid?"

Suddenly staring a hole through him, Reese wore a sideways grin. "I don't know, maybe because it seems as though you are planning to show up at your ex-wife's house and take your son," she pointed out to him. "But I am not going to let you do that."

Niles furrowed his brow. "What?" he uttered as they rolled past the office where Reese dropped off the bronze key with a different attendant than the one they met last night.

"The GPS says it will take us about four and a half hours to get from here to your house. I will get us there a little faster, but that still means we have several hours to figure out a better plan."

4

After toweling off their wet bodies, Eden, Kirk, and Riley left the opened cooler at the edge of the garage to air out while going inside to slip into dry clothes. Thankfully, Kirk thought ahead and prepared a bag with extra attire and a toothbrush in case Eden asked him to stay the night. Although when he mentioned having a fresh set of clothing, he made sure not to explain to Eden why he brought the bag, especially not in front of her little guy.

After nestling in on the couch and watching one of the local television stations for a bit, they listened as the weatherman commented about readiness supplies. Eden and Kirk instantly turned to each other and grinned. Last night, a similar comment by the same meteorologist sparked an impromptu grocery store trip when Eden realized she forgot ice for the cooler. Being a gentleman, Kirk offered to drive his vehicle, which required transferring Riley's car seat, but Eden quickly shot down the idea. Ever since the accident, she hated the thought of moving car seats from one automobile to another. She even convinced her mom and dad to purchase separate seats for each vehicle so neither would forget or fail to attach one of the straps properly during an exchange.

Ultimately, they drove Eden's vehicle, and when the three of them walked through a set of sliding double doors, Eden let a smile stretch across her face when Kirk reminded her that this was where they met. It quickly became evident that nearly everyone in the town decided to make one last trip to the market before everything shut down in preparation for the approaching hurricane. The aisles were busier than when Eden and Riley weaved through them earlier in the week, and the shelves were definitely emptier. Even the toilet paper supply was low. Kirk pushed the cart which kept Eden on edge as he drove it twice as fast as she did on a slow day. Riley seemed to love it, so she bit her tongue as much as possible while they snatched up a few snacks, a case of beer, and several bags of ice.

On the way home, they veered into a gas station parking lot where the lines of cars were as long as the ones filled with people at the grocery store. Eden decided either everyone was headed out of town or, like her, wanted to fill up to the brim in case tanker trucks were unable to make it into the county over the next few weeks due to flooding. This happened during past hurricanes especially in Kinston, a town to the west, where the main highway into New Bern became blocked for an extended period. A two-lane road leading in from the north was also prone to flooding. Usually, it ended up with more downed trees although those were typically cleared relatively quickly.

"It would be my pleasure to pump the octane," Kirk offered when Eden was finally able to ease the car up next to a pump.

Since she hadn't let him drive, Eden figured the least she could do was allow him to prove his manliness by pumping the fuel. "That's mighty kind of you," she replied, handing over a credit card with a smile.

Kirk hopped out, and Riley, watching from his car seat, followed his every step before eventually realizing he wanted to be out there with him. "Mom, can I get out and help Kirk?"

"No, there are too many cars around," she answered.

"Can you unbuckle me so that I can watch from the window?" he pleaded.

"You may not," Eden answered sharply. She never unbuckled her son when at the pumps unless they absolutely needed to go into a service station to use the bathroom. On hot days, she would roll down the windows so the vehicle's interior wouldn't become suffocating even though she despised the smell of gasoline. On this occasion, she rolled down the back window in case Kirk had any questions.

"I don't mind him assisting," Kirk announced through the open window.

"He's fine in here," Eden snarled. "We need to hurry so the cars behind us don't have to wait any longer than necessary," she mentioned. However, that was only a portion of her reasoning.

"Noted," Kirk responded, wrinkling his brow as he stared over the car into the dark sky beyond the well-lit gas station. A few seconds went by then he asked for the zip code associated with the card and which grade of gasoline she preferred.

A few minutes later, he climbed back into the car and Eden squirted hand sanitizer onto his open palm.

"Thanks," he responded while rubbing it into his skin.

A moment later, they were back on the busy road which led out of town, but Eden soon pulled off on the exit taking them toward downtown. As usual, she raked in the view of the Neuse and Trent Rivers while struggling to imagine what the scene on the other side of the windshield might look like once the storm began to wreak havoc on their little town. She hoped that the forecasters were wrong about the flooding they were still predicting, and she silently thanked God that the winds wouldn't be as destructive as initially expected.

Thinking back to their grocery and gas run last night, Eden found herself wondering if she had made the wrong decision about evacuating. The best thing about leaving was knowing the storm couldn't harm you, but the convenient part of staying was that she could take care of her home and wouldn't have to miss any work. Watching the effects of the hurricane was pretty cool, too, as long as it didn't take a significant toll on your property. She had always enjoyed witnessing the river rise from the massive windows of her parent's home on the water when she was growing up. Come to think of it, that was where she rode out every hurricane throughout her entire life even as an adult. She, Niles, and the kids hunkered down there a couple of times because it was safer than their home. For the first time since her parent's left town, this thought made her consider staying at their home tonight. The key was tucked away in her purse and she was confident her mom and dad wouldn't mind. They might be leery of Kirk being there with her, but she didn't have to share that bit of information and only anticipated allowing him to stick around until the storm started to flare up to the point where it was no longer safe to be on the roads. Of course, the reporters stationed downtown were already declaring some roads in extremely low-lying areas impassable and urging residents not to be out and about. Her parents were hundreds of miles away anyway and would never know the difference about Kirk. She would give it some thought, she decided, as the television showed footage of Union Point Park being overtaken by water earlier this morning. The park constantly flooded during hurricanes, but it surprised her that it filled with water so soon this time. Last night, as the wheels on her car made a thumping sound every few seconds as the vehicle rolled over the expansion joints on the drawbridge, she remembered staring into the park located off to the right at the foot of the bridge. She thought about how peaceful the popular local landmark looked as the pole lights lit up the area as though it was daytime, allowing a clear view of the lush green grass now entirely covered by murky river water.

"If the power goes out, don't let me forget to move the bags of ice from the freezer into the cooler a few hours later," Eden randomly mentioned to Kirk who helped stuff them onto the bottom shelf last night. After pouring the ice into the cooler, she would transfer every item from the fridge that would fit into it and possibly some from the freezer.

"You mean *when* the power expires?" he corrected with a smirk.

"Yeah, I guess it is pretty much a certainty, isn't it?"

Kirk shook his head. "Even though the winds won't be as fierce, the electricity will still blackout," he predicted. "I will remind you," he agreed, hoping he would still be sitting beside Eden at that point rather than texting or talking to her on the phone.

Over the next several minutes, the inside of the house slowly grew a little darker. A sudden downpour followed by a few strong gusts of wind pushing against the home's exterior forcefully enough to make a sound sparked Eden to pace frantically from room to room. She gathered all the flashlights and installed the new batteries purchased from the store. Then she plugged in her cell phone to maintain a full charge although after having it off all day it didn't really matter. Nonetheless, she planned to leave the device charging during the storm, so attaching it now made sense.

"Did you bring a phone charger?" she asked Kirk when dashing by the couch at a high rate of speed.

Kirk glanced away from the cartoon on the television in time to notice the blur that was Eden and then spoke to her back as she scurried into the kitchen. "A charger?" he queried, puzzled. It took Riley less than thirty seconds to convince Kirk to change the channel once Eden left them on the couch.

Over her shoulder, Eden explained why she asked as she pillaged through the cabinets, then Kirk uttered, "Crud. The thought never entered my mind."

He arrived home so late last night after being with Eden and

Riley all day that he went straight to bed. Upon waking, he quickly stuffed a few things into a drawstring bag and hurried out the door to help Eden move her outdoor belongings inside before the rain and wind became heavy.

"I think I have an extra," she called out.

Eden searched through a few drawers and eventually plugged a second charger into an outlet near the couch where Kirk could reach.

"What do you guys want for dinner tonight?" Eden asked.

Kirk glanced at Riley who hadn't heard a word either said in the past five minutes. "I guess ordering delivery or takeout is out of the question," he teased.

"Uh, yeah, I think every restaurant in town is closed."

"I have some chicken in the freezer that I can thaw out and make chicken fettuccine alfredo," Eden suggested, remembering Kirk saying he liked the dish.

Kirk lifted his eyebrows. "Sounds delectable to me."

"Riley loves that meal, too."

Riley's head swiveled at the sound of his name and Kirk nudged him with his elbow. "We are having chicken fettuccine alfredo for dinner," he shared.

Riley revealed a cheesy grin which made both Eden and Kirk laugh. Then, a loud clap of thunder shook the house and Riley nearly jumped into Kirk's lap. The rain was still pelting the rooftop and Eden, staring out the window, noticed the wind whipping the trees behind the house.

"Oh, no," she stated suddenly.

"What is it?" Kirk asked.

He and Riley quickly joined her at the window to discover Riley's swing flying back and forth nearly as fast as when he was on it pumping his legs earlier.

"I can dash out there and remove it," Kirk offered.

"There's no need to get your fresh clothes soaked." Eden had thrown his wet clothes into the dryer now humming in the background. "Maybe the rain will slack up and one of us can run out there."

A few moments later when Eden changed the channel back to the weather, Riley became noticeably upset even though she tried to explain the need to keep an eye on the hurricane. Based on the radar, it didn't look like the rain would let up anytime soon, and video footage showed the rivers beginning to rise into nearby neighborhoods. Maybe the destructive wall of this storm was closer than she thought, Eden suddenly realized.

5

The eastbound lanes on Interstate 40 were relatively clear as Reese's foot hovered above the gas and brake pedal. Set on cruise control, the vehicle traversed at the highest speed she was comfortable driving and so far they were making good time. Slouching in the passenger seat, Niles had been quiet for the most part and Reese had a good idea what was occupying his mind. She tried her best to start conversations that would keep his thoughts off Riley and the hurricane knocking on the door of his hometown. The meteorologist on the radio station informed them about portions of Eastern North Carolina beginning to be inundated with water due to one hundred plus miles per hour winds in the Atlantic Ocean pushing the water inland and high tides playing a role as well. It sounded like the conditions were worsening faster than expected even though the storm itself had slowed down, moving at less than ten miles per hour.

Hurricane Florence was more massive than Reese originally realized. Tropical storm force winds were about two hundred miles out from the center, and Cape Hatteras emergency management recorded twenty-nine-foot waves. A reporter announced the farthest storm clouds stretched 250 to 300 miles from the eye, which meant some of the clouds above their heads probably belonged to Florence. Letting her eyes dart up and down, Reese studied the puffy cotton-like formations for a moment against the blue backdrop but decided none really looked like rain clouds.

"That's crazy," Niles stated as he processed the information.

Reese wished she could turn off the radio. Technically, since the Humvee belonged to her department, she could. Plus, carrying a badge and gun gave her authority. However, she knew Niles wanted to hear updates on the storm and she found the stats fascinating although things weren't boding well for the area where her new friend lived.

"Hatteras is part of the Outer Banks, right?" Reese asked. Before leaving Chattanooga, she studied a map of the coastline but couldn't quite visualize each location being talked about now.

"Yeah, there's like a two hundred-mile stretch of barrier islands that cover most of the North Carolina coast."

"Those are a good way from where you live, right?"

"Somewhat, but Mickey, Riley, and I were literally standing on the Oceanana Pier Tuesday night, where the lady mentioned fifteen to twenty foot waves reaching the structure's deck."

"Wow," she replied. "Were the waves high then?"

Niles told her about the trip to Atlantic Beach, and Reese was glad to hear him talking rather than letting out the occasional huff and puff in response to the news.

"You know what I was thinking when we were in the park earlier and I was reading?"

"What?" he inquired.

"The author of the book I am reading is named Riley," she revealed. "Did you notice that?"

"I can't say that I did, detective," he said with a quaint smirk. "But that is pretty cool."

"I was going to mention it to you then but you were busy with your yoga."

Niles chuckled. "I don't do yoga."

"Then what were you doing?"

"Stretching," he decided.

"Yoga is a form of stretching," Reese laughed.

"Yoga is for women."

"That sounds like a Mickey comment," she divulged even though she only shared one conversation with the guy. "It's kind of sexist, don't you think?"

Niles turned his head to face her, and Reese glanced back and forth between him and the road as he spoke. "You are a detective, so I am sure you understand profiling. Would you say that more men or women do yoga?"

"Women," she answered without hesitation.

"I rest my case then."

"Wait a minute," she suggested, changing lanes to pass a slow moving semi. "Men practice yoga, too," she pointed out. Honestly, Niles's initial comment about yoga being for women didn't bother her one bit. She was all for equal treatment of men and women but facts were facts. "In fact, I once dated a male yoga instructor," she shared.

Niles raised his eyebrows toward the vehicle's tall ceiling. "Really?"

"Yep, so there you go, your case is unrested," Reese announced, happy about entertaining a subject unrelated to the hurricane.

"Is unrested even a word?"

"I don't know," she claimed.

Niles clenched his teeth at the first thought that came to mind as his thumb rubbed the bottom side of his ring finger: *Let me ask Eden.* "I don't think it is a word," he pleaded instead and then looked it up on his phone. "Nope, not a real word," he confirmed a moment later.

"So, unrested isn't a word and men practice yoga," she announced as her cheeks rose. "We both learned something new today."

"Something like that," he uttered.

"Are you telling me that if I asked you to perform yoga with me you would say no?"

Niles pondered the idea for a moment as he halfway noticed the billboards on the other side of the window, one advertising peanuts and the next fishing poles. "Maybe," he considered.

"Maybe you would practice yoga with me or maybe you would say no?" she asked for clarification.

"I would probably try yoga with you because you aren't a girly girl and I don't think you would make it all weird."

Reese snickered. "Weird?" she asked with a quizzical look flanking her face.

"Yeah, like play soft and sensual music and do chants and odd stuff like that."

Reese couldn't help but laugh again. "I like soft and sensual music," she revealed. "I actually went to a piano bar Tuesday night—probably while you were walking on the pier listening to the soft and sensual sounds of the ocean," she teased.

"Don't tell anyone, but I would like to visit a piano bar," he admitted openly then added his next thought before Reese could respond. "By the way, the waves were loud and powerful," he revealed in a purposeful masculine voice.

"One day, I am going to take you to a piano bar," she offered.

Niles shrugged. "I might agree to that," he replied, wondering if she meant as friends or on a date.

"What kind of music do you like?"

"Don't tell my guy friends, but I actually listen to classical music when no one else is around."

"Niles North, you have yet to cease to amaze me," Reese declared.

Niles smirked. "I like country also."

"Country and classical are probably my two favorites," she revealed, suddenly finding herself wishing she and Niles didn't live in two different states. She could seriously see herself dating this guy even though she had sworn never to date a man with a child.

"You have good taste," Niles commented.

"Thanks," she acknowledged appreciating the steady flow of their conversation as this one came particularly easy even though Niles had been in and out of that hard outer shell this afternoon. Then, as she began to think about where this might lead, his phone rang.

Niles's attention immediately turned to the screen in his lap hoping to find Eden's number on display.

"Hello, Grandyma," he answered.

"Hey, Son-In-Law," she responded. "Have you heard anything from Eden?"

"I have not," Niles said, wearing a frown. "I have been trying to get a hold of her ever since you and I spoke. Have you talked to her?" he checked, choosing not to tell Grandyma that he was heading back to New Bern at this very moment.

"No, I think she must have turned off her phone this morning after getting angry at me."

"Why would she be mad at you?"

"Honey, I gave her an earful about not evacuating."

Niles was pretty sure Grandyma mentioned this earlier; however, that whole conversation was overshadowed by the words *Eden and Riley are not evacuating*. Niles found himself wanting to give Eden a few earfuls. "I just want Riley to be safe," he declared.

"Me too, darling. I don't know why on God's green earth she decided not to evacuate."

"Me neither," Niles agreed although he had a good idea it would be harder for Eden to hide her addiction if staying with her aunt and parents for an extended period.

"She hasn't been the same person since the accident, Niles. We both know that."

Niles absentmindedly shook his head then realized Grandyma couldn't see him. "I know," he finally replied.

Reese attempted to focus on the three lanes of the road ahead, but the woman on the other end of the conversation with Niles was speaking so loudly she could hear every word being said as easily as if the call was on speakerphone. Thankfully, it sounded like the two maintained a good relationship regardless of what happened between Niles and the woman's daughter. Reese deciphered the same information from the phone call he received in the park and found this surprising and commendable. Unfortunately, most families didn't get along after a divorce.

Before the phone call ended, Reese heard the woman say she had been on her knees praying for her daughter and Riley.

"Where did the name Grandyma come from?" Reese asked Niles.

"The kids started calling Eden's mom that out of the blue one day and it stuck."

"It's cute," she mentioned.

"I've always been fond of it."

As they passed exit after exit, Niles didn't share anything about the conversation with his mother-in-law although Reese was pretty sure he realized she heard every word. She didn't ask any questions either like a detective was trained to do. She just took it all in and filed away that she admired Grandyma.

Along with Niles, Reese was bummed about the call not bringing good news. She was hoping for an update on Eden and Riley or to find out Niles's ex wised up and evacuated at the last minute. Now, she feared it was too late and found herself saying a silent prayer for her and Niles to make it into the hurricane that Eden and so many others might not be able to get out of soon.

Reese's goal was to reach New Bern before dark. She had never driven a vehicle or swift water rescue boat through a hurricane, but based on the violent storms in which her team saved lives, she knew navigating in the dark when flooding and high winds were present was much more complicated than during the daylight hours. They would have to stop for gas and maybe a quick bite to eat at some point, but she was pretty sure they could make it barring any major setbacks.

6

The power flickered off and on a couple of times as Eden and Kirk found themselves glued to the television. During a trip to the bathroom, she popped an extra pill hoping it would help calm her nerves. The rain steadied and the wind pushed against the house causing those creepy creaking noises to intensify. The local weatherman said New Bern was experiencing gusts in excess of fifty miles per hour and reports of flooding were being called in across the county. The news showed a video, captured by a citizen, of a sailboat in the Trent River breaking loose from its anchor and eventually being shoved onto the shore in one of the marshy areas. Thankfully, an emergency response team promptly rescued the two people on board, but the authorities continually urged people to stay indoors.

Ever since Eden switched the channel off Riley's cartoons, he had been in his room playing cars. Every five minutes or so, she wandered down the hallway to check on him. Kirk sat on the couch with his fingers wrapped around a beer as if it was just another day in paradise, and after Eden's last trip into the hallway, he fetched her a cold one from the fridge.

"Relax," he encouraged, handing over the can. "It is merely a diminutive storm," he breathed with ease.

"Little storms don't sound like they're about to push my house over," Eden pointed out.

"That is simply the pressure of the wind; your house will withstand such an amount of force without any notable consequences."

At that moment, every light in the house went out and all the appliances powered down, leading Eden to the sudden realization that dark storm clouds stole the daylight; she could barely make out Kirk's silhouette. The house was eerily silent for a brief moment when suddenly Riley burst into tears and screamed, "Mom!"

Eden quickly navigated a path she knew by heart, one she staggered down many nights to check in on her son, and she only felt for the wall one time. When she made it to Riley's room, he stood in the middle of it as though he was lost in his own home. Same as with Kirk, she could make out the silhouette of her little boy and in no time flat she scooped his trembling body into her comforting arms and assured him everything was alright. In response, he reached his short arms around her thin neck and held on tighter than he had in some time.

Eden slowly retraced her steps to rejoin Kirk in the living room where he abandoned the couch in search of the flashlight currently in his hands and now shining a path for her to follow.

"I didn't anticipate needing this so soon," he broadcasted.

Riley's cries turned into sniffles, and as Eden held him like a heavy sack of potatoes, she felt uncomfortable about the current situation.

"We are going to my parent's house," she informed Kirk abruptly.

"What would you prefer me to do?" he asked unsure whether *we* meant he was invited.

"I would like you to come with us, please," she pleaded. Eden realized she had never experienced a hurricane alone and although she didn't want to speak her thoughts in the presence of Riley's ears, she was suddenly scared.

"Certainly," he agreed without hesitation knowing Eden's parents were out of town because she told him all about the conversation with her mother this morning.

"I think we will be safer there," she stated. The idea of moving locations had been circling her mind ever since the initial thought popped into her head and she felt like the decision should be made sooner than later. It was highly likely that portions of the roads between her home and her parent's house would become impassable at some point this evening.

"Groovy," he accepted.

"They have a generator," Eden mentioned spontaneously feeling somewhat dimwitted for only now thinking about the generator which she knew from past experiences would power the lights and some of the appliances. "Do you know how to work a generator?"

"I believe I can figure it out," he presumed. "I watched my dad start one on several occasions."

"Great, because I have no clue how it works." During previous hurricanes, Niles and her dad were the ones handling the generator. They were both excellent with their hands when it came to using equipment and working with tools, and it seemed as though the ability came naturally. "We need to pack up some items to take with us," she announced.

"Just point me in the direction where my hands are needed," Kirk offered.

Eden grabbed a flashlight and then handed a small one to Riley. "I will pack bags for myself and Riley. Will you transfer everything you can from the freezer and fridge into the cooler?"

"I am delighted to tackle that assignment," he confirmed.

Eden let Riley down then held his hand as the two of them made their way to her closet while Kirk retrieved the cooler from the garage. She unearthed a couple of suitcases and quickly stuffed as many clothes as possible into the largest one. Riley sat on the bed, watched her, and played with his flashlight.

"Mom, can I bring my toys?"

"You can bring some."

"I want to bring all of my emergency vehicles," Riley pleaded.

Eden huffed. "We will bring as much as we can," she conceded.

"I want to bring Banana, too."

"You can definitely bring Banana," she agreed.

"What about my nerf guns?"

"No, no guns," she demanded. "My nerves are already shot."

"I want to bring my building blocks."

"Riley, just chill for a minute," she implored while pacing frantically around the room as the rain slapped against the windowpane. Earlier, she and Kirk took down the bird feeder, and now she found herself wondering where the birds were hiding. "Let me gather my things then we will head to your room and take care of everything you need."

"I need underwear," Riley announced.

Eden pushed out a laugh. "Yes, you sure do."

When they passed by the kitchen on the way to Riley's bedroom, Kirk was stuffing chicken and peas and jelly and all sorts of things into the cooler he'd layered with ice.

"The limited capacity will not allow everything to fit," he reported, "but I am prioritizing and meticulously organizing the contents."

"Thank you so much," Eden obliged, glancing over the packed items. "You know what, there are grocery bags in the cabinet beneath the sink. Anything that won't fit into the cooler, just put in those. My parents have a deep freezer in the garage and we can load it up." She knew her dad emptied the deep freezer before leaving town because he mentioned it yesterday when calling to inform her about his crew lifting Riley's ark from the dock with a trailer and securing it in the backyard.

Once in Riley's room, Eden felt as though she uttered the word *no* fifty times as her son begged to take literally every toy and stuffed animal he owned. He even asked to bring his bicycle which wasn't indoors for obvious reasons. Thankfully, she could pack his bag much quicker than her own, and to make things simpler, she eventually plucked a box from his closet and told him he could take as many toys as would fit but nothing more. Of course, it ended up overflowing and as they scurried back down the hallway, a loud clap of thunder rattled the interior walls and he dropped the box spilling out nearly everything he stuffed inside.

Hearing both sounds, Kirk hustled down the hall with his flashlight to help pick up stray toys.

"All the groceries are loaded and on the kitchen table," he informed Eden once Riley's box was put back together. "How else can I assist?"

"Drive us there," Eden requested. There was absolutely no way she was driving in these conditions. She didn't even like driving in heavy rain let alone high winds and who knows what else.

Kirk smiled on the inside because if they were only taking one car, he was pretty sure that meant Eden wanted him to stay the night.

"Oh," Eden asked, "will you grab my suitcase off my bed? It is kind of heavy."

Within a few minutes, they had everything Eden wanted to take to her parent's house grouped together in one area of the kitchen.

"I will start loading my vehicle," Kirk declared. "You and Riley can hang out inside and stay dry."

"My car," Eden stated firmly.

Kirk shrugged his shoulders. "Fair enough."

"We have to take mine because of Riley's seat," she explained.

Kirk packed the vehicle while Eden scoured the house for any last-minute necessities. She found herself wishing she had made a list of the hurricane items so she wouldn't forget anything during her haste to leave. Hopefully her parents would have any necessities she accidentally left behind.

When Eden and Riley walked out the front door, the wind was blowing the rain sideways. The streetlights were out; no cars passed by on the road; and no signs of life remained in any neighboring homes. It was an eerie scene, and Eden stood there taking it all in for a moment before popping open an umbrella. That boneheaded idea proved useless because a strong gust instantly turned the frame inside out, leading her to toss it onto the porch before running with Riley to the rear car door with flashlights clutched in their hands like batons.

Kirk hopped into the driver's seat and started the engine but waited patiently as Eden buckled Riley into his seat. As she made sure to fasten the belts securely, half of her body stuck out the vehicle getting soaking wet. When she finally made it to the passenger seat, she felt as if she was sitting in a pool of water.

"Ready?" Kirk asked, feeling bad for her. Then, he watched as her fingers combed her darkened hair back. Drenched from head to toe, she looked as sexy as any woman he had ever seen, and he knew if Riley wasn't in the vehicle, he would climb over the center console in hopes of sharing some body heat.

"I guess so," she uttered, experiencing the familiar uneasy feeling people often get upon leaving for a trip while sensing they forgot something.

When the reverse lights popped on, Kirk turned to navigate the driveway but before making it to the road, Eden hollered, "Stop!"

Kirk slammed on the brakes. "What?" he questioned looking at her then out the foggy, raindrop-filled windows wondering if he nearly hit something. The rain was pounding the windshield while the wind beat against the car and threw leaves across the driveway. "What is it?"

"Riley's swing," she announced.

Kirk didn't want to get back out in the elements, but he jogged into the backyard anyway and popped the chains off the hooks while rain pelted his body like rubber bullets. Eden feared the swing would end up flying through one of the windows if left attached; otherwise, she wouldn't ask him to remove it. A few moments later, Kirk emerged around the corner of the house then quickly tossed the swing into the rear floorboard.

"You're soaking wet," Riley pointed out.

Kirk laughed, and Eden did, too. "You just wanted me to know how you felt, huh?" he commented to Eden although he was already as wet as she from carrying the suitcases and food to the car.

"Yep," she agreed, watching Kirk pull back his hair with his hand while she unknowingly entertained thoughts similar to the ones he considered the last time a car door shut.

"Is there anything else you can think of before we depart?"

Eden racked her brain for a moment while still feeling uneasy about leaving in such a hurry. Finally, she shook her head side to side then Kirk navigated the vehicle onto the street where the storm drains on either side were overflowing. Before the storm, authorities advised residents to help keep those clean, but she forgot all about the suggestion.

Since no one else was crazy enough to be out driving in this mess, Kirk drove right down the center lines, slowly, while Eden prayed they would make it to her parent's house without a tree falling on the vehicle. There was no way they could see a hazard like that coming because even with the headlights on and the windshield wipers at full speed, they could barely see fifteen feet ahead.

7

Niles and Reese were roughly halfway to New Bern when Mickey's number popped up on Niles's phone.

"Where in the world have you been all morning?" Niles questioned although at this point it didn't really matter.

"Bro, I am so sorry," Mickey apologized. "Kristen and I just got back to the hotel room and found your note," he verified, holding the hotel-imprinted sheet of paper between his fingers while staring at the same ceiling as Niles this morning. "We were out roaming around Hickory. We grabbed a bite to eat and I showed her my family's old tree farm," he finally explained in response to Niles's question. "Are you really on the way to New Bern?"

For a moment, Niles wondered if they came close to running into one another at some point this morning. Again, that didn't matter now either. "Reese and I left Hickory about two hours ago."

"Dude, I hate I had your car when you needed to leave, but that chick must be really cool if she's willing to drive you all the way to New Bern."

"I know, right," Niles recognized, still shocked that Reese agreed.

"Is Riley okay?" Mickey asked, his voice lower than a moment ago.

"I don't know," Niles admitted with a stomach swirling with worry. "I can't get in touch with Eden."

"That sucks. How did you find out Eden and Riley didn't evacuate?"

As the white lines between the lanes flickered by like old movie reels, Niles shared a synopsis of how the morning transpired, catching Mickey up on everything leading to the present time.

"What do you want me to do?" Mickey inquired.

"I don't know, man; I have no idea how this will play out."

"If you need the truck once you get home, my keys are in my bedroom," he offered.

"Thanks, I'll probably grab it at some point. First, I just want to find Riley."

Niles could tell that Mickey felt terrible about the whole ordeal.

"I'll do whatever you need, buddy. I can head back home right now if you think that's best."

"I don't think that's necessary," Niles said. "My plan is to get Riley then head straight back to Hickory," he explained. He and Reese had been talking through a game plan and decided that was the best idea. Niles already had a room in Hickory, where Mickey would be until the hurricane moved out. Niles hoped Reese would agree to drive him and Riley back to Hickory, but he wasn't surprised when she said she didn't think it was a good idea to put the extra miles on the police vehicle even though he offered to pay for the gas both ways. When Reese had asked about a car to drive, Niles mentioned Mickey's truck, and he was now relieved to find out Mickey left the keys at home.

"Just keep me posted," Mickey requested.

"I will," Niles replied. "Make sure to keep your phone with you," he urged.

"Bro, I am so sorry," he mentioned for about the tenth time.

Before receiving the phone call from Mickey, as Reese and Niles talked during the trip, he decided not to give his best friend a hard time about the situation. It wasn't like Mickey did anything wrong and Reese mentioned several times how things happen for a reason. So, in Niles's mind, there was some purpose why she was the one driving him back to his son.

When the phone call ended, Reese smiled at Niles. "I am proud of you for taking it easy on Mickey," she shared.

"Thanks, Mom," he teased.

"I'm not old enough to be your mother, remember?" she laughed.

"You just sounded like her, though," he chuckled.

"She must be a smart woman," Reese considered, lifting her eyebrows toward the visor.

Niles shook his head. "She's pretty bright."

These comments led to a conversation about their moms. Niles explained why his mother moved to California and how he and Riley didn't get to see her as much as he'd prefer. Reese told him that she was fortunate to live so close to her mom but admitted the two of them probably didn't spend as much time together as they should.

"I think when my dad died, it almost pushed me away from my mom," she revealed. "I know that probably doesn't make sense, but we just don't have much in common. It was like my dad was the bond between my mom and me."

Contemplating Reese's words for a few seconds, Niles's eyes moved back and forth between her and the interstate. "That makes sense," he responded with sincerity. "My dad and I were closer than my mom and me," he shared. "She and I still talk frequently, but I think if my dad were alive and in California with her, I would visit more often."

"I understand that," Reese acknowledged. Both of her small hands rested on the large steering wheel when she shifted the conversation. "Have you checked your email recently to see if there is a response from the lawyer?" she investigated knowing he hadn't taken a call from the attorney's office.

Niles glanced at his phone. "I looked a little while ago but I will check again now," he responded eagerly.

As his finger tracked across the screen, Reese decided to pose another question lingering in her mind. "Do you think there is any chance Eden will consider evacuating with you and Riley?"

Niles's head popped up and he gazed at her intently. "I kind of doubt it," he answered.

"If she agreed to that, would you let her?"

Until now, the option hadn't crossed his mind. "I'm not sure," he contemplated. "That might be kind of awkward."

Reese turned her attention from the road to Niles for a brief moment. "I was thinking that might be the best opportunity to keep attorneys and law enforcement out of this dilemma."

Gradually, Niles's head bobbed up and down. "That's true," he admitted, recognizing the logic behind the idea. "I just don't know if she would go for it, and I am not sure how I feel about it either."

Reese shared an expression relaying understanding. "The way I see it, each of you has ground to stand on," she stated. "Eden's argument will be Riley is currently under her supervision and yours is she agreed to leave with Riley due to the mandatory evacuation." She paused for a moment to let that sink in while figuring out how to best articulate another idea simmering in her mind for the last hour. "I was thinking if a third party played mediator, maybe you two could reach an agreement that Riley leaving with both of you is in everyone's best interest; then the involvement of the authorities would be avoided."

Niles pondered the thought as the vehicle whizzed beneath an underpass leading to a variety of chain restaurants and retail stores on either side of the interstate. The scene beyond the automobile's windows vaguely reminded him they had yet to stop for gas or a bathroom break.

"Who would be the third party?" he questioned.

"Ideally, it would be your attorney," she suggested.

Niles held up his phone. "Still no email," he revealed.

"Do you all have a mutual friend who is relatively level-headed?"

He thought about the people they'd both remained in contact with. "I can't think of one I would trust to be neutral."

"How about Grandyma?" Reese mentioned.

"Maybe," Niles considered, "but if she wasn't able to talk Eden out of staying earlier, I doubt she could once I arrive on the scene. Honestly, I am not certain anyone without some sort of authority on the matter could," Niles expressed, ending that thought abruptly and jumping to the next. "What about you?" he asked. "What if you put on your uniform and showed up at the door with me?"

"Are you serious?" she questioned, nearly rolling her eyes.

"Yes," he declared. "Eden would most likely be intimidated by your badge."

Reese laughed all over herself. "If you show up at your ex-wife's house with another woman trying to make peace, I am pretty sure my presence would only escalate the situation even though I am a police officer."

"It's worth a shot," Niles suggested. "If she says no, then I just go back to the original plan of taking Riley."

"Niles, I wasn't planning on going to Eden's house with you," Reese revealed. "I'm already more involved in this situation than I need to be."

"Then how am I going to get to Riley?"

"I am taking you to get the mouse's truck, remember?"

Niles shrugged. "I guess in my mind I was thinking we would get Riley first then grab the truck."

"I'd rather not go to her house," Reese clarified. "At that point, my job would definitely be on the line."

8

Heavy sheets of rain blew sideways while Kirk slowly guided Eden's vehicle down each street as she gave him turn-by-turn directions. The headlights were basically useless and when he tried switching to the high beams, it only made matters worse. It wasn't helping that he didn't know exactly where they were going even though Eden explained it to him before they left the house and he somewhat knew the roads in the area.

"Are we in a car wash?" Riley asked from the backseat, shouting so his mom could hear his voice over the sound of the wind pushing against the car and the rain slapping against the windows.

"No. We are in a hurricane," Eden exclaimed realizing it sounded and felt a lot like the enclosed car washes of which this scene obviously reminded Riley. In all honesty it was an excellent comparison.

Kirk's chin hovered just above the steering wheel—about as close to the windshield as physically possible—upon determining any attempt at dodging the small tree branches flying across the road was pointless. Some slammed against the glass but thankfully weren't large enough to produce significant damage; what concerned him the most was the water covering the roadways.

"I thought the hurricane was coming later," Riley shrieked.

"Riley," Eden hollered into the backseat, "just close your eyes. We can talk about it when we make it to Grandyma's house."

If we make it to Grandyma's house was what she was really thinking. "Is the water on the road from the rainfall or is this area beginning to flood?" Eden asked Kirk as she attempted to look straight out of the passenger's side window to gauge the water's depth as it rippled around the vehicle.

He squinted his eyes. "I've been attempting to evaluate that myself," he explained as the water being kicked up by the tires made a constant roaring noise when it slapped beneath the wheel wells. Kirk guessed at least three inches stood on the road.

"It seems to be getting worse," Eden recognized. "Should we go back?" she questioned, talking above the outside noise.

"How much farther until we reach our destination?" Kirk investigated as the windshield wipers swiped at full speed but barely made a difference.

"We're a little over halfway there."

"I would be apprehensive about turning around now," he disclosed, thinking the car might stall out if forward momentum came to a halt. If that happened, he had no idea what they would do; it was difficult enough to drive in this mess let alone try to navigate these harsh conditions on foot.

Eden silently prayed they wouldn't get stranded out here. If such a thing occurred, would they attempt to walk back to her house? Continue forward to her parents where they didn't know what they might encounter? The latter was closer to the Neuse River. All this water in the roadway could be from the river and might only get deeper as they headed in that direction. Maybe they could seek refuge at the closest house? It was difficult to make out the homes with the power out even though she knew most stood within a stone's throw of the street.

"Are we almost there, Mom?" Riley asked in a panicked tone.

"It won't be long," she announced, concern underlying her voice as well even though she tried to hide it.

Soon after, the rain and wind began to calm down a bit. That was the good news, but the bad news was the water on the street wasn't subsiding. If anything, it got deeper as they turned onto the road where Eden's parents lived, and the churn of the wheels sprayed the water above the roof of the car as they eased forward. She knew undoubtedly that what they were driving through was river water, which scared her more than anything they encountered in this short drive, lasting way longer than expected. On a typical day she made it from home to her parent's house in a matter of minutes. She hadn't looked at the time when they ran through the rain to the car, but she was almost certain it took at least thirty minutes to reach their destination. When they pulled into the driveway, Kirk pressed the accelerator to climb the small hill which led to a closed garage door.

Both Eden and Kirk let out a sigh of relief when he shifted the gear to the park position. They were all safe, at least for now.

9

*N*iles and Reese began encountering rogue bands of rain when they reached the Raleigh area which meant they were only a couple of hours from New Bern, at least under normal driving conditions. Radio forecasters mentioned how the region recently began experiencing wind gusts of up to twenty-five miles per hour, and Reese could already feel the minor effects the weather was having on the vehicle, especially the boat trailer.

"We should probably stop soon for gas," she suggested.

Niles glanced at the needle and realized his body's tank needed emptying more than the vehicle's needed filling, but he understood Reese wanting to top off before venturing into the unknown. Earlier, to stay on the road, he climbed into the backseat to retrieve several bottles of water to keep them hydrated, and he appreciated her agreeing to that rather than stopping for beverages with more flavor which they both would have preferred. "Isn't this illegal, officer?" he'd mentioned as he worked his way over the center console. Reese laughed then told him to hurry up.

Now, both bottles of water nestled in the cup holders held a few last drops. Of course, there were cases on top of cases in the back, and the first time Niles looked at the supplies this morning, he couldn't believe how many items were packed into the vehicle. That surely impacted gas mileage, he thought.

When Reese exited the interstate and pulled into the closest gas station, she was and wasn't surprised when Niles offered to pump. Ever since telling him she wasn't planning on going to Eden's, he hadn't said much. Regardless, she took him up on the offer, but before heading inside the building to use the restroom and grab a snack, she couldn't help but notice how swiftly he was moving. She knew he was more than eager to make it back to his hometown, and if it were up to him, she doubted they would have even made this stop.

At a counter nearly her height, Reese paid for chips, candy, and sodas with personal money to avoid explaining to the captain why she snatched two of each item from the shelves. During her return to the Humvee, Niles scurried past her and into the convenience store then within a matter of minutes made it back to strap the seatbelt across his shoulder. Reese cranked the engine and jumped back on the interstate in less than ten minutes from when they veered onto the off-ramp.

"I grabbed drinks and snacks for us," she announced, glancing at the assortment occupying the console.

Niles had been in such a hurry he hadn't even noticed her carrying two of everything when she walked out. "Thanks," he remarked. "Which ones are yours?"

"I like all of the items I picked, so you choose which you want and I will eat the others."

"That's kind of you," he acknowledged reaching for a bag of sour cream and onion chips.

"It was sweet of you to pay for the gas, so buying drinks and snacks was the least I could do," she mentioned.

It didn't take long for them to devour the chips and candy, but the dialogue dwindled as they ate. Niles had been racking his brain about Reese's idea regarding Eden evacuating with him and Riley.

He wasn't sure if either he or a neutral person could convince his ex to leave nor was he very comfortable with that scenario. Even though he didn't want to admit it, Reese was right about it being a bad idea for him to knock on the door and snatch Riley. Of course, he would explain himself to Eden and bring his son along with him as gracefully as possible, but he could see how an unsolicited exchange might get ugly. At this point, though, he decided his son's safety was worth getting arrested if it was to come to that.

"I like the stuffed animal you were cuddling at the motel," Reese revealed randomly hoping to ignite a conversation.

Niles snickered. "It's Riley's monkey," he pointed out.

She glanced in his direction and smiled. "I hoped that was the case," she reported. "Does it have a name?"

"Banana."

Reese chuckled, "That's fitting."

"Riley talked me into taking Banana on the trip so that he could keep me safe from the hurricane," Niles disclosed with a sideways grin.

"That is so cute."

"He's a cute kid," Niles proclaimed, staring out the window and thinking about his son lying in their bed with his little arms wrapped around the monkey. He went on to tell Reese the history of Banana, how Riley ended up with two of the same stuffed animal because Grandyma bought one for both him and his twin brother Cameron.

As he shared the story, Reese found herself wanting to cry. She couldn't help but think about the tragedy he told her about in the boat last night, and now she was glad she hadn't teased Niles too much about cuddling with a monkey.

"That works out well that Riley can keep one at your house and one at his mom's," she recognized.

"It is one of the bittersweet things that came out of everything that happened to our family," he admitted. "Riley has two of a lot of items from toys to blankets to cups."

Reese continued fighting the urge to let her emotions take over and even found herself sniffling a couple of times as tears formed in the corners of her eyelids.

"You're a good dad," she reminded Niles in a tone as soft as the classical music she found out they both liked. She wanted to switch the radio to a station playing that genre of music, but the woman who was talking through the speakers began telling them that the rivers in the New Bern area were rising faster than expected. "We now have reports of several feet of water in some places, and homes along the waterfront are beginning to flood," she explained.

"That's not good," Niles groaned.

"Does Eden live near the river?"

"She's only a few blocks from it, but I don't think the water will make it to her house."

"What about your place?"

"Our land is on the river but we built the treehouse up high enough that water will never reach it."

"That's good, but what about Mickey's truck?"

10

When Kirk twisted the key to shut off the engine, Eden realized she hadn't even been able to hear the usual roar of a running vehicle. The weather was drowning out everything except her thoughts, and as they sat in the driveway, she took a moment to catch the breath she felt like she'd been holding since leaving home. She surprisingly remembered to ask Kirk to engage the parking brake when she found herself wishing she had her parents' garage door opener so the three of them wouldn't get more soaked than they already were. Of course, the rain decided to pick up as soon as they opened the car doors, and by the time everyone and everything made it through the large front entrance of the two-story Victorian style home, water was dripping all over the hardwood floors. If her mother were here, Eden knew she would be frantic at this moment and probably hollering for Eden's dad to bring towels quickly. Instead, Eden let the bright beam protruding from the end of her flashlight lead her through the quiet house and into the bathroom where she gathered towels for Riley, Kirk, and herself as well as an additional one to wipe up the entrance.

The house was dark but, thankfully, she knew where pretty much everything was kept. Riley hadn't particularly wanted to stay behind with Kirk but Eden knew if her son walked with her he wouldn't be mindful about not touching things or tracking water, grass, and whatever else collected on his shoes when they ran out of their house. By the time she made it back to them, she had heard Riley call out her name at least three times.

Eden handed Kirk a towel, set two on the floor, and used the last one to dry Riley while Kirk shined a flashlight on her son's trembling little body. Even though the power was out, the house was cold. She imagined her dad must have turned the thermostat way down hoping it would keep the space cooler when the electricity went out. However, she doubted it would make much of a difference in the long run.

When Eden finished toweling off Riley, she reached for the top towel on the floor and dried off her own clothes; while in the bathroom, she had taken a moment to wipe her face and arms dry.

"Let's leave our things here for now," Eden advised, noticing how lost Kirk looked. "I'll show you to the garage so you can check out the generator while I come back in and clean up this mess."

They all took off their shoes and left them near the front door before walking gingerly through the kitchen and into the pitch black garage.

"I think the generator is out here somewhere," Eden guessed as she and Kirk shined their flashlights around the large area housing her dad's pickup truck and a thousand other things from tools to a stack of antique furniture.

"Where is my flashlight?" Riley asked.

"You had it when we got into the car," Eden reminded him. She knew that for sure because she made him turn it off while Kirk drove through the monsoon. "Did you bring it inside?" she investigated. Riley shook his head side to side. "Then it's probably still in the car," she assumed.

It didn't take Kirk long to locate the generator in a small room attached to the garage which also housed the lawn mower, gasoline, and random chemicals. Eden took Riley with her to wipe off their bags, the cooler, and eventually the floor. Then, she and Riley each toed a towel and retraced the steps all three of them had taken since arriving. All the while, the rain pounded on the roof above the second story and echoed down the stairwell. Similar to the sounds at her house, the wind pushed against the wood-planked siding and caused creaking noises inside the home making it feel haunted. Riley stayed as close as a shadow while they cleaned and even clung onto one of her legs a couple of times when a heavy gust rammed the house.

"Riley, it's just a storm," she declared, trying to remind herself of the same.

"It's a hurricane," he clarified mimicking the word she used in the car.

When Eden and Riley checked on Kirk, they found him dragging the generator out the garage's exterior doorway where rain spray blew into the opening as they watched him finagle the large piece of equipment through the relatively narrow frame.

"Are you taking it outside?" Eden called out, her voice bouncing inside the four walls of the garage.

"Yes," Kirk responded, talking over the wind slapping against his back. "I vividly recall my father advising against starting a generator inside a house or garage."

"So where will you put it?" Eden questioned. She couldn't remember where the contraption hooked up when her dad and Niles operated it, but as soon as Kirk mentioned it needing to be outside, she recalled at least one instance when her dad and Niles emerged from the outdoors wet from doing whatever they did to make the thing run.

"While you were cleaning, I walked around the backside of the house and found a weatherproof outdoor outlet designed for the wattage." He also found that his bare feet dug into the completely saturated ground but thankfully Eden's parents' yard was covered with thick grass that kept him from sinking too far into the muck. "This has to be plugged up there," he explained, holding a heavy duty cord in the air as he spoke. "It appears your dad built a concrete platform where the generator will sit flush."

"Okay," Eden accepted. "It sounds like you know what you are doing." She hoped he did because she wanted to cook dinner, dry their wet clothes, and see what was going on inside the house. As for outside, it seemed like hurricanes always came at nighttime which made them even scarier because no one could really tell what was going on; people could only hear and feel the effects.

"It's one of the perks of being in a band," Kirk stated loudly. "We often work with power and cords and things similar to this unit." *Kind of,* he thought to himself, but he didn't want to take the time to explain further while his clothes dripped as steadily as if someone were ringing them out.

About that time, a gust of wind forced its way into the garage, strong enough that Eden and Riley could feel it from where they stood on the brick steps. Kirk grabbed a hold of the door jamb with one hand to keep his balance while his other hand held the handle on the generator.

"Good gracious," Eden sounded in response to the surge of wind. "Do you need help?" She hoped not because she didn't want to take Riley out in the extreme elements and she knew he wouldn't stay inside by himself.

"I think I can manage," Kirk answered then a moment later disappeared into the gray air which had taken over any hope of the remaining daylight that otherwise would have been.

The backside of the house faced the river, and although Kirk couldn't see the choppy water very well, he could hear it crashing into the seawall realizing the open space above the vast body of water allowed the wind to come through unhindered. The generator was heavy enough to help keep him grounded as he pulled it while walking backward as if playing a game of tug of war in the mud. Thankfully, the unit had wheels which made getting it to and setting it up on the concrete base less complicated than expected. When he plugged the heavy duty cord into the outlet, his cheeks pinched his eyes as he thought about the dangers of mixing electricity and water. Still, he figured this piece of equipment was designed to handle the elements.

Once it was installed outdoors, he realized he had forgotten to check the gas tank. Using one hand to unscrew the cap while the other shielded the rain from his face, he wasn't sure why he was surprised to find it empty. Trudging back through the soggy grass, he remembered seeing gas containers against one of the walls in that little room and he prayed to find one filled to the brim.

A minute later, Kirk carried a smile and a can of gasoline through the rain and the wind. After pouring, he screwed the cap on, cranked the unit, and went back into the garage to set the breakers to the position which would allow the generator to run power into the house. Staring blankly at the opened panel for a moment, he took in the cluster of light-switch-like levers as the flashlight in his hand illuminated the box. He was fairly certain the main breaker needed to be turned off for the generator to push power into the home but wasn't quite sure what to do next. That's when he noticed the switch labeled *generator* and saw a metal guard needing to be pushed upward to flip the lever. This was a failsafe designed to make sure the primary breaker which brought in electricity from the power company's lines wouldn't be on at the same time as the generator. As he slid the guard then flipped the switch, he hoped he'd done everything correctly.

Inside the house, Eden and Riley jumped when the power suddenly jolted to life. A few lights popped on in random rooms, the microwave made several beeping sounds, and the stainless steel refrigerator started breathing heavily. Eden felt a hundred pounds lift from her shoulders, and the smile on Riley's face helped calm her nerves even more. She knew having power didn't change the effects of the storm, but something was soothing about being able to see what was happening in the house.

When Kirk entered through the back door sopping wet and smelling like gasoline, Eden skipped toward him, put her hands on his shoulders, and, keeping most of her body at arm's length, leaned in and kissed his lips in front of Riley for the first time.

11

"Does anyone ever call you Reese's Pieces?" Niles asked Reese.

"Everyone," she huffed as her eyes rolled while a grin played out across her face.

Niles laughed. "I won't call you that then," he promised.

"Good because I might make you walk the rest of the way." Not that Reese had been counting, but she thought this might be the first conversation Niles started that didn't have something to do with the hurricane.

"Is the candy spelled the same way as your name?" he asked knowing he had seen the packages hundreds of times but couldn't for the life of him remember the spelling.

"Yes, it is," she confirmed.

"Is it your favorite candy?" Niles asked seriously but for some reason he couldn't help but snicker.

Reese shook her head at both him and his question. "No, Reese's Pieces are not my favorite candy," she answered, "but I do like them."

"What is your favorite?" he inquired.

"Milk Duds," she answered, picking up the empty box from the center console and throwing it at Niles. The nearly weightless container bounced off his chest and landed in his lap before he threw it back at her. "Hey, didn't anyone ever teach you not to throw things at the driver?" she queried.

"They taught me," Niles assured her, "but I guess I didn't learn."

"So it seems," she pointed out. "What is your favorite candy?" she probed.

"Probably Sour Patch Kids."

"That figures since you act like a kid," she teased, and Niles pretended to laugh. "I guess we should have had this conversation before I went into the convenience store," she mentioned.

The farther into Eastern North Carolina they drove, the more difficult it became to joke around. Reese found herself increasing the speed of the windshield wipers as the rain transitioned from sprinkles to steady showers to downpours. The wind became constant at some point although Niles wasn't sure when, and every once in a while surprise gusts caused them to check the mirrors making sure the boat and trailer were still attached to the Humvee.

"All of this equipment is designed for extreme weather conditions," Reese assured, but it still didn't keep her shoulders from tensing.

It wasn't quite dark yet but gray clouds covered the once blue skies, and Reese began to wonder how visible the roadways would be once they reached areas where potential flooding could be an issue. Having Niles beside her was a relief since he knew the terrain although she knew she wouldn't be driving in these conditions if it wasn't for him. The Hummer would have no trouble pushing through knee-high water but a strong current could quickly cause a major problem especially with the trailer and boat.

Niles still hadn't heard a peep from his lawyer, and he hadn't thought of any friends who could be a mediator when he arrived at Eden's house for Riley. Of course, Eden hadn't returned his calls or messages, and he was almost certain her phone was off since each call went straight to voicemail. He figured upon making it to her place in Mickey's truck, as long as the vehicle wasn't flooded and he didn't think it would be, he would call Grandyma and put her on speakerphone. Reese thought the idea was primarily solid but being a detective she also realized introducing another person to the scene would eliminate the fact of the situation being his word against hers which could prove positive or negative.

The closer they inched to New Bern, the more Reese realized how wrong things could go once Niles made it to his ex-wife's house, and she found herself questioning whether getting involved made any sense. From a professional stance the answer was absolutely not, but from a personal viewpoint she completely understood why Niles feared for the safety of his child. She ultimately told herself he had the right to keep his son out of danger, especially since Eden lied about evacuating. All this considered, the vast gray area was why dropping him off at his house and leaving felt absolutely necessary. The choices he made from there were on him. She wasn't sure exactly where she would go but decided against taking him up on the offer to fork the bill for her a hotel room in New Bern because that could look like he was paying for her help. At that conclusion Reese also realized letting him pay for the gasoline in the police vehicle probably wasn't a good idea. With that thought bubbling in her mind as small limbs danced across the highway, she reached for her wallet and handed Niles cash to cover the cost of gas. Knowing better than to attempt to avoid debris when driving this fast, she let the bulky tires crunch each piece while explaining her decision to Niles. She didn't want to dig any deeper into this situation, and she found herself wishing she wasn't so attracted to almost everything about this man from his rugged good looks to his quirky humor to his natural desire to protect his child at any cost.

12

ooking a meal with a hurricane brewing outside the kitchen
window seemed odd, yet Eden knew they needed food and
she would make sure to stay away from the window in case a
gust of wind decided to throw an object through the glass. Riley
kept mentioning he was starving even though at the moment the
Army figurines scattered about the kitchen table preoccupied
him. She was pretty sure Kirk worked up an appetite in the midst
of carrying their bags around and hooking up the generator.
Personally, she was almost too nervous to eat, so making sure they
all changed out of wet clothes and moved their belongings to the
bedrooms became her priorities. Then, she gave Kirk a quick tour
of the house before mentioning food.

"Kirk, will you move everything from the cooler to the
refrigerator while I start dinner?"

"I would be beyond ecstatic to help in such a manner," he
responded.

She giggled, unable to tell if his choice of words was humor or
just Kirk being Kirk. "If anything won't fit in the fridge, there is
a deep freezer in the garage."

Kirk gave her a thumbs up. "I stumbled upon that when I was
out there," he reported.

As he began plucking items from the cooler, Eden dug through a bag she placed on the counter. She set aside a box of fettuccine noodles, a jar of alfredo sauce, and a few herbs and spices she packed quickly before leaving home. "Oh," she mentioned to Kirk, "I will need the package of chicken from the cooler."

A few minutes later, Eden was dicing the meat and tossing the small pieces into a skillet. When Kirk finished putting away the cold items, he joined her at the counter and asked if she needed any help.

"No, thanks," she responded. "You can keep me company or you can play with Riley."

At the mention of Riley's name, they both glanced in his direction although he wasn't paying either of them any mind. Kirk took advantage of the opportunity by casually walking behind Eden and letting his hand slowly trace the low of her back. Feeling his touch, her stomach quivered and a smile stretched across her face as she let her wrists settle on the counter, temporarily letting go of the knife as her eyelids collapsed. Maybe she should have allowed Niles to take Riley, she thought as her mind imagined being alone with Kirk while the storm crashed into their little town. Something about that idea suddenly seemed romantic—the electricity off, candles flickering, and her body wrapped up safely in his arms and a warm blanket. A fire going in the background would be a charming touch, too, she considered. Maybe if she could get Riley to fall asleep early, she and Kirk could enjoy some alone time together.

While Eden hovered around the kitchen preparing dinner, Kirk bounced back and forth between touching her inconspicuously, playing soldiers with Riley, and watching her. He and the little guy set up two bases and acted out a battle while outside in the real world the wind picked up and the water rose. Every time a lightning bolt illuminated the sky, Eden could see the river creeping higher into the backyard. It overtook the seawall shortly after their arrival, and the dock was completely underwater by the time she finished cooking. These were regular occurrences during most hurricanes, but the thing was, this storm was just getting started. The water shouldn't be up so high already, and that's what had Eden on edge even though the house was nestled on a small man-made hill designed to keep the water at bay.

The three of them ate dinner at the kitchen table with their flashlights nearby although as long as the generator did its job Eden knew they should have power throughout the storm. Even though the ride here had proven treacherous, she was so glad she made the decision to ride out the storm at her parents' house. Knowing that Kirk would be here with them all night was also a relief.

For now, even with the hurricane flexing its muscles, Eden felt much safer than she had an hour ago.

13

The weather conditions worsened considerably as Reese and Niles made their way through the final stretch of the drive. Once they reached Goldsboro, hardly any vehicles were on the roadway and when they traveled through the small town of Kinston, the stoplights were flashing while swaying back and forth like a pendulum on a clock. The place looked like a ghost town as Reese took in the eerie sight with a tight grip on the steering wheel. Even though reports stated that parts of the area were experiencing flooding, they made it through after only coming across several spots where a few inches of water took over the highway.

Upon reaching New Bern, Reese couldn't see anything on which the headlights weren't directly shining and that's when she realized they hadn't met the goal of arriving before dark. Knowing what lay ahead, Niles warned that driving over the high rise bridge with the winds whipping fiercely would be a challenge. His heart was pounding primarily because of the unknown of what would happen upon making it to Eden's house but also because the gusts were pushing so forcefully against the Hummer that he and Reese could feel and hear the effects from the inside of the vehicle.

"You might want to get in the middle lane," Niles advised as the bridge came into view.

The windshield wipers swished at maximum velocity as Reese drove slower than at any point during the trip. Crossing the bridge looked risky, and it quickly proved to be just that. It felt like they were hovering above the Trent River—raging thirty or so feet below—as the wind was forcing the vehicle from lane to lane although Reese was still able to control the steering for the most part. In the rearview mirror, she tried not to watch the boat and trailer fishtailing as she prayed they would make it across without toppling over.

"Do you see what's happening behind us?" she asked, her eyes working back and forth between the mirrors and the bridge.

"I do," Niles stated with his eyes focusing more on the boat than the roadway.

Typically, when crossing this portion of the bridge passersby could take in a serene view of downtown New Bern and the lights illuminating the quaint town filled with bricked buildings and historic homes. Right now, though, the sight was eerie with only a few random lights still working. Niles assumed those homes or businesses must be powered by generators because it was apparent from this vantage point that the whole town was without electricity. Even the visible lights were faint due to the sheets of rain gusting above the river.

"Do you smell smoke?" Niles asked randomly, sniffing.

"I was about to ask you the same question," Reese answered.

As Niles surveyed all angles searching for the source, he couldn't decide whether the haziness in the air was smoke, fog, or cloud coverage. When gazing in the direction of downtown, the thing he noticed most was the fear mounting on Reese's face and he didn't have the heart to tell her they would have to cross this bridge again. At that point, they would be in separate vehicles which he hated. He wanted Reese to come with him to pick up his little boy, and he wished they were all riding back to Hickory together. He felt safer having her by his side, and he knew she would be a great mediator if she would go with him to confront Eden.

"Up here on the right, we are going to veer off onto an exit which will lead us to the portion of the bridge that crosses over the Neuse River," Niles explained. "We have another mile or so to go before we make it back to land."

"Are you serious?" Reese reeled off, still sniffing periodically. "We have to cross two rivers?"

Niles shook his head while clenching the handle on the door, but Reese didn't dare take her eyes off the road to look at him or help figure out the source of the smoke.

Somehow they made it to the other side, but the real danger lay ahead when they entered the small town of Bridgeton where Niles, Riley, and Mickey lived. Thankfully, the smell of smoke faded, but they soon discovered water had completely overtaken the roadway. By the time Reese realized the depth, the tires had dug straight in sending sprays of water in all directions. She immediately slowed the vehicle but before she knew it, they were a foot deep and the high beams were telling her it only got deeper. That's when Reese applied the brakes all the way to the floorboard then put the Hummer in reverse.

"Is there another way?" she asked.

Niles's gut sank right out of the vehicle and into the water. "Maybe," he said, although knowing that if this road was flooded his driveway was probably underwater, too. "This isn't good," he stated, shaking his head.

He guided Reese in another direction where the road eventually narrowed and towering pines bent like sea oats on a windy day at the beach. Reese steadied the Humvee straddling the double yellow lines and turned at each stop sign where Niles pointed. Eventually, they made it to the road leading to his property only to discover it too was covered by river water.

Niles buried his head in his hands.

"Even if I could get you in there, you probably wouldn't be able to get Mickey's truck out," Reese mentioned feeling defeated.

Niles couldn't believe how high the water rose in such a short time. The storm was barely here and nowhere near technically making landfall. This wasn't at all how he envisioned this scenario playing out. He imagined they would be able to drive right up to the treehouse, and within a matter of moments, he would climb the steps, grab Mickey's keys, and be at Eden's house in less than ten minutes. He knew the river would have already taken over the marsh behind his place but never imagined floodwaters would be consuming Bridgeton.

"This sucks," Niles announced, hitting his quads with his fists. "This really sucks," he reiterated.

"What do we do now?" Reese asked fearful of what Niles might suggest.

14

Eden cleaned up the kitchen while Kirk kept Riley company in the living room watching cartoons. When she turned on the back porch lights and saw that the river crept a few more feet up the hill, she decided to turn on her cell phone and call her mom. Before dialing the number, she discovered a slew of messages and voicemails from her mother, Niles, and friends checking to ensure her safety.

As Eden digested the messages from Niles, she found herself growing irritated not because he was asking why she hadn't evacuated but because someone notified him of her decision. Something in her gut told her that her own mother betrayed her. She was surprised Niles's tone didn't seem angrier; however, his texts stated he was calling his attorney and threatened to call the police. Eden huffed as she scrolled through the messages a second time. She knew the police couldn't do anything about her decision nor could his attorney, not now. This was something they would have to deal with later, she figured, but there was no way she was calling Niles tonight. She might text him but first she needed to figure out what he knew and how he knew it.

Eden immediately asked the obvious question when her mother picked up the phone. "Did you tell Niles I didn't evacuate?"

The line went silent for a moment although the wind slapping against the house provided plenty of noise on Eden's side of the conversation.

"Yes, I did," her mother eventually answered, honestly.

"Why?" Eden barked.

"Because Riley North is his son, too, and a father has a right to know where his child is during a devastating hurricane," she proclaimed firmly. "A mother also has a right to know where her daughter and grandson are," she added for good measure. All day, she had been sick to her stomach, worrying whether the two of them were safe.

"We are at your house," Eden revealed then turned the discussion back to Niles. "I can't believe you told him, Mom. He just wants me to make the same choices he makes."

"I can't believe you didn't tell him," her mother responded calmly then seemed to digest the part about Eden and Riley being at her house. "Why are you at my house, honey? Is everything okay?" she asked but didn't give Eden a chance to respond. "Oh, Lord, did a tree fall on your house?"

Eden shook her head as the rain outside the window blew back and forth. "No, Mom, nothing fell on my home. The electricity went out, and I decided we would be safer and more comfortable at your house."

"Thank God," she spewed. "Isn't the power off at our house, too?" she inquired.

"Yes, but you have a generator."

Grandyma furrowed her brow. "You know how to work that thing?"

"We figured it out," she answered.

"Be careful, darling; that contraption scares me."

"I will."

"I have been watching the weather stations," she mentioned. "New Bern is flooding all over the place, and they say the water could be up to ten feet high by midnight. Is it over the seawall?"

Eden stared out the French doors watching white caps splash into her parents' backyard. "Yes, it is."

"Oh, my goodness, sweetie. Are you all going to be safe there?"

Eden prayed they would. She could literally see the river drawing closer as they talked or at least it looked as though such was the case. "I think so," she guessed even though she had no idea. "Has the water ever made it up to the big oak tree in the middle of the backyard?" Eden asked.

"I think it's been close but I don't believe it's made it there," she said. "Please tell me it's not up that far."

"I don't think so," she lied for her mother's sake.

Eden walked through the living area making her way to the front porch and flipped on the outdoor lights on that side of the house. Kirk smiled and waved as she hurried by but he stayed put on the couch. Staring out the front windows, Eden could tell the water in the road was much higher now. In fact, she could no longer see the sidewalk in front of the house and panic began to set in when she realized they were basically on an island.

15

"**P**lease take me to get my little boy," Niles begged with tears brought on by a mixture of sadness and madness streaming down his face.

"Niles, I can't," Reese pleaded. "If your ex-wife reports me, I will lose my badge."

"If you don't take me, I might lose my little boy."

Reese shook her head violently. "Don't go there, Niles. Don't do that to me," she demanded. "That's not fair."

"Do you see this water?" he exclaimed. "If it's this high on my side of the river, it's probably up as much on the other side. That's where Eden lives; that's where Riley is right now," he proclaimed.

"I'm sorry, Niles, but we have to come up with a better plan," she demanded. "Under these circumstances, I can't go to her house with you, and I definitely can't let you put your little boy in this vehicle."

Niles dug his hands into his hair again. "A better plan?" he quizzed in frustration then a light blinked on in his head. "What if I take your vehicle," he suggested. "You can say I stole it from you; I don't care."

Reese's shoulders sank, her lips parted, and her eyelids collapsed as she conjured up a response. "Niles, you will go to jail for stealing a police vehicle, especially at the hands of an officer even if we are friends," she pointed out. "That's insane."

"Maybe from where you are sitting," he justified staring across the center console with determination consuming his green eyes.

Reese threw up her hands almost hitting the roof of the vehicle. "Then where am I going to end up?" she questioned. "Are you going to leave me here at the edge of this rising water in the middle of a hurricane?"

Niles let his head fall between his legs. "No," he uttered quietly, racking his brain for a better idea.

"What if I get you to Eden's but you have to promise to stay there?" she proposed. "Once you are there, you can do everything in your power to keep your little boy safe through the storm."

"What if Eden won't let me stay there?" he quizzed.

"If you show up at her front door with the river rising toward her house and explain you have nowhere else to go because a friend dropped you off, you don't think she will have the heart to let you stay? You think she'll leave you stranded on her front porch with no vehicle and no shelter?"

Niles shrugged his shoulders but said nothing as he absentmindedly held his ring finger with the tips of all the fingers on his other hand.

"She may not be happy about you being there, but I doubt she will turn you away," Reese claimed.

With a new plan, Reese turned the Humvee around. They trekked through the backroad and across the Neuse River portion of the bridge before exiting toward downtown where Niles headed every time he picked up Riley. For some reason, the wind didn't seem as bad this time, and Reese wondered if it let up or if experiencing it once helped her know what to expect.

When they neared the bottom of the exit ramp, Niles explained in advance that she would need to turn right and then they would cross over the short drawbridge. Then, all of a sudden, he hollered, "Watch out!"

Reese slammed on the brakes and the massive Humvee slid down the bridge with the boat trailer fishtailing behind. Niles grabbed the handle above his door and jammed both feet into the floorboard as though he was the one applying the brakes. Reese swiveled the steering wheel violently in an attempt to steady the trailer while a rockslide of supplies stacked in the rear came tumbling into the backseat.

When the vehicle finally came to a rest at the edge of what appeared to be several feet of water rushing across the bottom of the ramp, both Niles's and Reese's hearts pounded fiercely. They were mere moments from diving into water that would have probably yanked the boat trailer right off the hitch. The vehicle itself could ford through a few feet of water; it was even designed with drain plugs in the floor to release water once it reached dry land, but it wasn't made to defy the laws of physics. In training, Reese learned a flow of water at ten miles per hour produces the same force as 300 miles per hour winds, and she wasn't trying to experience that force of nature today.

What concerned Reese now was whether the boat hit the guardrail. With all of the foreign noises playing out as they spun sideways, she wasn't certain. She felt a few jolts but didn't know if any of those came from impact. After taking a moment to calm down, she climbed into the backseat just as Niles had earlier, but this time she retrieved two bright-colored rain jackets. Then, she and Niles jumped out to check for damage in the pouring rain. A moment later, they met at the hitch.

"Everything looks fine here," Niles called out, but Reese had to push her face nearly close enough to kiss him even to understand what he was saying. When he repeated the statement, she shook her head in agreement.

They each walked around either side of the boat—in which they had been lying together last night under calm skies—and studied both the vessel and the trailer making sure everything remained appropriately attached. They met at the rear where the motor was protruding and simultaneously gave it a once over.

"I think we avoided a catastrophe," Reese shouted into Niles's ear as she grabbed his arm to steady herself. Their rain jackets flapped like flags as they stood close and studied each other's faces for a moment as the raindrops pounded the hoods covering their heads. Even though the torrential downpour made them feel cold as it pelted their faces like a sandstorm, Niles swore he felt body heat between him and Reese. The sudden urge to kiss her felt stronger than Hurricane Florence.

16

When Eden hung up the phone after talking to her mother, she scurried back into the living room and nearly blurted out how they were trapped on an island. Thankfully, she recognized Riley wedged up against Kirk's leg and fast asleep before opening her mouth. All of the commotions must have worn the little fellow out, she figured. A smile stretched across her face for a short moment then she remembered the dilemma outside.

"Water is completely surrounding the house," she whispered urgently.

Kirk's head jolted. "Really?" he responded quietly.

"Yes, come see."

Eden grabbed his hand and led him to the front door then to the back. "Holy cow," he gasped as he took it all in.

"Do you think it will make it to the house?" Eden asked.

"I doubt it," he hoped. "It's probably high tide and the water will begin to recede shortly."

"You think?"

Although the hurricane was proving to be more intimidating than Kirk imagined, only one thing occupied his mind ever since the little dance with Eden in the kitchen. "I will keep you safe," he guaranteed, pulling her flush against his body.

"Will you, now," she replied, wrapping her arms around his neck and feeling his thighs pushing against hers.

Then, he kissed her and she kissed him back.

"The storm is going to do what the storm is going to do," Kirk conceded, sliding his hands up her back beneath her shirt. "The wind, the water, the rain, it's all outside and it won't harm us in here," he assured. "You just need to relax."

"How do you suggest I do that?" she asked, feeling a twinge more comfort in his arms already.

"I believe a pleasant massage would do the trick," he suggested, working his fingers around her tight shoulders causing her to shutter in a good way.

Eden let her eyelids collapse. "That might help," she agreed in a soft tone. A moment later she pulled back, grabbed one of his hands, and led him upstairs to the bedroom in which she grew up.

Stumbling through the doorway, Eden switched on the light then guided Kirk to the bed where they sat on the edge. They made out for several minutes, and Kirk began rolling his thumbs around her knotted back. Before long, Eden lay face down on the bed with Kirk straddling her while massaging slowly as her body fell deeper into the mattress.

Above their heads, a heavy band of rain beat on the roof and the wind howled as it blew in off the river, but somehow Eden and Kirk let passion drown out all the noises she didn't want to hear.

17

When Reese and Niles climbed back into the Humvee dripping wet, he wondered about her plan to get the vehicle turned around in such a tight spot. Before he could figure out how he might attempt such a feat, she began finagling the trailer like a Rubik's Cube and in no time flat solved the puzzle. Facing the wind head-on, the Hummer climbed to the top of the ramp they came down minutes ago, then Reese hung a right following Niles's instructions about another way to get into downtown. They traveled west across the bridge and just beyond the end of it Reese felt relief at the sight of an uphill exit. They turned down street after street avoiding both standing and moving water as Niles explained how they should be able to maneuver around the low-lying areas and make it to Eden's house. Thankfully, there wasn't just one way in and out of downtown on this side of town.

The stoplights lining Broad Street swayed like swings on a playground and the wind threw all sorts of debris across the road. Reese dodged a spinning trash can, a road sign ripped from the ground, and a random mailbox. She drove around, through, and over all sorts of other small items hoping nothing would pierce any of the tires. Reese asked Niles in advance to let her know when they made it to Eden's road, and when they did, she stopped the vehicle and spoke the words she dreaded.

"I have to let you out here," she uttered.

Reese guessed that the water standing in the street was about a foot deep, but that wasn't why she halted the Hummer. As she explained to Niles earlier, she wasn't going with him to Eden's house nor was she pulling into the driveway or coming within visible distance of the home.

Niles shook his head. "Thank you," he offered with tears of sadness and relief dripping down his face. Those replaced the raindrops present there a short while ago when out in the elements. Now, he was about to step into the unknown, and he found himself wondering if he would ever see Reese Kirby again.

"I owed you one, buddy," she proclaimed, remembering a fight scene that would be etched in her mind for eternity. "Go get your son," she encouraged, pushing his shoulder playfully.

Niles had the entire trip from Hickory to prepare for this moment but somehow it snuck up on him, and he felt like there were so many things he needed to say but hadn't. Surprising himself, he didn't say anything before hopping out of the jacked up Hummer. He simply stretched his upper torso across the center console and kissed Reese's lips as slowly and softly as a winter's snow silently falling to the ground. When he pulled back, he forced a smile then began to take off the rain jacket knowing it had the word POLICE written in reflective lettering across the back.

Reese grabbed his arm, stopping him. "It doesn't have my department's name on it," she revealed, assuming that's why he was giving it back. "So it's not evidence," she laughed as the rain beat on the windows.

Before watching Niles jump into a foot of water, realizing there could be dangers between here and Eden's house, Reese spoke her last words to him before driving away. "Don't forget to grab your bags," she reminded him, "and please call or text me once you're inside and know Riley is safe," she requested.

As Niles walked into the storm with a bag in either hand, Reese wanted to chase him down and kiss him again. She wanted to help him complete the rescue of his little boy. She wanted so many things but knew once she could no longer see him in the headlights shining in the distance through the rain and the wind that blew him away from her, she had to put the vehicle in reverse and head in another direction. She didn't know where she was going from here, but it made her sad to know Niles North wouldn't be there.

18

Eden and Kirk were half-naked under the covers when the electricity flickered off, but then it came back to life and they kept kissing. Not a minute later, it completely shut off.

"I bet the generator ran out of gas," Kirk assumed, wanting that to be the case.

"That quickly?" Eden wondered.

"I'll go check on it in a little while," he offered, kissing her neck as he talked.

The timing didn't seem to add up at the moment. Eden thought it wasn't a big deal for the electricity to be out because Kirk's body sure felt nice against hers and Riley slept soundly downstairs. She figured if he woke up she would hear him call out her name like usual.

Eden and Kirk rolled around on the soft mattress for several more minutes before a loud bang froze both of their bodies.

"What the heck was that?" Eden inquired.

"It sounded like a tree fell," Kirk guessed.

"We probably need to check it out and make sure the house is okay." Eden had heard stories about trees falling on roofs during storms and within a matter of hours a good portion of the home was completely ruined.

Kirk didn't want to interrupt the fun but knew it only made sense to check on Riley and the house. Something close by had definitely made a loud sound and he was certain it wasn't thunder.

In the dark, Eden and Kirk searched for each other's clothes. As they slowly unearthed them from beneath the covers, on top of pillows, and scattered on the floor, they dressed while only being able to see one another's silhouettes. When Eden stood up fully clothed, she realized she forgot to bring a flashlight upstairs.

"Did you bring a flashlight up here?" she asked.

"I didn't," Kirk answered.

"Follow me," she advised then the two tiptoed out of her room like she had on many nights when sneaking out of the house to see Niles. Sometimes she and Niles would lie in her backyard and gaze at the stars above the river and other nights they would hop in his car and take a ride around the town. Regardless of where they went, they usually ended up with at least half their clothes off just like she and Kirk tonight.

On the way down the stairs, Eden palmed the rail with one hand while Kirk's hand occupied the other. Unable to see anything, they moved cautiously.

"What's that sound?" Kirk quizzed hearing what resembled a noisy air conditioning unit.

"I'm not sure," Eden answered. "What's that smell?" she asked, wondering why it smelled like dead fish in her parent's house. She hoped she hadn't left out raw meat but it shouldn't have started stinking that quickly.

Thankfully, Eden knew the exact amount of steps on the staircase and with only three left she screamed when she felt her entire foot overcome by water.

"Oh, my God, the river is in the house," she shouted, nearly tripping down the final steps but, thankfully, able to steady her balance.

"What?" Kirk queried somewhat baffled then realized the

sound he heard was moving water sloshing against the steps and the walls.

At that moment, Eden's motherly instincts took over as she hurried down the remaining stairs and rushed through the moving river water to the couch where she left Riley sleeping. "Riley!" she shouted on her way there. The water slowed her progress, but it didn't take her long to reach the sofa, and when she did, she felt for her son's body but only found wet cushions.

"Riley isn't on the couch," she screeched, sending a surge of panic through her entire body.

Kirk found the back of the sofa with his fingertips and began reaching his hands down the cushions to double-check.

"Riley!" Eden repeatedly screamed yet he didn't respond and she couldn't believe this was happening.

"I'll find a flashlight," Kirk offered hastily, knowing he left the one from earlier in the kitchen on the bar.

Eden rummaged around the living room feeling like shackles were tied around her ankles. The water seemed thick as she kept running into furniture knocking things over but it didn't matter because the river was taking everything captive anyway. Her hands wandered around the cushions on the loveseat thinking maybe Riley moved over there then she made her way to the rocking chair where her mother often rocked him, but it too was empty.

A minute later, a beam coming from the kitchen illuminated the living room, and Eden couldn't believe the scene in front of her eyes. Even though she knew the area was inundated with water, she prayed the loud noise had been a tree falling on the house and that all the water came in through the roof but she knew better. Rainwater wouldn't fill up a room that fast. The water hugging her knees was from the Neuse River, and as Kirk made his way into the room she could see that the surge pushed open the French doors on the backside of the house flooding the entire bottom floor of the home.

After shining the light around every square inch of the room looking for Riley, Kirk made his way to Eden and handed her one of the flashlights he found on the bar.

"Let's search different rooms," Eden suggested quickly. "You go back toward the kitchen and check the laundry room, the mud room, and the garage," she ordered. "I'll check my parent's room and my dad's office."

Kirk simply said, "Okay," and moved as quickly as possible through the brackish water.

The water splashed all over the walls and up her body as Eden pushed through like a madwoman. The house didn't mean anything; all that mattered was finding her son. She first looked at her parent's bed, praying he went there for safety. She began crying harder when she didn't find Riley on the mattress or anywhere else in the master bedroom or in the walk-in closet. Her dad's office was empty, too, other than books and papers floating around like a scene from a nightmare. Still, she looked and looked and looked. She shined the light everywhere over and over and called out Riley's name a hundred times, but she didn't find him. As she worked her way toward the kitchen, she prayed out loud to God that her little boy was safe.

Kirk found Eden sobbing in the kitchen, but a flashlight was all he had in his hands. "You didn't find Riley," he observed with a shaky voice.

Eden's face appeared crumpled and frightened, and Kirk came to the stark realization that there was nothing he could do at this moment to comfort her. All either of them could do was keep searching for Riley.

"You check the places I just checked and I'll check the ones you did," Kirk mentioned.

Eden didn't know what else to do although she thought about searching upstairs and outside. They would do that next, she decided. Chances were he was somewhere inside the house, and if he made it up to the second story then he was relatively safe. He could have snuck up there when the lights went out and gone into the bedroom where he normally slept. Thinking about that, she prayed he hadn't been downstairs when the river barged through the doors.

When did the floodwater begin to come in and how had it come in so fast? Eden didn't feel like she and Kirk were upstairs for more than thirty minutes, but she obviously wasn't thinking straight then, and she didn't feel as though she was now either.

She searched the mud room, pantry, and garage although the water in the latter was deeper than in the house. She continued to call out Riley's name every few seconds and across the house she could hear Kirk doing the same. Every once in a while she would stop to listen hoping Kirk would quit calling out her son's name because he found him, but when they met in the living room she discovered that wasn't the case.

"Will you look outside," she begged Kirk, "while I go upstairs?"

Again, Kirk did exactly as requested. Imagining Riley would most likely go in the direction the water moved, he reached for the front door, but it wouldn't budge. He tugged hard and even used his body weight but it wouldn't move, and he knew if he couldn't open it then a five-year-old wouldn't have either. That's when he hustled through the water toward the backdoors, forced open by the raging river. Upon making it to the door frame, he tripped and fell onto the porch barely catching himself with his hands and knees. Gripping his flashlight tightly, he fought against the current to lift his sopping wet body and he lunged for one of the columns to regain stability. Holding tight, he shined his light around the backyard and called out Riley's name through the gusting wind and the heavy rain but the entire area had become the Neuse River. Unless the little guy was somehow clinging on to something, he wasn't out there. Even though Kirk was a grown man, he knew there was no way he could hold himself up if he attempted to walk off this porch into deeper water. Knowing that, he shined his light anywhere a little boy could possibly end up— into every tree and around the wood-framed swing set.

Upstairs, Eden ran in and out of every room several times shouting things like, "Riley, if you are hiding from me, come out now; this is an emergency." However, she never heard his voice, never saw his little body, nothing.

19

Reese's phone rang sooner than expected yet she answered with a spry voice optimistic that Niles was calling with good news.

"They're not here," he announced in a deflated tone.

"What do you mean they're not there?" Reese questioned. *How could they not be there?*

"There's no one at the house; it's empty," Niles confirmed.

"Do you think your ex is choosing not to come to the door?" she considered aloud.

Niles stared at the door as he talked. "I kicked it open," he informed her. He then peered down at the two bags he carried in, now sitting at his feet where he left them when searching the dark house for Eden and Riley.

Reese instantly whipped the Hummer and trailer around and headed for the drop spot. "I'll meet you where I left you in five minutes," she advised. Thank God she hadn't gotten far.

Niles stuffed his cell phone into his pocket and walked out of the house as the wind pushed the rain jacket flush against his chest. That's when he realized that while inside the water managed to climb nearly every step and began lapping onto the porch. Wondering if the busted door jamb would hold up in these conditions, he strained fighting against the gust pulling the door shut to create a barrier from the elements. The hardware didn't properly attach, but he forced it into the grooves as best as possible.

Returning to Reese, Niles stepped into the rapidly surging water where the bags draped over his shoulders nearly touched the surface. Pushing through the murkiness below, he was thankful for all the leg exercises he'd done throughout the years. It literally felt like he was walking with his pants around his ankles as the beam from the flashlight led him back to where Reese dropped him off.

Upon making it to the spot where he climbed out of the Hummer earlier, Reese wasn't there, but that's not the only thing Niles noticed. The water in that area of the road now touched his kneecaps. In the distance, he spotted headlights and realized the depth of the water was why she stopped short.

All sorts of debris flew everywhere and he did his best to dodge nature's bullets, but he primarily focused on moving forward. As he trekked the final distance, a small tree branch smacked him in the back of the head, but, thankfully, it wasn't large enough to knock him over. When he finally made it out of the water, Reese immediately hurried to his aid, pulling the bags from his sagging shoulders. Niles collapsed onto all fours a moment later, panting like a dog as he fought to catch his breath.

"Are you okay?" she asked, visibly concerned.

"I will be," he uttered as the rain pelted his back. Soaked from head to toe, he felt like he'd been fighting in the octagon for a few rounds.

Reese quickly ran the bags to the vehicle then reappeared at his side with a bottle of water. "Drink this," she instructed.

Niles began to suck down the liquid as if he had just completed a marathon. "Thanks, I needed that," he eventually gestured.

"Where do you think Riley and your ex-wife could be?"

Since bursting into Eden's house and finding it empty, the

present question gnawed at Niles even though it was hard to think straight when he couldn't walk straight. "My best guess is her parents' house which I should have thought of in the first place."

"Why is that?"

"They have a generator." Even though he doubted Eden knew how to work the equipment, it seemed like a good reason for her and Riley to be there. Plus, they always rode out hurricanes at her parents' home. She probably asked one of the neighbors to hook up and start the generator, he figured.

Using one hand as a visor to shield her face from the rain, Reese reached for Niles's hand with the other. "Let's finish this conversation in the vehicle," she suggested.

A moment later, they each battled the wind while shutting their respective doors, and even though it was by no means quiet inside the Hummer, Reese and Niles no longer needed to shout.

"I have to get to Grandyma's house," Niles claimed.

"Okay," Reese recognized, "where is it?"

Niles peered through the foggy windshield where the wipers swished at full blast and had been since they reached New Bern. "That way," he pointed in the direction from where he emerged a short bit ago.

"How far?" Reese asked.

"A few minutes by car," he explained, "but that obviously isn't happening today."

Reese snickered in agreement. "Is there another way in?" she questioned. "Maybe a route where water hasn't overtaken the roadway?"

Niles grimaced. "There are other ways in but I doubt any of them will be any clearer; Eden's parent's house is closer to the river than where we are now."

"We'll take the boat," Reese decided on a whim.

Niles mustered up the biggest smile possible under the circumstances. "Are you serious?"

"I didn't drive all the way from Hickory for you not to make it to your little boy," she declared. "But what you need to understand is once we get into the boat, I am in charge."

Niles shook his head. "Yes ma'am."

"Let's do this," Reese announced as she began calling out directions like a seasoned veteran. "I'm going to turn us around then back the vehicle into the water like at a boat ramp," she explained going through the literal motions while speaking. "Once the boat is in the water, I need you to drive the Hummer to higher ground. There was a parking lot next to a business on relatively high ground about half a mile away and I think the vehicle will be safe there. Do you know where I'm talking about?" She should have taken note of the establishment's name, but she hadn't known it would be needed for reference.

Niles couldn't believe Reese was so aware of her surroundings. "Okay, and yes, I know exactly where you're talking about." He'd driven these roads hundreds of times.

Reese stopped the vehicle just short of where the river was lapping, which changed every few minutes, and continued to explain her plan while climbing into the backseat. "I am going to put on my drysuit," she said, digging through the array of items beyond the second row. "Yesterday, I noticed Dominguez's gear back here next to mine, and you should be able to fit into it; you two are about the same size," she predicted. "There's no telling what we will encounter in the water. Everything normally on land and in the river is now on those streets, in yards, and everywhere in between. There will be hazards all around us. Downed power lines, sewage, snakes, sharp objects, large objects—get the point?" In a matter of minutes, Reese attempted to sum up what she learned during weeks of training. She tossed Dominguez's bag into the front seat then unzipped her own. "Here, put this on," she instructed as she began to slip on her drysuit.

Niles started pulling the gear out of the bag and held up the suit to figure out what went where. "Why didn't you give me this before I walked through knee-deep water?" he queried, half-joking but half-serious.

"It didn't seem like a good idea at the time," Reese insisted.

Niles shrugged and shook his head. "Better late than never," he responded, and it didn't take long for him to realize the difficulties of putting on unfamiliar, tight clothing in a vehicle being rocked by the wind.

Reese popped back into the front seat with a black suit covering her body from head to toe and helped Niles finish dressing. "Your suit is equipped with a PFD," she shared.

Niles furrowed his brow while trying not to stare at Reese in her drysuit which made her look sexier than most women in lingerie. "Which is?" he questioned.

"Personal flotation device," she spouted.

Reese quickly explained how to use the mechanism in case of emergency while they each pulled on a pair of waterproof boots.

"These fit and feel pretty good," Niles confirmed, referring to the footwear now taking the place of his soggy tennis shoes. A helmet was the last item in the duffle bag.

"It's your lucky day," she responded then shifted the conversation away from small talk. "I plan to drive the boat the entire time we are in the water, but in case something unpredictable happens, do you know how to handle a boat?"

Niles grinned. "Yes, I know my way around a boat."

"Good," she replied.

A few moments later, they were back out in the elements and pacing quickly as though they had previously prepared for this routine. Reese tossed a couple of weatherproof bags into the boat while Niles removed the straps holding it to the trailer, and then Reese jumped behind the captain's wheel.

"Now, back me down into the water," she instructed.

When the bottom of the flat vessel gripped the water, the

current instantly began to push the watercraft where it wanted, as Reese knew it would. In a swift motion she cranked the engine and felt the boat release from the bunks. Once entirely in the water, holding it steady was akin to riding a bucking bronco. There was an art to it and Reese quickly took charge of the raging river. She traveled in a circular motion while Niles parked the Hummer then jogged back to the water's edge. Watching him splash into the wake reminded her of a kid running into the ocean, and in no time he was waist deep and moving much slower.

When Niles reached the boat, he did a barrel-roll over the sidewall. The maneuver reminded him of workouts at the obstacle course surrounding the treehouse. Although out here, there would be no safety net so, hopefully, the helmets would help keep them from smashing their heads. In the boat they were completely exposed to the above-water hazards ranging from flying debris to the sheer force of the wind and the pelting rain. One of the instructions Reese gave Niles was to stay low and keep a firm hold on one of the grips on the boat designed for that purpose.

Niles pointed Reese down the same streets where Eden led Kirk earlier in the evening although now the roadways were completely covered with flowing river water. The wooden posts holding the stop signs were half-buried along with the street signs, and Niles couldn't believe how different the neighborhoods looked under water. His primary focus was on getting to Grandyma's house as fast as possible, yet he couldn't help but take in the surrounding scene. They came across people with flashlights standing on their front porches begging to be rescued and other residents yelling out from second-story windows.

"Swift water rescue teams will be here to help soon," Reese called out as they passed terrified people. Unsure if anyone could hear her, she purposefully didn't turn on the flashing lights, only the ones designed to assist with navigating. From experience, she knew rescuers would have to pick and choose who to rescue based on various factors. Residents in two-story homes would most likely be advised to stay in the second story and wait out the storm. "We are on a specific mission," she hollered out over and over.

The roar of the boat's engine battled with the sound of the wind as one flooded street led to the next.

"When we get to the house, I will identify a secure place to tie off the boat and then take the lead when we go to the door," Reese declared. "My plan is to convince Eden that she and Riley need to evacuate."

"Okay," Niles agreed.

"Is the house one or two levels?" she yelled through the rain as the watercraft bounced on the waves rolling through the city streets as though they were meant to be there.

Niles held up two fingers, deciding it was the easiest way to communicate the answer. Reese cringed, knowing that could pose an issue but hoping Eden would be frightened enough to jump into the boat without thinking twice. She couldn't imagine that anyone entirely surrounded by water in the middle of the hurricane wouldn't want to get out.

When they reached the house Niles identified as Grandyma's, Reese scanned the area for the best place to situate the boat. The river in its natural boundaries was behind the house. Now, it was rushing across the street, so she figured they could tie off to one of the large columns on the front porch which should hold the boat steady and keep it from slamming into the house.

Steering carefully, Reese put her hand firmly on Niles's shoulder. "Stay in the boat until I tell you to get out," she instructed while reaching to flip on the blue lights knowing they would immediately give her an edge. Her plan was to get as close to the porch as possible and let Niles jump out and secure the rope. Earlier, after finding out he could drive a boat, the next question she asked was if he could tie one off and she didn't mean like shoestrings.

As blue flashes bounced off the white house, Niles's mouth fell agape when he realized the water was rushing out the front door which meant it was coming in through the rear doors and flowing through the entire house. He vividly remembered riding out previous hurricanes in this home and the river never made it anywhere close to the back porch. It had to be at least six feet above normal sea level, maybe more.

Peering through the windows, he could see flashlights flickering around like strobe lights. A moment later, Eden and another person climbed out one of the front windows onto the porch acting way more frantic than Reese anticipated.

"Who's with her?" Reese hollered toward Niles's face realizing the second person appeared to be an adult. "And what are they shouting?" She began to wonder if they were high on drugs or drunk, and she started to second guess the idea of coming here with Niles.

Once Reese maneuvered the boat within earshot, Niles nearly fell out when he deciphered the words coming out of Eden's mouth.

"Thank God you got here so quickly," Eden exclaimed.

Reese furrowed her brow as she studied Niles's face and felt almost certain his ex-wife didn't realize her ex-husband was one of the people in the boat.

The words that attacked Niles's heart as sharply as the lightning bolts striking around them were "He's not in the house; we can't find him anywhere. He has to be out there in the flood somewhere."

20

iley. Niles immediately realized Eden was referring to Riley. Even though she hadn't spoken their son's name, at that very instant he understood the meaning of the intense gut feeling he had been experiencing since the beginning of the week. His worst nightmare was now a reality.

Without thinking twice, Niles flung his body over the side of the boat and into waist-deep water. Within a matter of moments, he stood on the porch face to face with Eden and some guy he didn't know.

"Riley is missing?" Niles asked for clarification purposes, his voice roaring above the sounds of the wind and the waves as he steadied his balance as best he could.

Eden's face instantly fell apart. She didn't say anything, just shook her head up and down as tears streamed like rain.

Edging the boat closer to the porch, Reese watched this event unfold. Like Niles, she quickly realized what was happening and who Eden and the man thought were in the boat—the police. Of course, she was a detective and they were driving a swift water rescue boat, but they were not the authorities Niles's ex apparently called.

Kirk, realizing Eden was at a loss for words yet unaware Riley's dad was the man on the porch, spoke next. "We've looked everywhere in the house and we can't find him."

"Who are you?" Niles shouted, growing angrier by the moment.

"Niles," Reese hollered from behind, purposefully interrupting. "Catch this line," she demanded, throwing a knot of rope that looked like an oversized ball of yarn directly at him.

The heavy duty rope cut through the air but unwound rapidly as it pierced the elements. With two hands, Niles caught it and quickly circled the braided strands around the column at the corner of the porch. In less than ten seconds, a secure knot held the boat in place as the force of the water pushed it as far as possible, stretching the line tight.

Both watching, Eden whispered into Kirk's ear. As he processed the identity of the man tying the rope, his eyes bulged.

Reese lowered herself into the water and used the taut line to steady her balance on the way to the porch where Niles lowered his hand to pull her up. Once there, she knew taking over the situation before it spiraled out of control was imperative, realizing they didn't have time to play games. "I'm Detective Reese Kirby," she stated authoritatively. "Who is missing?" she quizzed Eden and Kirk needing precise confirmation.

"Riley," Eden confirmed. "My little boy."

"Our little boy," Niles added bluntly.

Everyone held onto something for balance while emotions took over the scene as the wind fast danced to an erratic melody.

"Niles," Reese requested, firmly glaring at him, "focus." Then she turned her attention back to Eden. "Where did you last see Riley?"

"On the couch," Eden answered, then she and Kirk went through how the last thirty minutes of their lives played out, omitting the fact they were half-naked in the bedroom when the power went out; nonetheless, mentioning the two of them were upstairs.

"Why in the world did you leave a five-year-old downstairs by himself in the middle of a hurricane?" Niles yelled.

This time, Reese turned and grabbed Niles by the shoulders. "You two can argue later," she hissed. "Right now we have to find Riley." She didn't want to tell anyone standing on this porch about the time clock for kids who went missing, and a flood in the middle of a hurricane only diminished the chances of finding him.

Normally, Reese would have an entire team to assist with rescuing this little boy. On a positive note, she skipped many of the preliminary questions—age, height, weight, haircut, and a request for a recent photo. She could vividly remember Riley's facial features from the image of him carrying the leaf blower.

Given the conditions, there was no telling how long it would take local authorities to arrive even though Reese knew this case would be granted the highest priority. Considering the unknown, she began to call out instructions. "You two stay here at the house," she told Eden and Kirk. "Keep searching inside and calling out his name from the porches. Look everywhere. If Riley is hiding in the home, someone needs to be here when he comes out; otherwise, he will freak out." Ordinarily, some of the search and rescue crew would head into the house at this point to comb through every square inch, but Reese had to trust that Eden and Kirk had already searched high and low like they explained. She turned to Niles. "You come with me," she instructed.

"I am going with you, too," Eden declared, her motherly eyes begging Reese. "My little boy is out there somewhere and I can't stay here and do nothing."

Reese cringed. Under normal circumstances the answer would be *no, absolutely not*; an additional passenger without gear became a liability. She would have explained to Eden the vital role of searching the house, but she understood Eden had already gone through every room a couple of times if not more. It wasn't like the woman could walk around the yard or neighborhood searching for her child. The flood made this situation unique, and Reese decided to break protocol and let Niles's ex into the boat knowing full well it could be a big mistake.

"I'll get you a life jacket," Reese expressed to Eden, "but only on one condition," she added, her eyes darting between Eden and Niles as she spoke. "Out there in that boat you two are on the same team, and if either of you starts arguing, I'm bringing one of you back which will cost us precious time that isn't on our side."

Niles and Eden quickly agreed, and in a matter of minutes Eden was fastening the buckles of an orange life vest Niles retrieved from the boat. Reese gathered everyone's phone numbers explaining that they all needed to stay in contact in case anyone found Riley or a clue that might lead them in his direction.

Getting Eden off the porch and down the rope line took a little extra effort but soon she was gripping two of the handles inside the boat as it rocked like a buoy in the surf. Niles swiftly untied the line and joined them.

Kirk looked like a lost puppy as they backed away from the porch.

"What was Riley wearing when you last saw him?" Reese asked.

Eden's eyelids sank as she recalled taking off Riley's wet clothes; then she explained replacing them with camouflage pajamas.

"Knowing what he is wearing is helpful," Reese shouted, unsure of any other positives about him wearing camouflage given the situation. "We're going to head to the backyard first," she mentioned then pointed to a cubby asking Niles to retrieve high powered flashlights for Eden and himself. "I want the two of you looking at places where the water could have taken him—where he could be clinging—the exterior of the house, trees, any object he could hold onto," Reese advised.

Niles gave a thumbs up and Eden shook her head. As the watercraft navigated through a cluster of crape myrtle trees in the open yard next to the house, Niles could tell the wind became stronger as they headed toward the mouth of the river. He studied every tree limb as each fought to stay attached as the force of Florence's heaviest winds of the evening shook them like pompoms. He knew how well Riley could climb, and he kept expecting to catch a glimpse of his little boy holding onto one of the branches for dear life. A couple of times something caught his eye, but it was only that everything looked different in the dark with rain blowing sideways and winds shifting nearly every object within sight.

As they made it into the large opening between the back of the home and the raging Neuse River, Eden shined her light toward the house and spotted movement near the deck. She squinted her eyes praying it was Riley but then realized the generator was wedged up against the wooden frame shifting with the current and slamming into freshly tattered boards. The heavy piece of equipment must have been shoved there when the water pressure forced the plug out of the outlet, simultaneously shutting off every light in the house. She hated herself for going upstairs with Kirk and leaving Riley downstairs alone. If those few moments of pleasure led to a lifetime of suffering, she knew she would never forgive herself.

"Niles," Reese hollered. "I'm going to get us as close as I can to the shed then I want you to take the rope line into the water and search around in there as best you can," she directed. "Don't forget the hazards that will be below and above the water."

The wooden shed wrapped with the same color siding as the home was larger than Niles's treehouse and it housed Eden's dad's construction equipment, or at least it normally did. Now, the garage door was ripped off one side of the track and dangling from the other making an ear-piercing screech like fingers scraping a chalkboard as it rocked against the open frame. Loose boards floated out of the opened structure along with random objects like PVC pipes and insulation.

Reese positioned the boat where it was least likely to be in the path of the door in case it became detached entirely. She couldn't help but think that this looked like one of those places a boy might come for shelter if he wandered out in the storm when the water was ankle-deep in this area.

Earlier, while standing on the porch examining the scene and the surrounding evidence, Reese's training guided her to search in the direction the water moved which meant the front yard and beyond. However, with no one knowing how high the water was when Riley wandered out of the house, her gut told her to go to the furthest point toward the river that he could have made it and work back from there. Kids usually went somewhere familiar: a playhouse, down a trail they often walked, a friend's house. At this point she had no reason to consider abduction, and she prayed Riley wasn't still asleep when the water rose into the home like Eden thought. If the flooding caught him off guard on the couch, he was most likely in the house somewhere, and unless he was playing the best game of hide-n-seek of his life, she didn't want to tell his parents where they might find him. However, just before leaving, she whispered into Kirk's ear to search below the water's surface, especially against the house's interior walls.

Before the river barged in, Reese knew Riley could have walked out the front door as easily as the back. However, based on Kirk mentioning being unable to open it, she knew the little guy hadn't exited that way after a few inches of water accumulated. Upon arrival, when Reese watched Kirk and Eden climb out of a window onto the porch without Riley was the moment she feared something was wrong.

Reese glanced at her phone and found it hard to believe it was already after ten o'clock.

As Niles worked toward the shed, Reese began asking Eden questions while keeping her eyes on Niles and working the wheel to control the watercraft. "Does Riley have friends who live in the neighborhood?" To be heard, she screamed louder than at any point this evening.

"Not really," Eden hollered back. "Mostly old people live in this area."

"Where does he play when he's here?"

"The backyard," Eden answered, glancing around at what was normally a large open area with luscious green grass and a magnificent view of a relatively calm Neuse River. "On the swing set," she added, shining her light in the direction of the wooden frame which was one of the few objects not completely submerged in water. Either her dad or the storm removed the swings, she immediately noticed. The monkey bars were still attached but Riley wasn't dangling from them like he regularly enjoyed. He loved to hang on them with his feet, and the moment that thought entered Eden's mind she could see his face, his smile, and his hair sticking straight up, or technically down, because of gravity.

Niles quickly realized the current on the riverside of the house was fiercer than when he walked to Eden's earlier and when he transitioned from the boat to the front porch upon arrival at Grandyma's. Here, the water was above his waist and he thanked God for the drysuit and the snug boots. He was surprised he didn't lose his tennis shoes earlier and now they were probably stinking up the Hummer, but everything that happened prior to arriving at Grandyma's no longer mattered.

Once inside the shed's four shaky walls, Niles thought about all the nails kept on the lower shelves and he wondered if some of them were what felt like darts pricking his legs as he trudged in here. Temporarily sheltered from the rain and the brunt of the wind, his flashlight lit up the enclosure as he shined it from right to left level with the surface of the calmer water. Thankfully, the back wall ran parallel with the river. This allowed him to maneuver more easily as he shifted his light toward the rafters, calling out Riley's name over and over, praying for a response.

A tractor Riley loved to play on was wedged against the front wall, and Niles saw the top part from the seat and steering wheel up which was where he figured his little boy would be if in the shed. With no such luck, he double-checked the higher shelves where pretty much everything above waist level remained unscathed for the time being.

From the boat Eden continued to shine her flashlight at every object in the backyard like the detective suggested. She had no idea how Niles knew this attractive woman or why they showed up here together. Until the moment she saw her ex's face, she assumed he was still in Hickory with Mickey. Eden wanted to ask Niles these questions yet tried to focus on the critical task at hand like the lady demanded when putting Niles in his place earlier as he slung insults.

When Niles made it back into the boat empty-handed, Reese circled the backyard several times while the three studied the area like hawks. Staring toward the wide-open river, Reese contemplated the distance to the other side although she could conjure up no reason to venture any farther in that direction. Heavy rain and dark sky limited the view but the tree line explained where the water crested on a typical day.

Through the massive windows flanking the rear of the house, they could see the beam from Kirk's flashlight bouncing off the walls, reminding them he was doing the same thing indoors as they were outside. Niles wondered again who the man was and why he was at Grandyma's house with Eden and Riley during the hurricane. He turned to his ex-wife and was about to ask when a voice interrupted.

"Does Riley know how to swim?" Reese queried.

Eden shook her head.

"Very well," Niles confirmed with rainwater pouring into his mouth as he spoke.

Swimming in raging water like the river pushing the boat

around the opposite side of the house toward the front yard was nearly impossible for an Olympic swimmer. However, Reese knew that kids who could swim also knew how to stay above water much better than kids who didn't. Being Niles's kid, she assumed he was probably agile, steady on his feet, and able to climb like the real version of his little monkey Banana.

Once in front of the house, Reese drove around while Niles and Eden shined lights at everything within sight just like in the back and side yard areas. There were several large oak trees and a vehicle she assumed belonged to Eden. Earlier, after Reese climbed into the boat from the porch, she shined her light into the car and spotted a pink lei dangling from the mirror. This time, Eden pointed her flashlight through the front windshield and every other window as Reese skimmed around the car again. Noticing the top half of Riley's empty car seat, Eden nearly burst into tears then suddenly the sheer force of the water began to move the vehicle. Seeing this out of the corner of her eye, Reese immediately gunned the engine to clear the path the water determined.

"Holy crap!" Eden screeched.

The three of them held on tightly as gravity pushed stronger than the wind, and then they watched the car float slowly toward the road and eventually into the neighbor's yard across the street where it slammed into a thick maple tree. The automobile rested there for a short moment before the current twisted the backend and sent it spinning into the front porch where it became stuck. Reese headed the boat in that direction, not to check on the vehicle but to make sure Riley wasn't on the porch or anywhere in that yard.

Hearing the violent impact, a man inside the house popped open a second-story window and called down to them.

"Have you seen Riley?" Eden yelled upward through the downpour toward a relentless black sky.

"No," the guy shouted.

Reese gave him a very brief synopsis of what was going on and asked him to be on the lookout but to stay indoors. The last thing she needed was more people to rescue, and she prayed another swift water rescue team would soon come bouncing up the street. She knew there were probably a handful of crews deployed in the New Bern area, but there was no telling where they were upon receiving the call. Some watercraft probably carried citizens onboard who were evacuating to higher ground; others might be in the middle of a rescue; and some were possibly searching for other people reported missing. In severe weather conditions like this, the authorities regularly received calls regarding missing people. Sometimes those reports were accurate but often a concerned party called simply because they couldn't reach a friend or loved one by phone and they feared the worst. Regardless, the police and fire departments investigated every call seriously. Reese knew this area would be swarming with patrol cars if it wasn't for the flood. A perimeter would have already been set up and officers would be searching every inch of each yard within several miles.

Niles and Eden, whose voices were nearly hoarse from calling Riley's name, were on opposite sides of Reese who inconspicuously glanced at her watch. The three of them had been searching out here for about twenty minutes. So far, no messages from Kirk, and that was good and bad news. They traveled up and down the neighborhood streets where Reese felt most comfortable driving the boat. Even though anything could be in the water, hovering above the roadways basically eliminated the worry of running over a stump, a utility box, a fence, or any number of inanimate objects found in people's yards. Of course, debris floated everywhere as she continued to maneuver around everything from tree limbs to bicycles to floating vehicles.

Reese couldn't believe the devastation although with her mind honed in on finding Riley there was little time to think about the damage her eyes were witnessing. He had to be out here somewhere, but where? Where would a scared five-year-old go or try to go?

"Is there a park around here?" Reese suddenly asked.

"Union Point Park," Niles answered looking across at Eden.

"It's not close enough that he could have made it there," Eden chimed in, her voice fighting the sustained wind.

"True," Niles agreed, "and it's on the river so the water would be flowing in through the park making it nearly impossible to walk in that direction."

As beams of light from the boat shone from yard to yard, tree to tree, and house to house, the looks on the faces of Niles and Eden grew more desperate with each waning minute. Alongside raindrops, tears constantly streamed down Eden's face since climbing into the boat. Even though Niles had yet to shed a tear, his heart was ripping apart as violently as the homes being shredded by the flood of a lifetime. Niles and Eden had already lost one child, which haunted every waking moment of their lives. Losing Riley, their only living son, seemed absolutely unbearable.

21

Unbeknownst to Niles and Eden, the word was already spreading through social media about the five-year-old boy who'd gone missing in the floodwaters of Hurricane Florence. It didn't take long for Riley's name to surface in some of the posts, and people who knew the family instantly began asking questions. Most said kind things but not all. Some brought up the horrifying accident that took Cameron's life and a few began to question the parents' ability to keep their children safe. Others questioned why the family didn't evacuate and how such a young boy could go missing during a hurricane. Many shared prayers and several initiated an online prayer chain which spread like wildfire across the United States and beyond. People from all over watched the weather channels which were covering the storm around the clock but no reports about the missing child aired on television yet.

It didn't take long for local residents to decide to pitch in to aid the rescue efforts. A group of fishermen made plans to meet downtown where they intended to put a boat in the water and begin searching. Another man and his two adult sons, who were already in a boat in the area helping evacuate people, posted they were heading toward the boy's last known location.

In Kentucky, Grandyma, with layers of tears streaming down her rosy cheeks, helplessly absorbed this information. She didn't care much for social media but decided to log in to read updates and see pictures of what was happening in New Bern. Never in a million years did she expect to find out her grandson was missing and her address was being plastered for all to see. She tried to call Eden over and over, and she couldn't believe that she hadn't heard the news straight from her daughter's mouth. When Grandyma spoke those words to her husband and sister, that's when she began to wonder if Eden was missing, too. Eventually, she came across a post mentioning that the mother's whereabouts were uncertain. Another claimed the mom was out searching for her son.

Grandyma didn't know who or what to believe and eventually decided against responding to messages other than the private ones coming in from family and close friends. She tried calling Niles but had no luck getting through to him either. As she read comment after comment regarding her daughter, grandson, and son-in-law and about how horrible the conditions were in New Bern, her husband stood over her shoulder with his phone against his ear. She begged him to keep calling Eden and Niles until one of them answered.

Parents of small children posted how upon learning the news of a missing boy, they held and hugged their children tighter this evening as the storm continued to surge. Many realized it could have easily been their own child. In contrast, others continued to criticize letting a five-year-old out of sight, especially during a catastrophic hurricane that brought unprecedented floodwaters. Citizens with friends in law enforcement reached out to see if more information could be shared. Eden's father tried calling a few firemen and police officers he knew, but no one answered their phones.

22

Two swift water rescue boats barreled down East Front Street heading toward the one operated by Reese Kirby. Blue and red lights swiveled and bounced off the homes, the choppy river water, and everything else all of those onboard could barely make out through the treacherous conditions. At the sight of Reese's boat, the others slowed to a halt and she released the throttle simultaneously.

Reese quickly introduced herself as Detective Kirby from the East Ridge Police Department. However, she instantly sensed that the three members on each boat became confused by the presence of her watercraft along with the appearance of her crew. She was well aware these teams were likely briefed as a collective unit within the past twenty-four hours and assumed each person was thinking a boat from Tennessee hadn't been mentioned. As all eyes drilled her, Niles, and Eden, she imagined the others quickly realized Eden wasn't a professional—her casual clothing, especially the fact she wasn't wearing a drysuit, gave that away. Reese glanced at Niles out of the corner of her left eye already knowing he looked the part yet glad to see he wore the confidence as he stood tall next to her while she explained the extent of the rescue mission without going into much detail about what brought her to the scene in the first place.

In the midst of hasty introductions, Reese learned the red and black boat was being operated by the New Bern Fire Department's team and the blue and white watercraft belonged to a group from Kentucky. After the task force leader of the local boat discovered Eden was the missing boy's mom and had been with the child at the time of his disappearance as well as the one to make the 911 call, he respectfully demanded that Eden climb into his watercraft to accompany his team back to the house where he would begin the investigation Reese unofficially started. Of course, he didn't state the latter but Reese realized he didn't know her, and if he took her word for what was going on at the initial scene, his job would be on the line if something was overlooked. She knew her career was on the line, too, and for more reasons than one. She dreaded having a conversation with her superior, Captain Lawson, about what led to her ending up in New Bern, but she was beginning to think it was inevitable. That feeling punched her in the gut the moment she lowered the swift water rescue boat into the rising waters earlier, and now that she was part of an actual rescue mission, it pretty much sealed the deal. Questions would be asked and documents would be filed.

Reese and Niles could both tell Eden didn't want to get into the other boat but amid the commotion Reese inconspicuously explained that no other option was on the table. "I am no longer in command," Reese pointed out.

Thankfully, moving Eden from one watercraft to the other proved less difficult than transitioning her from the porch. It helped that this time highly trained personnel assisted on each side of the transfer. Reese found out there were other swift water rescue teams deployed in various parts of the county and that evacuations had been rapid-fire since about eight o'clock. One of the men mentioned how around that same time the fire department started fighting a structure fire in Old Town—which Niles explained was near where they smelled smoke earlier when driving across the bridge—and then he said when the firefighters made it to the scene the water was at their ankles yet the latest report stated it was above their waists.

"You guys continue to search the area where you were heading," the task force leader instructed once Eden was safely aboard. The gentleman's southern accent was the thickest Reese had ever heard, way more obvious than hers or Niles's, and it had been one of the first things she noticed when he introduced himself and the others earlier. "There's no chance the boy could have made it to the park, but I like the idea that he might have tried to head in that direction," he divulged. "If you find him or anything that might help the search, let us know immediately," he asked then disclosed the communication channel in use. "My crew will head directly to the house so that we can start at ground zero," he explained before turning to the group from Kentucky. "You all search in the opposite direction, and let's find this kid," he ended.

Alive was the missing word Reese heard loudly and clearly. *Let's find this kid ALIVE.* Of course, any professionally trained rescue person wouldn't dare say the word in front of the parents but that was what he meant. It was rare when a child wasn't found; the terrifying part was whether they were found before it was too late.

"His name is Riley," Reese shared, making it personal even though she had yet to meet the little guy but was determined she would.

The others nodded respectfully, and a moment later the three boats headed in different directions. Reese appreciated how the task force leader hadn't demanded she come back to the house or park her boat and stay out of their mission. He possessed such authority and she would have completely understood if that stance was taken under the circumstances. Whether she would have followed the order was another thing altogether, but thankfully, they hadn't gone down that road. Honestly, she was impressed that he quickly realized the addition of her experience would be beneficial in this rescue.

With the radio tuned to the channel provided, Reese slowly navigated the boat in the direction of Union Point Park. She overheard the task force leader relay to the command center that they crossed paths with her, and she knew the authorities stationed there would be investigating her background immediately and most likely contacting her department. A moment later, she felt a vibration in her pocket and prayed it was Kirk calling to say he found Riley hiding in an upstairs closet. Thankfully, she remembered to set the phone to vibrate earlier because even though the ringer was on max volume, she still couldn't hear it while staring at the waterproof screen. Realizing it was her boss, Captain Lawson, Reese squeezed the phone and winced although she knew there was no way the local authorities could have contacted him that quickly. She momentarily contemplated ignoring the call but decided things would probably end better if she was the one to share the news of her whereabouts. "Yes, Captain," she answered as the heavy wind blew into the receiver.

"Why the heck are you in New Bern, North Carolina?" he quizzed, ignoring the sound of gusting wind blaring through the earpiece.

How did he already know that? "It's a long story," Reese answered, "but the short version is I am assisting with the rescue of a lost boy."

"Who is Niles North?" he probed rather than directly responding to her comment.

Reese's eyebrows climbed to the top of her forehead as she realized the captain really did know every move his team made. "He is the father of the missing child," she revealed.

As Reese conversed with Captain Lawson, Niles guided the spotlight into every nook and cranny he could find. He checked bushes Riley could have been swept into, the tops of road signs protruding above the water where he might be holding on for dear life, and a few porches high enough where the water hadn't climbed onto them yet. All the while, he listened to Reese's side of the conversation with her boss while praying he hadn't gotten her fired.

"You have a lot of explaining to do, Kirby," Captain Lawson insisted.

Reese pursed her lips as her jaw tightened. "I know," she agreed.

A few other questions were asked and comments made, but ultimately the captain was wise enough to realize that at the moment she was doing the right thing by helping search for the missing child. She gave him a heads up that he would likely receive a phone call from the local authorities soon and she asked for his full support regardless of what his decision would be once this mission was complete.

After Niles watched Reese shove the phone back into her pocket, he timidly asked, "Am I going to need to help you find a job after we find my son?"

"That's to be determined but let's focus on finding Riley," she encouraged, staring straight into the storm. "Nothing else matters right now."

He could tell she was angry although still resolved, which he appreciated more than she would ever know. In all honesty, he was scared to death they wouldn't find his son, yet Reese's confidence was contagious. He had been feeding on her positive energy since discovering Riley was missing.

At that moment, Niles slipped his arm around Reese's waist and hugged her for a hundred different reasons. Reese let her head collapse onto Niles's shoulder and for a brief moment she closed her eyelids as the rainwater rushed over her face. Two seconds later, she was back in search and rescue mode although she could still feel the lingering presence of his touch.

This mission was more unique than any in which Reese had ever been involved. In a typical swift water rescue, she knew an approximate location of the person or persons needing help. She often rescued whitewater rafters who fell out of canoes; however, their friends were almost always able to pinpoint their whereabouts. She rescued people from floodwaters similar to these although not as strong because the hurricane was a force to be reckoned with, unlike any flash flood she encountered in Tennessee. Even in those situations, someone who called in the danger could usually point the team in the right direction. When there wasn't a strong storm present, a helicopter could aid in the mission flying overhead and helping with locating the stranded person.

During rescues not involving water, a large number of highly skilled people could disperse in every direction and cover ground rapidly. Lost children were typically found within a mile from where they went missing, often closer. In those cases, one team could work from the center out and another from a designated exterior radius inward. Everyone involved could call out the child's name, but Riley was unlikely to hear the limited number of people calling for him in a storm like this. Audibly, nothing worked in their favor yet they continued shouting his name so much their voices became hoarse. The rain and the wind weren't helping in that regard either.

Thankfully, the air wasn't cold but it was cool enough that the temperature played a part in this process, more so for Riley than for those searching. The professionals were dressed for the conditions but Riley wasn't. He only wore a pair of pajamas and most likely didn't even have shoes on his little feet. He would be cold and uncomfortable especially if soaking wet, and Reese could hardly imagine a scenario where he wasn't completely drenched from head to toes. Thank God, hypothermia and frostbite weren't issues of concern right now although the temperature would drop as the night wore on making it more of a factor. The water was relatively warm, probably warmer than the air; however, the wind also played a part. An FBI agent once told Reese a true story about a man who went missing in the mountains of West Virginia at one of the coldest times of the season. One night that man lay down to sleep sure that during the night he was going to die of hypothermia, but when he woke up, a pack of wolves was nestled up against him sharing their body heat. Many people didn't believe this story but no other possible explanation existed. The man should have died, but apparently nature, God, or perhaps both made other plans.

Visibly, Reese knew the boat's flashing blue lights were working in their favor. Most kids loved emergency vehicle lights, and Reese remembered from listening to Niles's stories that Riley was enamored with police cars and fire engines. Children felt safe around police officers and firefighters unless their parents taught them otherwise, and during her time as an officer, Reese came across a few of those situations as well which made her upset. There were some unfit emergency workers in this country. She had even met one, but 99.9% were amazing people who would lay down their lives to protect any citizen, law-abiding or not, especially children. She hoped if Riley saw the blue lights, he would do everything in his power to bring attention to himself. It was heartbreaking how many lost children searchers walked within a relatively close distance of but didn't see. Kids become scared in situations like this, and they often panic or freeze when they have an opportunity to be found. They see someone they don't recognize after being taught 'stranger danger' their whole lives. It was one of those rare catch twenty-two situations.

Reese was part of one search where a child was lost in a large wooded area near the family's home, and the authorities blared the child's favorite songs from loudspeakers, and eventually the little girl walked right into their hands. All kinds of strategies could be used, but conditions like what they were facing now limited those opportunities. Glancing at her watch inconspicuously, Reese was reminded time wasn't on their side.

23

Two local swift water rescue crew members helped Eden onto the porch after securing a rope line much like the one attached by Reese and Niles earlier. Kirk, hoping for good news upon their arrival, crawled through the open window. He instantly noticed a new set of people and wondered why Eden switched boats. He was relieved to see her face because the thought of being alone at the house when the authorities showed up made him nervous. He was afraid they would blame him for Riley going missing, and if the child's mother wasn't present, they might think he had something to do with her sudden disappearance as well. It didn't seem legitimate that a police officer on a boat showed up with her ex-husband; he had been trying to wrap his mind around that. What if they arrested him? A hundred thoughts erupted in his brain while alone at a home in which he was a stranger.

Eden wished so badly for Kirk to tell her that he found Riley after they left, but, unfortunately, no one shared a favorable report. All Eden then wanted was to be back on the water searching for her son with Niles and Reese even though she had been completely terrified the entire time on the boats. The water was so choppy it felt like they might capsize at any moment. Everything about this situation was frightening, including the urgency of the two men scurrying into the house to search for her missing child.

On the ride here, Eden explained the situation from the beginning as best as possible like on the phone when initially calling 911. The rescue guys said their first step would be sweeping the entire home even though she and Kirk had done so repeatedly. It was their job, she understood that, and she prayed they would find Riley hiding somewhere they hadn't thought to look. Inside the house, she surprisingly watched the places the professionals searched both above and below the water's surface. They opened cabinets, dug through closets, and even went into the attic. All the while, the task force leader fired questions at her and Kirk in the upstairs portion of the home. He explained he did not want the two of them in the floodwaters due to hidden dangers which could lie beneath the surface. It made sense, and she noticed the water was higher and rougher when they walked through it to get upstairs. The ferocious wind slapped the house from every direction especially on the river side which made the entire structure sound like it could collapse at any time. She'd heard similar sounds during previous hurricanes, but something about the excessive flooding and Riley missing magnified everything.

Eden hated answering many of the same questions Detective Kirby already asked although she understood the purpose. She showed the man recent photos of Riley, described his camouflaged pajamas, shared approximate height and weight, and told them nearby places he might wander including their home. During nicer weather, they made the walk from time to time for exercise. She hadn't thought of that earlier when talking to Reese but it made sense that Riley might try to go home. However, it didn't make sense that he would leave the house in the middle of a hurricane. What child would do that and why? Letting her mind travel these roads made her burst into tears because she was afraid that rather than leaving the home voluntarily, the floodwaters swept away her little boy.

"You have to find him," Eden cried, slamming her fists on her legs just above the knees as she sat sopping wet on the same bed where she'd been fooling around with Kirk when Riley went missing. Now, her hair dripped as much as her eyes and she felt her body begging for something to take the edge off. She wanted to wash a handful of pills down with a bottle of whiskey, pass out, and wake up in the morning to find out this was all a horrible dream.

"We will find your boy," the man pledged as a light attached to his helmet lit up the room along with a flashlight which Kirk was pointing toward the ceiling where the fan and light fixture rattled. After responding to Eden, the task force leader relayed the information she and Kirk shared to the command center.

Eden's flashlight sat wedged against her thigh, then she turned it off because she grew weary from holding it, and the others provided adequate light. "You promise you will find him?" she begged as a voice came over the radio confirming receipt of the information and announcing another swift water rescue team was en route.

"My team is combing through this residence, the Kentucky crew is searching the immediate area around the property, and as you just heard on the radio, a third swift water rescue team is heading to your home to search there then work their way back to this house," he clarified. "Plus the two folks from Tennessee who you were with are working the space from here toward Union Point Park."

"Niles isn't from Tennessee," Eden revealed.

"Who is Niles?" the man asked calmly but with a slight wrinkle in his brow.

"The man who was on the boat with the detective from Tennessee," Eden answered. "He's my ex-husband."

The task force leader cocked his head. "I am confused," he admitted. "Is he not part of Detective Kirby's team?"

"No," Eden hissed. "He cuts grass for a living."

"Oh," he responded. "He looked the part so I assumed he was swift water rescue since he was wearing a drysuit and all of the other gear we wear."

Eden shook her head while Kirk's eyes darted between her and the man asking the questions. "I have no idea why he is with her," Eden shared. "I've never met her before tonight."

The man's face became a little more puzzled although Eden could tell he was trying to mask the surprise while thinking through this new information. "Were either of them in this house when your son went missing?" he questioned.

"No, they showed up not long after we called you all," she announced.

"I'm glad Detective Kirby is here to help, but I need to inform my superiors of this bit of information," he commented then changed the channel on the radio before talking into the receiver.

24

iles and Reese came across a boat occupied by a middle-aged man and his two adult sons who stated they had been in the floodwaters all evening helping rescue stranded people.

"When we heard about the missing boy, we decided to help," one of the sons shared.

"What can we do to be of assistance?" the other asked.

Reese knew the authorities frowned upon citizens helping with swift water rescues although many greatly appreciated the gesture. She wasn't in the position to accept or deny assistance; therefore, she figured the best option was to explain such and share essential knowledge with them as she did earlier with Niles and Eden.

"Thank you for your willingness to help but you are risking your lives by being out here," she pointed out as kindly as possible. If this were her mission she would probably also tell them they were risking the lives of the swift water rescue team members who might eventually have to pull them from the floodwaters. "Stay on the streets as if driving a vehicle and don't get out of your watercraft for any reason other than to save a life," she advised. "There are many dangers in the water, some visible and some not."

Reese went on to list some of the hazards most people didn't consider including fire ants which attacked Niles earlier when he hopped out of the boat into the water to check something they saw on a porch which ended up being a statue of a little boy that had been knocked over by the wind. Thankfully, she saw the critters swarming his suit in time to tell him how to get them off and get away from them. Niles hadn't panicked which was often the difference between staying safe and getting injured.

Within ten minutes of meeting those folks, a boat with several fishermen came up the road and the men stated they were at home when the story broke.

"We all have kids," one of them offered. "We knew if it was one of our children out here, we'd want people to help."

Niles thanked each group several times although he wondered how random strangers knew his son was missing. As with the first group, Reese pointed out the dangers and let them know she was not in charge and that the local authorities may ask them to get themselves to safety. She also shared her phone number in case either of them came across Riley or any information that might lead to his whereabouts.

"Niles, all it takes is for one person to leak information about a missing child and it spreads like wildfire," Reese reported. "It could have been a friend or family member who Eden reached out to, a spouse of one of the emergency workers involved, or even one of the people we've talked to in this neighborhood."

"I guess that makes sense," he replied.

"If this water wasn't here, there would be a flood of TV crews, volunteers, and nosy neighbors," Reese mentioned, "which can be both helpful and distracting."

As Niles digested the information, he found himself praying that Riley wandered out of the house when the water was ankle deep and eventually found refuge in a neighbor's home which would be the best-case scenario. Reese mentioned she'd heard similar storm stories, and that is when the two of them began going door to door asking if anyone saw Riley. Of course, it wasn't as simple as stepping out of the boat, walking up a sidewalk, and knocking on the door. Reese steadied the boat at each residence and one of them called out until someone came to a door or, more commonly, opened a window on the second story since most porches along with the first floors of the homes were covered with waves of river water. On a positive note, pretty much every home in this neighborhood was two or three stories so people found safety upstairs.

Niles and Reese hoped if someone took in Riley they would notify the authorities; however, Reese pointed out that many lines of communication were likely down. They came across downed power lines along their search route, and Reese figured some were phone lines. Cell phone towers were bound to experience trouble connecting devices in this area although Reese's phone worked when talking to the captain. At the homes where no one responded to their shouts, Niles jumped out of the boat and swam as hard as possible to the doors on the river side of the road. On the other side, the water instantly pushed him right to the house. He rang doorbells and beat on doors, but not many people answered. He and Reese assumed most of the residents from the apparently vacant homes evacuated before the storm. At the very first house where no answer came, Niles thought about breaking in to look for Riley in case he took shelter there but then realized his son would have had to break in to get inside in the first place. So, he struggled back to the boat and went to the next home. The people they talked with all promised to keep an eye out, but none had seen Riley. Many pleaded to be rescued, but Niles and Reese explained time after time why they couldn't help in that capacity. Thankfully, so far, no one made an attempt to force their way onto the watercraft.

When Niles climbed into the boat after the last house where no one answered, he collapsed on the floorboard near Reese's feet, completely wiped out. He felt like he fought a hundred rounds in the octagon and doubted he could throw a punch now if his life depended on it. However, Riley's life depended on it, so he forced himself to climb to his feet and press onward.

"Sit down," Reese urged. "You need a break or you're not going to be able to finish this search."

Niles's body dropped to the seat where the two of them sat the night they met. So much had changed in such a short time, Niles realized. Then he remembered that it was only last night when they were sitting side by side in this boat before sinking beneath the tarp to hide from the motorcycle gang. In a way, he felt like he'd known Reese Kirby his whole life. The situations they battled together in the past two days were enough to fill a book.

Reese wished she could let Niles drive and do some of the in-water work herself, but she knew that could be dangerous and definitely highly frowned upon by the powers that be although she wondered if it even mattered at this point. "After you rest for a few minutes, you're going to take over the wheel and I'm going to get into the water," she suddenly demanded.

Knowing the risk this meant she was taking, Niles thought about questioning her but didn't. He feared drowning if he jumped out of this boat one more time, and if he died what good would that do in this search to save his son?

Before Reese and Niles could switch spots, the radio crackled.

"Detective Reese Kirby," an unfamiliar voice called out before stating that he was the emergency operations director.

Reese picked up the radio and pressed the talk button. "This is Kirby; go ahead," she replied.

"I need your vessel to report to the National Guard trucks stationed on Simmons Street near Ruth's Chapel immediately."

Reese's heart skipped a beat. This wasn't happening. They weren't pulling her from this search and rescue, not now. Not after how hard she and Niles had been working. He might not have any more in him at the moment but she did. She wanted to be in the water not sitting in a truck or eventually the command center talking to the local authorities about why she wasn't authorized to be here. How about those other boats operated by untrained citizens who could be anyone from saints to pedophiles? No one seemed to be forcing them out of the water.

With heavy rain slapping Reese in the face and wind blowing the boat sideways, she turned to Niles and instantly saw his head shaking east to west. He wasn't going to give up, and she knew that before she even turned around.

25

The search and rescue team cleared Grandyma's house and decided it would be most beneficial for them to hop back into the boat and help the others search the neighborhood. With the floodwaters so high, there was no need to set up a command center there as would be done if flooding wasn't an issue. In these conditions, the child wasn't going to wander back to the house nor would an array of emergency personnel show up to assist with the investigation. The only people who could help at this point were the swift water rescue teams, and half of the ones in the county were now devoted to this mission.

"I want to go with you," Eden insisted.

The task force leader's face cringed. "The safest place for you is here at the house, ma'am," he professed.

"My son is out there somewhere," Eden declared. "I want to help find him."

"I understand, but if I allow you on board, we can't focus on finding your son the way we are trained," he divulged.

Eden grabbed his arm. "Please," she begged. "I will sit in the boat and stay out of your way; I just want to be out there. If I remain here and do nothing, I am going to go crazy."

As a dad, he felt her pain. "If you don't want to be here, I can evacuate you to one of the National Guard trucks at the waterline, and they can take you to our command center where there will be people who can help you work through this situation," he offered. "But in all honesty, we will be wasting precious time."

Kirk grabbed Eden by the shoulders and pulled her away from the man. "Let's let them do their job," he suggested, knowing she might not be in the right mind to make the best decision for her son at the moment.

Eden turned into Kirk and fiercely shoved him onto the bed where she so tenderly touched him earlier. "Your child isn't lost out there in the middle of a flood," she shouted pointing toward the window as he stared up at her in shock. Quickly she turned to the other man standing in the bedroom. "Just go," she cried. "Find my son," she pleaded as he hastily walked out the door.

A moment later the light leading him down the stairs disappeared, and Eden fell face first onto the bed next to Kirk. "I am a terrible mother," she cried.

Kirk was afraid to touch her again but he took a chance and gently draped his arm across the low of her back. "You are a terrific mother," he declared. "You were brave enough to endanger your life out there in the hurricane to look for your son," he reminded her.

"It's my fault he's out there," she howled. "It's the least I could do. If he dies, I want to die with him," she admitted.

"No one is going to die," Kirk said, although he feared the entire house might collapse at any minute and who knows what would happen then. The storm worsened; it had been ever since Eden left the house with her ex and the police lady.

"You don't know that."

"I hope that," he clarified.

"I can't do this," she groaned. "I need alcohol. Will you go downstairs and bring back all the drinks you can carry?"

Kirk furrowed his brow. "With all that water down there, I doubt I can even pry open the refrigerator door," he articulated.

"Just try," she screeched.

When Kirk walked out of the room, Eden turned on her flashlight then dragged herself across the bed before reaching into her purse on the nightstand. She plucked out three prescription bottles and grabbed two pills from one and a single capsule from each of the others. If she was going to have to stay in this house not knowing what was happening out on the water, she didn't want to feel the pain so sharply.

Downstairs, Kirk waded through the nearly waist-high rancid water searching for alcohol. As expected, the refrigerator door wouldn't budge. He about gave up then he spotted the cooler they brought, and he remembered packing the entire bottom of it with beer that thankfully hadn't been transferred to the fridge. He meant to ask Eden if it was okay to store alcoholic beverages in her parents' fridge, but they got caught up with dinner and he forgot. The small waves slammed the cooler and an array of other items into the kitchen wall at the front of the house. He grabbed the handle and floated it across the top of the water until he got to the staircase where he lifted it and began walking gingerly up the slippery steps. Nearing the top, he lost his footing and suddenly realized he and the cooler were falling and there was no way to stop the momentum.

In the bedroom, after popping the pills, Eden decided to look at her phone to pass the time. She found dozens of missed calls and text messages as well as a full voicemail inbox. Upon noticing her mother's and father's names repeatedly on the caller ID, she couldn't believe that in the midst of all the commotion, she forgot to reach out to her own parents. She dialed her mother's number with trembling fingers then began frantically telling her everything. While talking, she heard a crash but assumed it was like one of the many others she heard since the hurricane started throwing things around. Trees were falling, limbs were slamming into the house, and all types of debris were flying everywhere. Also, the downstairs furniture set scattered all over the home along with everything else not bolted to the floor.

A few minutes later, Kirk staggered into the room with blood oozing from his face.

At the sight, Eden's jaw dropped. "Mom, I have to call you back," she screamed, jumping off the bed swiftly.

"Did someone find Riley?" Grandyma asked hysterically.

"No, no one found Riley," she clarified, wishing that was why she needed to end the call. She hadn't told her mom about Kirk and now wasn't the time. "It's something else," she shrieked then hung up.

26

Niles could barely manage the weight of the spotlight, but as Reese turned down street after street, he found the will to shine it in every nook and cranny his weary eyes spotted. After a conversation with her, they agreed it would take more energy to steer the boat than operate the light.

"I still don't think going to the National Guard trucks is a good idea," Niles professed.

"Niles, it's what I have to do," Reese reminded him for at least the third time.

After the call with the emergency operations manager ended, they debated what was best and, ultimately, Reese made the final decision.

"We need to be out here searching," Niles argued.

"We are," she insisted, using the tops of road signs and stop signs to navigate the waters and avoid potential hazards although some of the signs were ripped completely off the poles. Many dangled, and the ones still holding on for dear life spun like weather vanes.

"I don't think Riley would have made it this far," Niles challenged.

"Niles, the water can take nearly anything or anyone it wants as far as the surge flows; we've already seen it move cars," she reminded him.

Not three seconds after those words exited Reese's mouth, a cracking sound erupted, and without further notice the top half of a massive oak tree began falling toward the path directly ahead. Reese hastily assessed the two available options: attempt to outrun the tree with which they were on a direct collision course or whip the boat around and risk flipping or throwing both she and Niles overboard.

"Hold on," she screamed at the top of her lungs knowing if they didn't make it past the tree before it hit the water, the impact would likely kill them instantly. That's why she chose to release the throttle and spin the wheel as fast as her hands would move.

Niles lunged for something, anything to clutch, but his reaction time was much slower than usual and the sheer force flung his body clear across the boat.

A half a second later, the tree made an enormous splash sending a new set of waves directly toward the vessel which was now parallel with the line where the tree fell making the watercraft more susceptible to flipping. Reese was just about to gun the engine to clear the obstacle when she realized Niles was no longer in the boat.

Unsure of where he would surface, she immediately cut the motor knowing the blade spinning below the water became the most dangerous threat with Niles unaware of his surroundings. Watching for her friend to surface, Reese snatched the flotation ring and the moment his head emerged, she flung it in his direction. As the attached rope followed the lifesaving device, she yelled for Niles to grab hold knowing time wasn't on their side. The waves pushing them away from the fallen tree, now half-submerged, would soon give way to the rushing current, and if she didn't crank the engine at that point, they would end up stuck in a web of large branches.

Niles gasped for air while trying to take in the cloudy environment. Following Reese's voice, he turned his head and spotted the orange ring bobbing up and down less than ten yards away. "Swim to it," he heard Reese yell out. He flailed his arms and kicked as hard as possible, and a moment later he hugged the flotation device like a teddy bear.

Steadying herself as best as possible, Reese pulled the rope with all her might as the boat shifted toward Niles and the tree. She didn't want the watercraft to end up in the branches, but even more so she didn't want Niles to become pinned between the boat and the tree. Life seemed to move in slow motion for a few moments as Niles paddled relentlessly and Reese tugged with every ounce of energy within her small frame.

When Niles was close enough where she could grab his hands, Reese positioned herself as trained and used her bodyweight to pull him over the sidewall of the watercraft. Their momentum sent them falling into the floorboard where Niles landed on top of her. In the movies, it would have been the opportune time for the escaping-near-death-kissing-scene but in real life, Reese recognized she had mere seconds to find her footing and gun the engine. "Hold on," she announced once again to Niles as she turned the key and slammed the throttle down.

The engine came to life and overcame the violent current just in time, somehow avoiding getting tangled up in the large limbs which Reese could have literally reached out and touched before the boat finally jolted away from the fallen tree.

Niles sprawled out at Reese's feet grasping one of the attached ropes for dear life. She felt terrible for him but had never seen anyone fight the way he fought this evening. Every time it seemed he was down for the count, he staggered back to his feet and asked for more. He did the work of two professionals, even without a single day of training, and she would take him on her team in a heartbeat. Somehow, he sat up and helped her navigate to the rendezvous point where the emergency operations director promised two trained swift water rescue firefighters would be waiting to hop aboard Reese's watercraft to aid in the search and rescue.

"Aren't you glad now that we are on the way to pick up help?" Reese asked knowing Niles sat whipped.

Niles nodded his head ever so slightly and spoke for the first time since being pulled from the raging water. "Maybe," he uttered, praying this wasn't a setup to get them out of the water.

"That's not the way police officers and firefighters operate," Reese advocated earlier when he made a comment about a setup after the call ended.

The emergency operations director said that after speaking to Captain Lawson, who vouched Kirby was one of the finest rescuers he'd ever worked alongside, he knew they needed her on the water. At that moment, she grinned real big even though she knew her job was still on the line, then replied, "I will let your guys join my team on one condition," she acknowledged with confidence. "Niles North is my right-hand man until we find his little boy."

27

Eden led Kirk by the arm to the bathroom attached to her room, and a trail of blood followed them there. When she first noticed him standing in the doorway, the sight reminded her of a horror movie. The beam from her flashlight cast shadows making the blood glisten. The gooey substance was all over his face and hands, and his fingers drew haunting red lines on the white door frame.

"What happened?" she shrilled, instantly regretting sending him downstairs for alcohol.

When he spoke, blood spewed from his mouth. "I fell," he answered using the counter surrounding the double sinks to hold himself up.

Eden grabbed a towel that just happened to be white and gently dabbed his face. She couldn't locate the cut but didn't want to hurt him any worse.

"How did you land?" she asked.

"Face first into the steps," he mumbled.

Eden ran water over another towel and used it to clear more blood from his face, discovering a cut across his lower lip as well as a gash near his ear. She couldn't tell yet if either would require stitches, and the poor lighting wasn't helping.

"I'm so sorry," Eden stressed for the first time after thinking those three words over and over.

"I'm sure I'll be fine," he murmured as she carefully wiped the skin around his lip.

"Hold this towel there," she instructed as she dug through the drawers for bandages.

"My head is throbbing," Kirk announced.

"I imagine," she responded. "I have some pain medication in my purse if you need it," she offered.

"I might," he admitted, although he didn't want to come across as weak.

Eden unearthed a roll of gauze, a tube of antibacterial ointment, and a box of bandages. She grabbed a third towel and cleaned Kirk's face better before rubbing some of the cream on the wounds then wrapped the gauze around his head like a headband to cover the cut near his ear.

"I don't think you'll want me to wrap gauze around your mouth," she laughed, hoping to lighten the mood for both of them. She felt like the medicine she took was starting to kick in but adrenaline might also be playing a role. "Put pressure on your lip with this washcloth," she suggested grabbing one from an open drawer then running a little water over it. "We can monitor your mouth until the bleeding stops."

Kirk eyed the cuts in the mirror, and they honestly weren't as bad as he thought when he first slammed into the steps. "Are all my teeth still there?" he asked, displaying a cheesy smile like a little kid posing for a picture.

Eden looked close. "I think so," she reported, "but there is blood all around them."

"I can taste it," he divulged, which for some reason made him think of the alcohol. "The beer cooler went flying," he shared, "but on a positive note, I don't think it fell down the stairs."

"So you saved the beer but busted your face?"

"Just for you," he snickered.

Eden spent a little more time in the bathroom doctoring up Kirk, and he washed his hands and arms before they returned to the bedroom.

"Do you have another shirt in your bag?" she asked. "My mother will kill me if we get blood on the sheets."

"Considering the condition of her dwelling at the present moment, I think that will be the least of her worries, but, yes, there is a shirt in there," he confirmed, pointing to the bag he tossed in the corner earlier in the evening before everything went haywire.

Eden slid the zipper and pulled out a black t-shirt. She watched Kirk pull the blood-stained shirt over his head but for some reason the sight of his bare chest didn't do much for her this time. Too many other things encompassed her mind, namely Riley Cameron. She still wanted to be out there searching for him. She also wanted the medicine to kick in another notch so that maybe her mind would stop churning a million miles a minute. Being stuck in a house because of a hurricane was miserable enough but being quarantined in the upstairs portion of her parent's home while her son was somewhere out there lost in the storm was pure torture. She hated that Kirk had been injured, but in a way taking care of him temporarily took her mind off the reality that her five-year-old son was still missing.

Eden and Kirk ended up in bed together then she remembered the beer. She found out he was right; the cooler sat wide open near the top landing of the steps with cans of beer scattered throughout the hallway. She grabbed as many as possible, brought them back to the bedroom, and put them on the nightstand near her purse.

"Want one?" she offered.

Kirk furrowed his brow. "I'll try," he uttered.

"Oh yeah, your lip," Eden remembered. "That might make it difficult to drink."

"Maybe it will help take the pain away."

"Let me get you some medicine for that," she reiterated opening her purse and pulling out the bottle.

Kirk gently slid a pill into his mouth then gingerly washed it down with the taste of nominally cool beer as the wind continued to torment the outer walls of the two-story house. The rain pounded on the roof and the smell of river water drifted upstairs. As Eden took pulls from a beer can, she held her phone in the other hand, checking it constantly for calls and messages from Niles, Reese, and the authorities. Instead, there was only a slew of texts and voicemails from everyone else asking questions she didn't care to answer. Eventually, to pass the time, she began responding to her friends and parents telling everyone the same story over and over. She didn't want to relive the evening, but it kept her mind occupied and so did conversations with Kirk as they sat against the headboard in the flashlight-lit room.

Interestingly, Eden found herself wishing Niles was here. He had been her rock when they lost Cameron, and even though she blamed him, he had been the one to comfort her rather than her comforting him like she probably should have. There were times when she wished she hadn't left him, but the pain became too hard to bear and she ran away from nearly everything. She didn't even know why; she just did. Somehow, she managed to hold on to Riley . . . at least until tonight.

In tears Eden pressed the phone to her ear after dialing Niles's number but he didn't answer. When the voicemail picked up, she absorbed his voice.

A few beers later, Eden asked Kirk to hold her.

28

Picking up the two new crew members at the waterline, where the National Guard trucks waited for citizens evacuated by the other swift water rescue teams, ended up going smoothly. When the firefighters hopped aboard, Reese was pleasantly surprised that one of them was a female around her age. The other was a burly man in his early forties. After brief introductions and a discussion about the search, they headed back into the danger of the floodwaters.

Reese forced Niles to stay in the boat and let the others tackle the in-water searches that arose. At first, he didn't like the idea, but he conceded after she reminded him about five times how he needed to regain strength for when they needed him the most. His primary duty became the spotlight.

As the night wore on, the winds picked up and so did the waves. Reese predicted that the swells regularly lapping into their boat were two to three feet in height. If they were in open waters, climbing the white caps wouldn't have been as tricky, but in a downtown area with very little wiggle room, it took every ounce of energy Reese could muster to keep the boat from capsizing. Reports came in that the floodwaters exceeded eleven feet high in some areas and traveled all the way to the county courthouse on

Broad Street. At least ten feet of water had overtaken either side of the drawbridge, and the wind and storm surge pushed once-anchored boats at its leisure into homes and buildings. A sailboat and a couple of other vessels lie wedged against the large yellow Shriner's building, a well-known landmark in New Bern.

As Niles listened to these stats being broadcast over the radio, he found them hard to believe even though he was in the middle of the hurricane itself searching one of the worst impacted areas. Many of the sights he'd already seen firsthand at some point during the evening. Phone service was in and out, but a line of communication remained open with Eden who texted and called him more frequently than he could respond. He stopped answering calls because he couldn't hear a word she said due to the torrential rain and winds.

Reese maneuvered the boat around block after block. When she felt like they searched every inch of the flooded area in the vicinity of the house from where Riley went missing, they kept going. They crossed paths with the other swift water rescue teams several times and it was apparent everyone was worn out. One of the boats occupied by citizens decided to abort the mission after taking on more water than they could handle and the local authorities asked the other group to head home for safety reasons. Reese wasn't surprised when they didn't put up a fight, and she was relieved to know the trained teams wouldn't have to rescue those who bravely came out to help.

All three crews searched into the wee hours of the morning even after the other swift water rescue teams suspended their missions due to what the emergency operations director called deadly conditions. In all honesty, Reese knew they were facing life-threatening situations the moment she launched the boat in the water.

When the call came across the radio for all teams searching for the missing child to cease the search until the hurricane let up,

Reese watched Niles deflate emotionally although physically he seemed to shift into an even higher gear.

"We can't stop searching," he pleaded.

"If we don't, none of us might make it out of this flood," Reese responded. She knew that the staff at the command center watched the conditions closely. She also knew they'd gone out on a limb by allowing the teams searching for Riley to stay out longer than the others.

"She's right," agreed the man standing next to her. Having a child himself, he could relate to what Niles must be feeling but at the end of the day, he knew he owed it to his little girl to come home safely like he promised.

The other lady chimed in, "As soon as things lighten up, we will be right back out here looking for your son," she assured.

It took all three of them to convince Niles that temporarily halting the mission was the best thing for everyone.

"Do you want me to drop you off at the house so you can be there with Eden?" Reese asked. "Or would you rather stay with me?"

Niles studied her evergreen eyes as he weighed out the options. If he went back to Grandyma's, he could search there until the storm weakened. However, Eden and that guy—Niles still hadn't figured out who he was—had searched and so had the local team. The task force leader even guaranteed that Riley was not inside the house. Still, Niles hoped his son would turn up in the home unharmed.

"I'd like us to stay together so we can get back in the water as soon as it's safe," Niles finally answered.

Reese wasn't exactly sure what he meant by that. Was he saying he wanted her to go back to the house with him? That could bring about a whole new set of problems even though Niles's ex had been relatively cordial so far. If they were stuck in the same house for hours, questions would indeed arise and tempers could flare. The more she thought about it, the more she realized that even taking Niles back to the house alone could add to the issue at hand.

"Good, it will make things simpler if we don't have to make an extra stop at the house," she responded, deciding to imply her interpretation of his statement that the two of them staying together meant loading up the boat and heading to wherever they would spend the coming hours.

"True," Niles agreed. Plus, if he went back to Grandyma's, he was afraid he and Eden would end up arguing the rest of the night, and if that dude got in the middle of it, it wouldn't turn out well. As much as he'd like to drag the guy around by his ponytail for letting his son disappear, he knew doing so would only make matters worse. Maybe after this was all over, he'd get a chance to punch him in the face.

Relieved, Reese figured that she and Niles were on the same page even though she didn't realize he'd thought about some of the same potential problems as she.

Rather than drop off the firefighters at the National Guard trucks where they picked them up, they agreed it made the most sense to head toward the Humvee and put the boat back on the trailer. From there, they could ride together to wherever they would be stationed while waiting for the hurricane to let up. Upon arrival, they found the parking lot where Reese left the Hummer entirely surrounded by water.

"I think I can get it out as long as we can secure the boat on the trailer," Reese said, quickly assessing the scene as the wind threw her words around.

Knowing that getting the boat onto the trailer would be a feat in itself, she asked all three of them to hop out and assist with the placement. Then, she handed Niles the keys. While he backed the trailer into the edge of the water, she steered the boat in circles.

Once everyone was in place, she piloted the boat toward the trailer then cut the engine letting the surge and the wind do the rest. Still, the forward section nearly ended up in the vehicle's back window. Thankfully, all three people standing on land grabbed the boat simultaneously, one pushing from each side and Niles hugging the bow like a teddy bear or more accurately a grizzly bear.

Holding on tightly with one hand, Niles grabbed the winch line. At the same time the others began attaching straps in unison as if they'd performed this task a hundred times together.

After snatching the key and securing all items in the boat, Reese hustled around the watercraft double checking all the lines.

Soaking wet, all four people opened a door and climbed into the vehicle. Being out of the elements felt refreshing, yet it reminded them how tired their bodies were after hours of fighting against one of nature's most potent forces. Niles let his face collapse into his hands; the passengers in the backseat relaxed against the headrests; and Reese grabbed the steering wheel while releasing a strong sigh.

"If you all hadn't been with us, I'm not sure we could have secured the boat on the trailer," Reese professed looking into the rearview mirror.

"I'm glad we were with you," the woman replied with a grin.

"That was more difficult than I imagined," the man responded.

At least two feet of water climbed the tires of the Humvee as Reese maneuvered it down the flooded road. The wind pushed hard against the vehicle but steering it proved much less of a workout than the boat. The windshield wipers worked overtime as rain pelted the windows, and Reese watched carefully for hidden dangers such as water rushing across the road from a different direction. The last thing they needed was to be swept into the floodwaters they were trying to escape.

Reese felt her grip relax a little when they made it to the part of the road that wasn't completely covered in water. However, she still fought the wind and the rain as they headed toward the command center at the fire department where hot showers and a bed would be waiting.

29

When Eden received the message from Niles stating the swift water rescue teams were temporarily out of the water, a sense of hopelessness flooded her body. They texted back and forth several times, and even though he explained the boats would redeploy as soon as conditions let up, she couldn't help but think the rescue crews were giving up on finding Riley. She wanted to go back out there herself and search but knew she couldn't. In all honesty, she could barely stand after drinking so many beers that she lost count. Unfortunately, the alcohol hadn't seemed to take away the pain occupying her heart, her head, and pretty much every inch of her drained body.

After Eden's final message to Niles, she went into the bathroom, stood amidst the bloody towels scattered around the cold tile floor, and swallowed enough pills to knock her out for good. Holding her eyes open the last few hours proved difficult but somehow she made it to this point. Kirk tried to keep her mind off reality by telling her stories about his band and childhood, and he even sang her favorite songs. She appreciated him especially for focusing on her while dealing with his own physical pain, but she knew she wasn't showing gratitude all that well. While he grimaced anytime his face moved a particular direction or if anything brushed the wounds, she fussed and complained the whole night about everything from how dumb letting Riley out of her sight during a hurricane had been to how she wanted to be out there searching to how she wished she'd never been born.

Eden felt as though she sent a thousand text messages, and she talked to her mother and father on the phone several times. Her mother prayed with her which seemed to help temporarily until she began to wonder where God was when her little boy disappeared. Why had He let this hurricane devastate their town and her life? Why hadn't He let them find Riley? She found herself wondering why it couldn't be someone else's kid especially since she had already lost one child. It didn't seem fair. It wasn't, she decided. She questioned whether she would ever pray to God again. One moment, she wanted to quit believing in Him altogether but the next she found herself wondering if He was her only hope.

The posts she read on social media broke her heart and made matters worse. She knew she made a colossal mistake this evening, but some people basically made her out to be a killer while others said she was careless, worthless, selfish, and a conglomeration of other words that stabbed her heart. Many of the people sharing their thoughts openly had never even met her. She wanted to reply to every one of them and tell them they didn't know her or her family, but in a way she felt like they were right. It was her fault and she should have evacuated with her son. Niles even urged her to leave. He offered to take Riley and then begged to take Riley. Her parents asked to evacuate him. She had so many opportunities to make the right choice and she missed every single chance. She made the wrong decision, and now she knew it but could do absolutely nothing about it. She couldn't even enjoy being with Kirk—the main reason she decided to stay in New Bern in the first place. If she had let Riley leave with his dad or her parents, this situation would be so much different. Instead of lying here nestled beside Kirk with tears leaking onto the pillowcase after the worst night of her life, they could be having fun. If none of this happened, maybe they would have shared different conversations in the dark and made out into the wee hours of the morning. She might have even made love to him.

All these thoughts kept Eden's mind spinning and eventually they circled back to Niles. Again, she found herself wishing his arms were the ones holding her right now. She hoped he would come back to the house to be with her although she wasn't sure how that would have worked with Kirk stuck here. She saw the way Niles looked at Kirk like he wanted to pummel him into the ground. She had no idea what type of fighter Kirk was, but she had seen her ex in action enough times to know she always feared for the guys she dated if they ever crossed Niles.

30

Reese wasn't sure how she and Niles would be received at the fire department, but she imagined a lot of questions were awaiting each of them. Per instruction from their passengers, she parked behind the two-story red-brick building in which they would hunker down for the time being. Before entering the station, she sat in the Hummer with Niles after the others exited the vehicle. Even though they were on higher ground with no flooding in sight, the wind and the rain still wreaked havoc all around them. Trees bent like pool noodles and the rain traveled in sheets across the parking lot.

"When we walk inside, we need to be on the same page in order to get back out there to search for Riley as soon as possible," Reese prepped. "These truths are important: I brought you back to New Bern to check on your son after you found out he wasn't evacuated as planned. You wanted to make sure he was safe," she asserted, emphasizing the words with her eyes. "These are the things you've been telling me since we met. No one needs to know you had thoughts of evacuating him. That didn't happen and it's no longer relevant. If it comes up, it will only hinder our chances of being involved in this rescue."

"I'm with you," Niles agreed. "Riley's safety *is* the only reason

I came back," he confirmed. "But I thought you didn't want anyone to know you brought me here."

"That ship has sailed," Reese admitted. "We both need to be honest about everything that has transpired since we met although I don't suggest bringing up the condom incident that led to the biker gang fight," she mentioned, hoping to lighten the mood an inkling.

Niles snickered but barely revealed a grin. "I'll keep that between us."

"I don't think anyone will question you as a suspect or else they would have already yanked us out of the water," she explained. "If it was to happen, remember you have the right to remain silent and the right to an attorney."

"Why would they think of me as a suspect?" Niles rebutted.

"When a child goes missing, foul play is always considered," Reese explained. "Anyone involved should be questioned so that they can be ruled out as a suspect. Obviously, this situation is unique because of the hurricane and the flooding, but I can guarantee you background checks have been pulled and red flags are being investigated from every possible angle."

"Thanks for the heads up," Niles mentioned.

"Remember, your plan was to stay with Riley and Eden as long as she agreed and I was going to find a hotel room," Reese reminded him. "If anyone asks what our plan was if Eden said you needed to leave, we were going to take shelter wherever we could find a safe place. That's what we would have had to do."

"What if they ask why I busted open the door at Eden's house?"

"I don't think that question will arise for a while if ever," she responded. "If it does, tell the truth. No one answered your knocks and you were afraid they were in danger."

"Okay."

"Based on everything that happened after we arrived in New Bern, you have the opportunity to be completely honest about the entire situation," she reminded him. Telling the truth was the most crucial piece of this puzzle. "If they question us together, let me take the lead."

Reese wanted to lean across the center console and kiss Niles North but she knew this wasn't the time nor the place. There was no telling who was watching from one of the windows or doors, and she didn't want to have to explain anything she didn't have to.

A few moments later, they grabbed their bags, hurried through the rain, and entered the building using the same door they watched the others use. Inside, there were small clusters of first responders scattered haphazardly, but two in particular stood out as they made a beeline toward Reese and Niles as if they'd been waiting for their entrance.

"Detective Kirby, I presume," a tall, solidly built man greeted as the gentleman to his right handed each of them a dry towel. Both looked exhausted.

"Yes," Reese answered, reaching out her hand to meet him after toweling off her face and arms.

Within twenty seconds, they found out this man, Captain Jensen, was with the fire department and currently in charge at the station although in emergency situations like this the police and fire departments shared unified command. The other gentleman, Captain Stark, was the ranking police officer at this location, and the two of these men explained that the fire and police chiefs were at the command center on the other side of town with the emergency operations director.

"This is Niles North," Reese introduced.

"Mr. North, I am terribly sorry that your son is missing," Captain Jensen pleaded. "Please know that every member of our team is doing everything in their power to bring Riley home safely," he promised. Reese appreciated the gentleman calling Riley by name, and she knew Niles would, too, if his mind was clear enough to realize it. "While you all have been out there braving the elements, we have been helping support here with research, planning, and prepping for whatever it takes to complete this rescue."

"Thank you," Niles offered sincerely while still holding a dry towel in his hand as water dripped from every inch of his body creating random pools near his feet.

"I imagine the two of you are cold, hungry, and sleepy," Captain Stark assumed. "We have hot showers, warm food, and beds available. Just let us know which you need first and we'll point you in the right direction."

Reese was relieved that they were receiving true southern hospitality instead of a barrage of questions.

"I just want to find my son," Niles responded.

"I understand," Captain Jensen replied. "A little bit of rest and nutrition might give you the needed energy to get back out there once the storm allows."

"I'm not hungry," Niles uttered.

Reese chimed in, knowing Niles needed to make as few decisions as possible right now. "Maybe you can show us the showers and beds, then after we settle in we can nibble on some food if that's okay," she mentioned, hoping she could talk Niles into at least snacking on something.

The two men gave a brief tour of the firehouse. None of them stepped into the rooms housing the showers, but it sounded like they were similar to gym locker rooms based on the descriptions given. There were a couple of sleeping areas with bunk beds lining the walls on either side as well as a stack of cots in one of the corners. Niles and Reese learned they could each grab one at any time and set it up wherever felt most comfortable. Even though the lights in those rooms were off, enough trickled in from the hallway to make out that people occupied some beds. Reese knew no matter where they slept, if they even attempted to sleep, it would be difficult to drown out the constant noise of the hurricane as well as the hustle and bustle of the busy fire department. Regardless, it would be nice to close her eyes and rest although she had no idea if Niles would be able to stay still.

When they made it to the commons area where there were tables surrounded by chairs as well as two long rectangular-shaped tables covered with food, the ranking officer nonchalantly said, "Once the two of you eat a bite and freshen up, we'd like to ask some questions which might help with the rescue. It won't take up much of your time then you can get some shut-eye."

A few moments later, Reese and Niles stood alone together for the first time since entering the building.

"Let's take showers," Reese suggested. Even though the drysuit kept the outside water at bay, the clothes beneath were pasted to her body with sweat making her feel icky. After all the in-water work Niles did, she could imagine how much better he would feel to tear out of his soaking wet clothes.

"I guess a shower will help pass the time," Niles huffed, knowing he didn't want to stand around and talk to the strangers in the room.

Niles and Reese headed to separate showers and peeled their respective clothes off one piece at a time. Standing below a stream of warm water, Reese felt the tension pouring off her shoulders and spiraling into the drain below. On the opposite side of the blocked wall between him and Reese, Niles stood underneath a steady spray with his hands flat on the walls barely holding up the weight of his own body as tears streamed down his face before falling near his bare feet with the hot water. He tried not to let his cries, rising with the steam, become audible but a few times he could not hold back the sounds of a father who felt as helpless as the babies he once held. He had no idea Reese was within five feet of him on the other side of the cinder blocks swallowing his sobs. He tried praying but wasn't sure what to say at first. Eventually, he begged God to let his son be safe—somewhere, somehow. He pleaded with Him to comfort Riley wherever he was at this very moment. With his eyes closed, Niles imagined his son being pelted with rainwater but knew it wasn't warm like the shower above his own head. He knew the winds were whipping, and he wondered where the storm took his child. Sniffling, he asked God to let the hurricane lighten up so they could restart the search.

Suddenly, Niles felt a calm come over him, and the image of a rainbow flashed through his mind. He wasn't sure of the meaning or if he even liked feeling anything other than a desire to search for his son; nonetheless, it seemed as though God was listening because he instantly felt a sense of peace.

After slipping on a fresh set of clothes, Niles met Reese in the hallway where he wrapped his arms around her. He wanted to kiss her lips, but his thoughts mirrored her earlier ones, so he fought off the urge.

"Feel some better?" she asked in the softest, sweetest voice sounding more like a librarian than a police officer.

"A little," he proclaimed.

"Let's grab a couple of cots, find a spot where we can camp out later, and leave our bags there while we grab a bite to eat," she suggested.

"That works."

After trekking around the fire station for a few minutes, Reese and Niles discovered a small nook where they nestled their cots and left their belongings.

"You think our things will be safe here?"

"The only thing that isn't safe in a building full of firefighters and police officers is doughnuts," Reese laughed.

Niles snickered and a faint smile fell across his face. "That's funny," he laughed. "However, I am surprised to hear those words out of a cop's mouth."

"Doughnuts are something we joke about amongst each other just as much as citizens tease us about them when we're not around," she admitted. "I figure tonight you are one of us."

Niles appreciated her words more than she knew. "Thanks," he offered simply. "I have a funny story about a cop and doughnuts that I'll have to tell you sometime."

"Now seems like a good time," Reese mentioned, hoping to keep the conversation flowing so Niles's mind could relax.

A couple of officers walked by and said hello before making their way around the next corner.

"Maybe later," Niles suggested.

"Let's grab some food," Reese offered in response then started walking toward the buffet-style table they saw earlier. It wasn't quite Wally's—the buffet restaurant in East Ridge that her dad loved so much—but there were options from barbecue to ham sandwiches to chips.

"I'm not all that hungry," Niles claimed, standing over food he would normally devour.

"You need to eat something," Reese encouraged handing him a paper plate even though she could tell he didn't want it.

"I'll try," he agreed.

As Niles and Reese worked their way down the line, a couple other people stepped up to the table for a bite to eat as well. They greeted one another with a friendly *hello* and then filled their respective plates. Niles placed a handful of chips on his plate along with peanuts and crackers.

"The peanuts will give you a little protein," Reese pointed out.

"This is what I need the most," Niles revealed, reaching his hand into a cooler filled with ice and plucking out a soda.

"Caffeine, huh?"

"Yep."

"I better stick with water," Reese decided.

A few minutes later, they worked their way back to the cots where they each sat cross-legged holding their plates in their laps.

"This barbecue tastes different from what I'm used to," Reese pointed out as she held a bun filled with stringy meat in her hand after taking a couple of bites.

"Eastern North Carolina barbecue has a vinegar base," Niles educated.

"That explains a lot," Reese responded, staring at the sandwich.

"Do you like it?"

"The jury is still out," she answered with a smile.

Niles smirked. "It's the best barbecue in the country."

"If you say so."

"What type of barbecue is your favorite?" he inquired.

"I like what we have in Tennessee," she divulged.

"Memphis-style barbecue?"

Reese shrugged her shoulders. "I guess," she answered after taking another bite. "I'm not an expert on the subject."

"If it's served in Tennessee, it's most likely Memphis style. In the United States, there are four primary types of barbecue: Carolina, Memphis, Texas, and Kansas City," Niles shared. "There are a number of subtypes linked to particular geographical areas but those are the main ones. Different styles can be found in each area, but it's typically based on geography."

"How do you know all of this?"

"Well, barbecue is pretty popular in Eastern North Carolina. In fact, Moore's Olde Tyme Barbecue in New Bern is in the Guinness Book of World Records for making the largest open barbecue sandwich."

"That's pretty cool."

"I even had some of the famous sandwich," Niles shared.

"Really?"

"Moore's held the event in conjunction with New Bern's 300th Anniversary celebration," he explained. "I think I was about ten years old at the time."

"You are a part of history," Reese pointed out with a smile.

"I've never thought of it that way but I guess so."

The conversation ebbed and flowed as Niles nibbled on the contents of his plate while Reese finished the sandwich, baked beans, and hush puppies. She could tell he didn't have much appetite, but she was glad to see him eating something. The soda seemed to give him a surge of energy, and he mentioned several times how he was ready to get back to the search.

"Will you tell me the doughnut story now?"

"Sure," Niles agreed.

"I bet Mickey is involved," she guessed.

"Of course."

"This should be good."

"It is," Niles guaranteed. "Mickey, me, and some other friends once participated in a big mixed martial arts tournament in Atlanta. When we left the arena, all of us decided we wanted doughnuts after eating healthy for months. While sitting in a traffic jam in the parking lot, our mouths basically salivated. Mickey drove and I sat in the back. As we came up on a parking attendant directing traffic, I told Mickey to ask for directions to the closest Krispy Kreme," Niles snickered as he thought ahead in the story. "The guy had his back to us as Mickey slowed the vehicle to a halt and then asked, 'Hey man, do you know where Krispy Kreme is?'" Niles said, laughing harder all of a sudden. Reese grinned in response to the anticipation and because seeing Niles laugh made her feel good inside. "When the man turned around, Mickey noticed what I'd realized before asking him to stop: the guy he thought was a parking attendant was a cop," Niles revealed, then laughed hard enough that he had to pause the story to regain composure. "The officer turned around and asked, 'Is that a cop joke?' Mickey doesn't usually get embarrassed, but his face turned as red as a raw steak that night. He stumbled over his words, saying, 'No sir, it's not.' Without missing a beat, the policeman responded with, 'Is it a fat joke?'" Niles explained doubling over and nearly falling face-first into the crumbs on his plate. Reese laughed nearly as steadily, temporarily forgetting the seriousness surrounding them. "You see, the man was overweight too but I hadn't even thought about that when I tricked Mickey into asking a cop for directions to a doughnut shop. Fumbling over his words again, Mickey pleaded, 'No, no, I promise, we just want doughnuts.' He explained that we fought in the tournament and had been on a strict diet for a while. Luckily, the guy believed him because he quickly let his face relax and gave us turn by turn directions to the Krispy Kreme he guaranteed served the best-tasting doughnuts in town."

"That's so funny," Reese laughed. "I can't wait to tell your story to Dominguez, Brown, and Johnson."

"He was the coolest cop I've ever met," Niles noted, "except for you, of course," he added with a wink.

"Awe, you're so sweet," Reese declared.

"Just like the doughnuts."

Niles and Reese shared a few more laughs, and she found herself wishing the laughter would lull them to sleep, but it didn't although she placed her guardian angel's shadow box near where she rested to comfort her as always. The mood soon became somber again as reality settled in and kept them from sleeping even though they tried. The noises in the station weren't as bad as expected, but the noises in Niles's head were so loud Reese could see them in his aqua green eyes every time he opened them and stared at her without speaking a word. She wanted to cuddle up next to him like a teddy bear and hold him tight or let him hold her, but once again the moment was perfect but the setting wasn't. When Captain Jensen and Captain Stark showed up with clipboards in hand, she remembered exactly why it wasn't.

31

"Detective Kirby, would you mind accompanying Captain Jensen while I go over some questions with Mr. North?" Captain Stark requested.

Assuming this question would arise, Reese looked him in the eyes as he spoke. If she were in his shoes, she would want to separate the two of them as well. Not because of suspicion but because Niles's answers would likely be a little different based on her presence plus she possessed the skills to deflect if he became stumped. She knew the captain understood that.

"Mr. North is having a rather difficult time at the moment, and I would prefer to remain with him if that is acceptable."

The officer looked at her for a moment then at Niles and eventually at Captain Jensen. "It's fine by me," he agreed.

His response surprised Reese as she expected a push in the other direction. Maybe he realized how comfortable she and Niles were on the small cots only separated by a couple of feet of floor space.

"I'll get straight to the questions so we don't keep the two of you up," Stark said. "When was the last time you saw your son?" he asked Niles.

"A couple of days ago before I evacuated."

"Can you be more specific?"

"I don't even know what today is," Niles admitted frankly before shuffling beneath the thin blanket covering his aching body.

"Technically, it's Friday but it kind of still seems like Thursday since none of us have slept," Stark pointed out.

Reese wanted to interrupt and give the answer for him yet decided to let him handle the first question independently.

"I saw him Wednesday morning," Niles finally articulated after counting back the days in his mind.

"Where did you last see him?"

"At his mother's house where I dropped him off."

"Where did you go then?" Stark asked as he scribbled a couple of notes.

"I headed to Hickory."

"Hickory, North Carolina?"

Reese smirked on the inside thinking about details.

"Yes."

"Was anyone else with you at that time?"

"My friend Mickey."

"What is Mickey's last name?"

"Banks."

Reese continued to smile on the inside, knowing the officer already knew Mickey's last name along with his birthdate, arrest record, and a lot more.

"So, Mickey Banks would be able to verify you dropped off Riley with his mother Eden Franks on the morning of Wednesday, September 12th?"

Niles furrowed his brow. "Yes, of course."

"Where is Mr. Banks now?"

"In Hickory as far as I know," Niles testified.

"You and Mr. Banks drove to Hickory together?"

"Yes."

"Whose vehicle did you take?"

"Mine."

"Where is your vehicle now?"

"In Hickory."

The officer peered up. "How did you get from Hickory to New Bern?"

Feeling a sense of guilt as though he was about to rat out Reese, Niles glanced in her direction.

"I drove Mr. North here," Reese chimed in confidently.

The officer looked at Reese then back at Niles. "Is that correct, Mr. North?"

"Yes."

"Can you explain how and why you drove your vehicle to Hickory to evacuate Hurricane Florence yet ended up coming back to New Bern as a passenger with Detective Kirby on the day of the hurricane?"

"I found out my son hadn't been evacuated as I'd earlier been promised he would."

"How did you discover this news?"

"From Grandyma," Niles explained. "Riley's grandmother," he clarified.

Reese felt the need to add to the answer. "She is Ms. Franks's mother."

"Is this correct, Mr. North?"

"It is."

"How do you know Detective Kirby?" the officer asked changing the subject as he wrote on his clipboard.

For some reason, Niles immediately thought of the condom comment Reese made earlier and if things didn't seem so serious he would have laughed. This guy started to remind him of his drill instructors and he didn't like it even though he knew the man was just doing his job as Reese mentioned he would.

"We met in Hickory."

Niles and Reese spent the next few minutes explaining how they met, leaving out the previously discussed parts.

"Detective Kirby, is your superior aware that you transported Mr. North to New Bern today?"

Reese's eyes met the officer's eyes. If this question had been asked earlier in the day, she would have been forced to answer no, but since the truth came out on the phone with Captain Lawson tonight, she was able to say, "Yes." She was fairly certain her captain already told the local authorities this same information, and she only hoped they hadn't asked him nor would they ask her if she had his permission.

"Mr. North, when you arrived in New Bern earlier today, how did you plan to help keep your son safe during the hurricane?" Stark asked.

Reese felt the urge to point out they technically arrived in New Bern yesterday since he was so specific about the days earlier. However, she decided to let it slide because his interrogation had been relatively cordial.

Niles explained the plan to ask Eden if he could stay there with her and Riley.

"Do you think your ex-wife would have let you stay?"

Niles shrugged. "There was only one way to find out," he answered. Earlier, he explained about trying to get through to her on the phone on the way home from Hickory.

"What if she declined? What would you have done then?"

"I would have found a safe place to stay," Niles responded.

"Detective Kirby, where were you planning to go if Mr. North stayed with Ms. Franks and his son?"

"I was contemplating finding a place to stay in New Bern or heading to Wilmington for my hurricane assignment if the weather allowed."

"Thank you for coming to North Carolina to assist with hurricane rescues," he observed.

"My privilege," Reese offered.

"If Mr. North's ex-wife denied him the right to stay with her and their son, where would you have gone then, Detective?" Stark asked, adding a twist to the previous question.

"I would have given Mr. North a ride to a safe place to stay."

"Would you have stayed at that same place?"

"That's impossible to speculate," she answered. "It depends on the place, the weather conditions, and other factors I can't know given that this did not occur."

"I understand."

Reese was glad he didn't continue barking up that tree because she wasn't going to budge any more than this building budged for the hurricane currently pushing against its sturdy foundation.

"What made the two of you decide to put the swift water rescue boat in the water and head to the grandparent's home?" Stark quizzed while Jensen continued to watch the back and forth like a spectator at a ping pong match.

Reese noted that he didn't address either of them specifically so she chose to jump on the answer. "When Niles discovered no one was at Ms. Franks' home, he assumed they went to the grandparent's house to ride out the storm as they'd done in the past," she explained. "The only way to get there was by boat."

"I would ask why you didn't call the authorities but considering your training, I understand why you felt comfortable taking Mr. North to his son," he mentioned. "However, I am not sure it was a safe decision."

"I made what I thought was the best decision at the time based on the circumstances," Reese acknowledged.

"Fair enough. Mr. North, when you arrived at the grandparent's home, was your son there?"

Niles's face became as tight as the rope he tied around the porch column upon arriving at Grandyma's. "No," he responded simply with clouds covering his eyes.

"Detective Kirby, you never saw the child either?"

"No, sir."

"Who all was at the home?"

"Eden and some guy," Niles answered.

"Do you know his name?"

"I don't recall," Niles answered.

"Kirk Donaldson," Reese confirmed.

"Have you previously met Kirk Donaldson?" Captain Stark asked Niles.

Niles shook his head east to west. "I don't think so."

"Do you know if Kirk Donaldson has been around your son in the past?"

Niles shrugged his shoulders. "I'm not positive but I don't recall ever hearing his name from Eden or Riley."

"Once we finish up here, if you happen to remember meeting Kirk in the past or hearing anything about him, please let me know."

"I will."

Captain Stark asked a handful of other questions related to the timing of the evening, and Reese answered each without hesitancy. Her job was to remember every minute detail possible in situations like this. It was often the little things that led to the big answers, and this rescue was the most important one in which she'd ever been involved. Even though she didn't know Niles North well, she now considered him a friend, possibly more, which made finding Riley personal just like finding the man who killed her father had been personal.

When Captain Stark and Captain Jensen walked away with the answers they came looking for, Reese felt confident about the responses provided. She thought Niles handled himself appropriately especially considering the circumstances. However, there was one red flag jumping around in her mind. It was the way Stark posed the questions about Kirk Donaldson.

"Do you have any idea where Eden would know Kirk from?" Reese asked Niles.

"No. Why?"

"Just curious," she answered before plucking her phone from her pocket. This wasn't her investigation but it didn't mean she couldn't do some digging of her own she decided as the light from the screen illuminated her face. Within a couple of minutes, Reese pulled a background check on Kirk Donaldson and as she read through the profile, she soon discovered why the ranking officer was so interested in this man.

32

"Niles, I need to use the restroom," Reese shared before lifting her body off the cot, somewhat surprised her muscles cooperated after finally relaxing.

"Okay," he responded with his eyes wide open.

Reese wandered down the darkened hallway heading for the commons area. Once there, she searched the faces in the room but didn't see the one she hoped to find. Thankfully, she spotted the woman who assisted in her boat earlier.

"Have you seen Captain Stark?" Reese asked.

"He's probably in Captain Jensen's office," the lady presumed.

Reese then followed the woman to an office near the front of the building.

"Thanks," Reese offered, then knocked on the closed door as the lady walked away.

"Come in," she heard a voice call out.

After opening the door, Jensen greeted her with a smile. "Detective Kirby, I figured your eyes would be shut by now," he assumed out loud.

Sitting at the other end of the desk in a padded chair, Stark stared at a laptop screen until the moment he heard her name.

Reese directed her next question at him. "What do you know

about Kirk Donaldson?" she asked.

"Why do you ask?" he probed.

"You seemed to show an interest in him," she pointed out.

"As you are well aware, my job is to have an interest in anyone associated with this case."

"Have you pulled a background check on him?" Reese asked even though she knew the answer.

"This isn't my first rodeo," he responded with a faint snicker.

Quietly, Jensen's eyes danced between Reese and the officer as the two went back and forth.

"Mine either," Reese reciprocated. "Which is why I'm wondering why you haven't questioned him face-to-face."

"You can rest assured that Mr. Donaldson has been questioned," he shared.

"By whom?"

Captain Stark furrowed his brow. "By me," he declared. "I spoke with him on the phone hours ago while you all were out searching for Riley."

"You are comfortable with him being at that house?" she investigated with concern in her eyes.

He swallowed. "I am not comfortable with much of anything about this situation," he informed Reese. "We are searching for a lost five-year-old in the middle of one of the most devastating hurricanes New Bern, North Carolina, has ever experienced. So, if you are asking if I would have rather questioned Mr. Donaldson face-to-face, then yes, I would have."

"Does Eden know about the other investigation into Kirk Donaldson?"

"I would assume she doesn't; at least not unless he has told her himself," he shared. "As you know, the information we are privy to is confidential."

Reese instantly realized that *we* meant he knew she pulled a background check. "You don't think the mother of the missing five-year-old needs to know that the man who was in the house when her son went missing has been linked to kidnapping cases?"

The officer remained quiet for a moment and the look covering his face made Reese believe he'd been contemplating the same question. "The lead singer in the band in which Mr. Donaldson plays has been linked to two kidnapping cases; therefore, the entire band is under the umbrella of the investigation," he clarified. "It doesn't mean Donaldson is guilty of anything." After that statement, he paused for a moment and shifted his lips. "That said, of course, I think Ms. Franks would want to know," he agreed. "Believe me, I asked her every question I could think of that might possibly surface a red flag in relation to Kirk Donaldson's situation. None of her answers led me to believe he is involved in any criminal activity regarding this case just like none of the answers she gave about Niles North raised concern," he shared. "Your friend's background, or more specifically his military record, isn't flawless either, you know."

Reese's nostrils flared. "I realize that but he is the child's father and the ding from his past has nothing to do with minors."

"That's why I didn't pull him out of the water although many would argue his presence on your boat was a bad idea."

"I can promise you Niles is equipped for the job."

"I believe you," he commented with a nod of his head. "Does Mr. North know about Mr. Donaldson's background?"

Reese pursed her lips. "If he did, I can promise you he would be on the way back to that house right now regardless of the severity of this hurricane."

The wind blew so hard outside that from inside the fire station it sounded like they were in a vacuum.

"If you tell Mr. North the information we are discussing, I can't allow him to go back out on the water."

"That's the only reason I haven't told him," she acknowledged, "although he deserves to know just like Eden does."

"I agree."

"Based on what you know, you're confident Kirk Donaldson doesn't have anything to do with Riley's disappearance?" Reese asked specifically, honing in on his eyes while awaiting the answer.

"If I did, I guarantee you he would be in handcuffs right now," he revealed, then exhaled slowly before speaking again. "I believe the boy is in the water," he added with a disparaging look.

Although Reese wasn't completely sure what Stark meant by the latter statement, she was glad he hadn't made it in front of Niles. If Riley was literally still in the water, his chances of survival were slim. All along, her gut told her Riley was alive, but she began to believe there was something she was missing. "Let's pray he's safe," she finally uttered as her brain moved a hundred miles an hour.

The officer folded his arms and cocked his head. "You crossed paths with Mr. Donaldson, did anything about him stand out to you?" he probed.

Reese recalled their encounter. At the time, she didn't know Kirk's past but that hadn't stopped her from watching for abnormalities. "He seemed frightened and concerned," she shared. "He was cooperative and gave his first and last name as well as his cell phone number so we could stay in touch during the rescue."

"Did he contact you at any point?"

"No, he didn't. He texted Eden some while she was on the boat with us but just to check on how things were going."

"I can tell you cross your t's and dot your i's," Stark referenced. "Did your gut tell you this could be anything other than a missing person's case?"

Reese slowly guided her head from side to side. "No, nothing," she confirmed but now she was second-guessing herself. What if she missed something? Things at Grandyma's house were so chaotic upon arrival. The hurricane wreaked havoc and Eden acted hysterically on the front porch.

"If you think of anything, just let me know," were the words he left with her.

On the way out Reese pulled the door closed then inched her way through the unfamiliar hallways. How could she not share the news about Kirk with Niles? He deserved to know. At the same time, she knew it would only intensify his worry. His knowing wouldn't help the investigation; in fact, it would probably hinder it. If Niles knew, there was no doubt in her mind he would plead with her to take him back to Grandyma's house immediately, and when she disagreed, she wouldn't put it past him to attempt to take the boat on his own. Parental protective instincts were stronger than hurricanes, and Niles's seemed to be on steroids.

When Reese made it back to the cots after a pit stop at the restroom, she hoped to find Niles fast asleep, but instead he was sitting up with his back propped against the concrete wall staring into space with so much focus that Reese wasn't sure he saw her standing there.

"Niles," she whispered.

His eyes rose but his body didn't budge. "Yeah," he offered.

"Are you okay?" she checked then realized it was a dumb question.

"No."

Reese settled in near him but made sure not to get too close even though she wanted to hold him again and promise everything would be okay. "What's on your mind?" she asked gently.

His cheeks lifted as his eyes bubbled over. "He's out there somewhere and we're in here, doing nothing."

"We're waiting out the worst of this storm so that we *can do something*," she reminded him all the while realizing the inadequacy of the response.

"What if I never see my son again?" Niles considered out loud through a sniffle.

At that instant, Reese's emotions controlled her body and

before she knew it, tears streamed down her chapped cheeks. The wind took a toll on them although she hadn't realized it until standing beneath the showerhead earlier thinking about what the wind could be doing to a vulnerable five-year-old. She'd thought about having kids one day, hoped to, but this was one of those moments in life where something clicked and she knew she wanted to know the kind of love this man felt for his child. Even though this was literally one of the saddest moments she'd ever experienced, Niles's love for Riley radiated off him like the scent of a breathtaking bouquet of flowers.

Letting go, Reese draped her arms over his shoulders and hugged him tightly. "I'll do everything in my power to make sure you get to hold Riley in your arms again," she whispered into his ear. It was relatively dark in their little nook, and the moment she decided that one of them would hear if anyone approached, she let her lips settle on his cheek and rested them there as she squeezed a bit tighter.

Niles's eyelids collapsed as the warmth of Reese's body spread across his own like a fire jumping from one house to the next. He could feel the moisture on her lips as they lingered on his face tracing his skin like a tender massage. There was something he loved about her confidence, something about her touch that set him at ease even while the inside of his body screamed at the top of its lungs. He wanted out of here, wanted to fight the storm and all of his demons together with this woman whom he barely knew. She was strong yet soft, forceful yet calm. He never met anyone like Reese Kirby in all his life, and he couldn't help but think God sent her to him at just the right time. A piece of him wanted to be selfish and wonder what tomorrow might hold for the two of them, but all he could think about at the moment was how grateful he was that she was willing to risk her life to help him find his son.

Somehow, eventually, Niles and Reese both fell asleep beneath separate blankets. Under an extra sheet Reese plucked from the pile earlier, their fingers hid intertwined like two strands of rope. Staring at one another, they whispered until neither of them could hold their eyes open any longer. Reese thought Niles would never let his body rest, but she made a pact with herself to talk to him until he did. She knew his mind wouldn't wander as much if she could keep a conversation streaming. In a way, it felt like they were in the boat again, and as she drifted off to sleep, Reese couldn't help but think about how hiding seemed to be their thing.

33

Niles nearly swung his fists when a loud voice startled him awake. Upon moving the fingers on his right hand, he realized just in the nick of time they were still attached to Reese's, and as he glared up to discover Captain Stark's face, his eyes instantly darted to the sheet between him and Reese. Like laser pointers, Reese's eyes met his at that very spot. Thankfully, it appeared their hands somehow remained covered for however long they slept, and upon realizing such, each of them simultaneously glanced back up at Captain Stark and Captain Jensen as the two stood over them.

Niles didn't care what these people thought about him and Reese, but he didn't want them trying to tell him he couldn't go back out into the water. There weren't enough first responders in this building to keep him from searching for his son once the conditions were safe.

"The hurricane has let up slightly and we're almost ready to deploy the swift water rescue teams," Jensen announced hastily.

Seconds later, Niles's and Reese's fingers became untwined carefully as though they practiced the maneuver.

"We'll be ready in just a few minutes," Reese announced, lifting her body from a cot that seemed way more comfortable last night when she was completely wiped out.

Niles followed suit, and his eyes, like Reese's, were still half asleep but adrenaline was already kicking into high gear.

"Everyone is meeting in the conference room for a briefing in ten minutes," Stark shared. "Visit the restroom, grab a bite to eat, and meet us there."

Niles and Reese each darted to the locker rooms where they'd left their respective gear. In a matter of minutes, they fully dressed and sat around an oblong table with the members of the other teams. Reese found herself wishing Dominguez, Johnson, Brown, and Captain Lawson were here. In a way it felt like she'd taken a job with a completely new department; she even began to learn the faces and a handful of the names.

Niles felt awkward sitting around a table with a group of strangers. He never held a position where he met in a conference room although something about the structure of things reminded him of his brief time in the military. Taking in the surroundings, he nibbled on a granola bar Reese threw at him as they hustled through the buffet line on their way here.

Several televisions mounted to the front wall showed hurricane footage from various stations although the audio remained muted. When Jensen and Stark walked in and stood at the head of the table, the rest of the room suddenly fell silent. Captain Jensen spoke first: "Florence made landfall near Wrightsville Beach at 7:15 this morning," he announced.

Reese reminded herself that landfall meant the eye of the hurricane reached land, and upon glancing at her watch she realized it happened only fifteen minutes ago. The storm itself obviously ravaged the North Carolina coast for quite some time.

"We have probably experienced about half of this monster," Stark declared, pointing at a screen showing still images which he began to click through as he talked. "The good news is the storm is weakening as it moves inland. The bad news is it's moving slowly, so we're going to be fighting against deadly conditions most of the day."

Niles stared at the screen where the radar image showed the storm covering eastern North Carolina. When he saw the hurricane symbol in the bottom corner, it reminded him of Mickey's comment about using it as their landscaping company's logo. He wondered what Mickey was up to now. He found himself wishing they evacuated Riley when they had the chance, then all of them would be having fun in Hickory now or maybe dodging the police. At almost any other time in his life such a thought would have made him snicker because at the moment a police officer literally gave him a report and instructions while he sat next to a detective who was now his friend and maybe something more as well as being surrounded by a room full of first responders. Last night he and Mickey messaged back and forth several times, but he hadn't found an opportunity to tell his best friend anything other than what everyone else knew—they were still searching.

"Today, there will be new hazards," Jensen revealed. "Obviously, no one has been able to clear the roadways other than the National Guard who has been clearing the direct route being used to evacuate people who walked out of flooded areas over the past few hours. They patrolled the waterline which pushed its way into our city. So, things are going to look a little different. You're going to encounter additional obstacles, but you've trained for pretty much everything out there."

Except for me, Niles thought to himself but no amount of training could have prepared him for what Hurricane Florence was putting him through. On the contrary, no obstacles would stop him from searching for his son. He would have never halted the search if these people hadn't forced it, regardless of the conditions.

Jensen and Stark went over assignment details that would disperse teams all over the county and outlined the areas that experienced the worst flooding. "As expected, countless rescue calls have been coming in around the clock from the neighborhoods I've shown on the screen," the officer explained. "Pretty much everyone in town is without power and a large portion of the city limits are flooded. Rescues are expected to take place all day."

Niles listened but in all honesty he didn't care much about the random people who were stranded. They were dumb enough not to heed the warning to evacuate in the first place. However, his five-year-old son hadn't been allowed to make a decision. His careless mother who must have decided to stay in town to be with the punk rocker-looking dude made the choice for him. Niles still wanted to punch him in the face. More so, he longed to get out of this stuffy room and into the water.

Thankfully, moments later, the meeting adjourned and Reese's team was the first out the door which ended up meaning they were the first to come across a downed tree covering the entire roadway. Reese jammed the brakes and by the time the Hummer came to a stop, Niles sprang into action. Yesterday, he spotted a chainsaw in the rear of the Humvee, and now, once he hopped out of the vehicle it only took him a few seconds to yank the cord, instantly setting the chain into motion.

Watching Niles work the piece of machinery with precision—cutting chunks of wood for the others to roll away while slicing the next—Reese found it hard to believe how the sounds of the hurricane nearly drowned out the chainsaw's roar. In addition to that, the wind whipped the sawdust around, shooting some of the pieces like BBs. Thankfully, everyone wore headgear and goggles at this point, so they didn't have to dodge the particles of wood although the impact still stung a little. Their biggest concern was another one of the bending trees snapping or giving way to the overly saturated ground. Still, they didn't have time to monitor every potential hazard. Even if they did, every tree mirroring the roadside looked as though it could fall at any time.

When they first started clearing the roadway, the rain pelting their bodies seemed colder than the last time they were out, but the feeling diminished as their body temperatures climbed with movement. A couple of other teams showed up, and with so many hands and two more chainsaws, it didn't take long to remove a section of the tree large enough for the vehicles to fit through. Thankfully, that was the last time they had to come to a complete stop although Reese steered around several trash cans, a large sign, and a stray dock near the waterline.

When they reached the new entry point, the distance the flooding came into the city in just a matter of hours astonished the teams. Getting the boat into the water went like clockwork, and once again Reese became impressed with how well Niles and two other people she never practiced with before worked together on what was by no means an easy task for even the most experienced crew. Although reports said the hurricane decreased slightly, the conditions still seemed severe. Waves rolled across downtown streets, the wind tossed objects in every direction, and the rain made it hard to see fifteen feet ahead.

Reese carefully guided the watercraft through the familiar streets as they once again began to search every nook and cranny as they had throughout the night. Even though it wasn't as dark as it had been the last time they were in the water, violent gray clouds covered the sky and the rain they dispensed made it hard to see. Niles still used the spotlight and yelled out his son's name as often as possible even though his voice was hoarse.

"Have you heard from Eden?" Reese hollered out to Niles.

Before they left the station, he texted Eden to let her know the search was continuing, but she hadn't responded as of the time he stepped out of the Hummer. He rechecked his phone. "No," he answered.

Reese pushed the throttle a little deeper and kept the boat heading in the direction of Grandyma's. Although she hadn't clued anyone in on her plan, she wanted to stop there yet make it seem random. She needed to ask Kirk Donaldson a few questions and study his eyes as he responded. However, she would need to get him alone, which might not be a simple task given the circumstances.

34

pon reaching Grandyma's house without any major disturbances along the way other than the new normal—randomly floating objects, flying debris, and choppy water—Reese steadied the boat near the porch. The river's surge still flowed through the backside of the home and out of the front although the water level had risen to the point where it gushed out of the lower portions of the same windows people climbed in and out of up to this point. The front door was completely off its hinges and Niles wondered if it was the one they passed floating on the surface a few hundred yards down the street. All types of items were in the water; things a person would never imagine like porch swings, plastic playhouses, and gardening tools. The scene surrounding them was surreal.

Niles hopped into the nearly chest-high water and carried the rope line toward the house ultimately tying it off on the same column as before. Eventually, he and Reese ended up on the porch together in knee-deep water while their team members remained with the boat to keep it secure.

"We won't be in there long," Reese told them before jumping out. "I just want to check on Eden and Kirk since we haven't heard from them this morning and find out if they have any new information that might help the search."

After entering the opening where the front door once stood, Reese inched as close to Niles's ear as possible. "I am going to pull Kirk away so that you and Eden can talk uninterrupted for a few minutes. The two of you are battling the same emotions right now, and I think it would do both of you some good to connect on that level. Even though you are divorced, she needs you," Reese reminded Niles, knowing he probably needed her too even if he wouldn't admit it. However, she couldn't help but wonder if they'd spend the time consoling one another or arguing. Regardless, she needed to question Kirk Donaldson.

Niles furrowed his brow then it eased back a little. "Sure," he agreed, shrugging his shoulders.

A moment later, both Reese and Niles began calling out Eden's name. Reese called out Kirk's name as well, but Niles didn't seem interested in doing so. She knew from experience that people should never enter a house other than their own without letting the occupants know who they are and why they are there. Looters would likely take advantage of this hurricane's devastation when the winds and the flooding calmed. Still, she didn't want herself and Niles to be mistaken as intruders. If the bottom floor wasn't covered in floodwater, she would have started calling out names the second they came through the entrance.

Trudging through several feet of water in the house was a leg and abdominal workout; however, Reese and Niles eventually made it to the staircase but without a response. With openings on either side of the home allowing the wind to whip through, Reese wasn't surprised Eden and Kirk couldn't hear their voices. When talking to Niles moments ago, Reese could barely make out his response. As their flashlights lit up the stairwell, Reese noticed a trail of water leading to the top of the steps and beyond, then she caught a glimpse of something glistening a different color—red. Blood, it looked like blood, she quickly analyzed, and at that moment she immediately shifted her shooting hand to her pistol.

Seconds later, a head popped around the corner of a door frame on the right side of the hallway. Simultaneously, both Reese's and Niles's eyes darted in that direction, and as Reese aimed her flashlight directly at the person's face, she gripped her firearm, ready to pull if needed.

"Who's there?" the voice asked, apparently blinded by the beam of light.

It was Kirk.

"Detective Kirby," Reese stated loudly and clearly, realizing he must not have heard them up to this point; he'd probably only come out upon seeing the lights. "Keep your head where I can see it and show me your hands," she demanded, knowing she didn't want to take any chances.

"Okay," Kirk clamored as he complied.

Reese kept her eyes on Kirk as she imagined the expression on Niles's face was one of confusion based on her aggression. She wasn't sure if he'd seen the blood, and she hadn't had time to show him or say anything.

"Is Eden in there?" Reese questioned with a few more steps to climb. Niles was two steps behind.

"Yeah," he hollered down with his empty hands raised toward the ceiling which was already caked with moisture.

"Step out into the hallway and then slowly walk backward a few steps for me," Reese insisted. She could see the fear and the question in Kirk's eyes.

A moment after Kirk followed her instructions, Eden emerged from the room. Although Reese didn't suspect her to be involved in any foul behavior, even if Kirk was, she still shifted her eyes between the two of them watching for any signs of aggression.

"What's going on?" Eden asked, realizing something seemed abnormal.

"Why is there blood on the steps and the door jamb?" Reese

quizzed. By now, she'd taken note of the bandage on Kirk's face and assumed a connection which was hopefully harmless but she wanted to be certain.

Kirk and Eden spent the next couple of minutes explaining Kirk's fall, then Reese herded everyone into the bedroom to check out the rest of the scene and ultimately decided the evidence appeared to line up with the story.

Once that surprise was out of the way, Reese continued to steer the conversation filling Kirk and Eden in on the morning briefing. She really had very few new reports to share, but she tried to be as positive as possible.

"Kirk, can you show me around the rest of the upstairs portion of the house while we give Ms. Franks and Mr. North some time to talk about their son?" Reese eventually asked.

Kirk turned to Eden. Reese positioned herself to watch his eyes closely to see if the look he was sharing with her was one of hostility, but it appeared as though his eyes asked for her permission. That was a good sign.

A few moments later, Reese and Kirk stepped into the hallway then began going from room to room.

"I don't think there's any chance Riley is in this house," Kirk stated. "Eden and I, as well as the other search and rescue team, searched every inch of the dwelling a dozen times."

"Where do you think Riley is?" she asked bluntly.

Staring at the floor, Kirk shrugged his shoulders but didn't respond audibly.

"How long have you known Eden?" Reese quizzed. She figured that Niles was probably asking Eden the same question about Kirk right about now.

"We just met."

"When did you meet Riley?"

"A couple days ago," he answered, shining his flashlight into a closet.

"Do you think there is any chance the boy could have been kidnapped?" Reese asked, and based on Kirk's body language, she could tell instantly how the idea made him uncomfortable.

"No."

"Do you know how easy it is to kidnap a child when a parent is distracted?"

Kirk shook his head left to right but once again said nothing.

"There are certain things I am not going to say in front of Ms. Franks," Reese stated, "so I need to make sure you and I are on the same page since you were the only other person here when Riley North went missing."

"Like what?" Kirk asked defensively.

"I'm not going to say anything which might make her think her child was kidnapped, but if you know anything, I need to know it right now."

"I've already told everyone all I know," he claimed. "Eden and I were upstairs. When the power expired, we hurried downstairs to check on Riley. The river was already in the house and he was gone."

"Have you told Eden everything?"

Kirk furrowed his brow. "What do you mean?"

"Have you ever been questioned in connection to a child abduction case?"

Kirk's face turned a shade of red as deep as the blood on the staircase. "I didn't have anything to do with that or with this," he objected.

"Have you told Eden about it?"

"No," he answered, his chest rising and falling as violently as the wind. "That's not something you share with someone when you first meet them."

"Not even when their child goes missing?" she quizzed with her brow furrowed.

"I am an innocent bystander in all of this," he declared.

"Maybe, but if she and Niles find out, they're going to think their child was taken and assume you had something to do with it."

"It's not my fault he went missing," Kirk protested.

"I didn't say it was but you have to admit this looks suspicious."

"I get that," he agreed.

"Why are you still in the band?"

"Because I don't think Benny or anyone in the band has anything to do with what we've been questioned about."

"Then why do you think Benny and the other members of the band including yourself have been questioned?"

"For being in the wrong place at the wrong time," he announced.

Reese had read the report. The child of the owner of a bar where Benny played a solo gig went missing after his performance there. The last time he was seen was helping Benny carry equipment to the van. After an investigation, authorities discovered that a year prior another child in a different city went missing when the entire band played a gig at a festival where the mother's food truck parked.

"There's a lot of coincidences involved," Reese pointed out.

Kirk closed his eyes. "I get that but we're all innocent."

"You better hope so," she demanded. "We're going to find Riley, and I'll spend as long as it takes to figure out exactly how he got to wherever he is."

"I have been helping, too, and I will continue to help in any way I can," Kirk declared.

Reese studied everything: the tones in Kirk's voice, the movement of his blue eyes, and his neurotic body language. She quickly determined he either lied really well or he told the truth. Although she could tell her questions intimated him, nothing he said or did set off any alarms. However, this was a strange case. Analysts would probably claim they had a better chance of finding Riley alive if he had been kidnapped. In her own way, Reese hoped she would pick up on something that would lead her in that direction. For now, though, it seemed like the best thing to do was head back out on the water.

35

hile Reese wandered the upstairs portion of the house with Kirk, Niles and Eden fired questions of their own at one another.

"You look like you're hung over," Niles initially commented when he and Eden found themselves alone for the first time since their son went missing.

"I barely slept last night," she hissed. "You don't look so great yourself," she observed while looking at his wind-chapped face and weary eyes.

As soon as they stepped into the bedroom, Niles caught a glimpse of the beer cans scattered around the room; some on the nightstands and others tossed on the floor in the corner near the bloody towels. Reese studied those while Niles thought about giving Kirk a bloody nose. He hadn't initially noticed the trail of blood on the staircase, maybe because of the water or perhaps because Reese flipped the switch to complete cop mode.

"Riley is missing, and you're busy getting drunk with your boyfriend," Niles yelled.

Eden glanced at the beer cans and found herself wishing she cleaned them up before anyone arrived, but honestly she hadn't expected visitors again until the hurricane let up. "I'm stuck in a house with nothing to do but think about my missing son, so yeah, I drank a few beers," she snarled.

"A few? It looks like you drank a whole case."

"Don't judge me, Niles, not now," she pleaded.

"This whole thing happened because you and this dude were being irresponsible," Niles claimed. "I think I have the right to judge you. Anyway, who is this guy and why was he staying the night with you and Riley during the hurricane when you were supposed to be in Kentucky?"

"Plans changed."

"Oh, they sure did," Niles clamored. "Who is he?" he pressed.

"He's my friend."

Niles's eyes shifted to the ruffled sheets on the bed. "Looks like a little more than your friend to me."

Eden glared at him. "Your police friend seems like a little more, too. Where did you meet her? Who is she?" she quizzed with her hands on her hips.

"She's here to help find Riley."

"Where did she come from?"

"That's none of your business."

"Kirk's none of your business."

"Well, if we don't find Riley, I'm going to kick Kirk in the other side of his face so that he'll have matching cuts."

"Why do you always want to fight someone?" Eden quipped.

"I only want to fight idiots."

"Kirk's not an idiot. He's actually pretty smart, but you wouldn't know that because you're judging him just like you're judging me."

"You're both irresponsible."

"Says the man who shows up with some detective from another state who you probably just met at a bar when you and Mickey were hanging out in Hickory."

The accuracy of the comment stunned Niles momentarily.

"She's here to help," was all he could think to say.

"Kirk is helping, too."

"Kirk is in the way."

"He searched through all the nasty water down there for hours looking for our son."

"But he didn't find him; he only helped you lose him."

"That's a low blow, Niles."

Thankfully, Reese and Kirk stepped back into the room at that moment, causing Niles and Eden to temporarily forget why they were even arguing.

"I want to get back on the boat and search with you all," Eden implored, looking to Reese for approval.

Reese glanced around the room once again taking in the sight of the beer cans she noticed earlier as well as a pill bottle sticking from the top of Eden's purse. She'd also been close enough to both Eden and Kirk to smell their breath. "I'm sorry but I can't allow someone who has been drinking alcohol to be in the boat unless I am evacuating them to safety," Reese explained. "If you want to go to a shelter, I'd be happy to take you. There are probably professionals there who can help talk you through all of this."

"Absolutely not," Eden answered, knowing she didn't want to talk to a random therapist who never lived a moment in her shoes, especially the sopping wet ones she pried off her cold feet late last night. "I definitely don't care to be surrounded by a bunch of strangers packed into a gymnasium or some uncomfortable place like that."

"I understand," Reese responded.

"Yeah, they probably wouldn't let you get drunk there either," Niles jabbed.

Eden glared at him, and Reese pressed her lips together and stared in his direction.

"That's mean, dude," Kirk announced.

Niles immediately stepped in his direction. "You want to see me be mean?" he sneered.

Standing between Niles and Kirk, where Reese purposefully positioned herself every time the two men were in the same area, she moved toward Niles and put her hands on his firm chest. "Stand down," she instructed.

"I'm not going to let this jerk talk to me like that," Niles asserted, pressing his chest into Reese's hands and forcing her to plant her back leg on the floor to counter his strength.

Reese knew Niles wasn't the type of man who would let a woman hold him back if he wanted to fight someone. At the same time, she wasn't the type of woman whom he might be used to holding him back. "Niles," she hissed, holding him steady for the time being. "If you don't collect yourself, I'll take you to the shelter."

With his face puffed up, Niles fought the urge to push Reese aside and land a few blows on Kirk before she could attempt to drag him off. Glaring at the man, he eventually forced himself to pull back while hoping to find another chance to take his anger out on this guy's grungy face.

36

Still inside Grandyma's house, Reese removed herself and Niles from the bedroom and shut the door behind them. Standing in the hallway, she quickly sent a text message update to Captain Lawson. Knowing every moment was precious, she asked him to please pass along the information to Johnson, Dominguez, and Brown. She wished they were here helping with the rescue but was thankful for the help from the others.

Niles noticed Reese standing between him and the door leading to Kirk. He wanted to rush back in and take out all his anger on that guy but instead looked down from the top of the staircase into the home's first story and couldn't believe this was happening. Seeing the house in ruin, Niles felt in so many ways that his life headed in that direction, too. His eyes eventually wandered to the steps where he spotted the trail of blood for the first time, and even though he knew where it came from, he couldn't force himself to feel bad for Kirk.

A few minutes later, Reese and Niles joined the other two team members in the boat and began searching the area surrounding the house once again. They went up and down streets that Niles didn't even remember existed because everything looked different from this perspective. Typically, he drove in a vehicle at street level or walked on the sidewalks which were no longer visible. Beneath the surface, the water uprooted many of the walkways as well as trees, and they noticed some that fell on homes overnight.

The day moved along much like the storm—slowly. Some hurricanes were a sprint but this one was a marathon. Niles grew weary mentally and physically. Reese tried to keep everyone inside the boat as much as possible knowing that more water rescuers died from culverts and manholes than anything else. Niles constantly wanted to jump out and search behind bushes, trees, and anything possibly hiding his son, yet Reese reeled in his desires frequently.

The radio constantly buzzed with rescues taking place across the county while the winds kept pushing and the rain continued to pound. On a positive note with the storm now mostly over land, it weakened even though moving at a snail's pace. The downside was the rain showed no signs of subsiding, and the longer the hurricane sat atop them, the more water they had to deal with. Reese prayed the backside winds would soon take over and begin to push the flood water out of downtown; however, she knew that could present new problems. As of right now, there was absolutely no way Riley or anyone else could have been pulled into the normal boundaries of the river.

Last night, Reese dreamed Riley climbed into a boat, but that was all she remembered other than waking up later and recalling seeing a rainbow. This morning in the briefing, the captain happened to mention the impossibility of a vessel with no power crossing from the New Bern side of the Neuse River to the Bridgeton side. Even a boat with a motor would have had a hard time and would likely capsize due to the heavy winds and ferocious waves. So, to this point, there hadn't been a need to search in that direction. However, whenever the water did decide to shift, it wouldn't be a good thing for their chances of finding Riley if it moved him out into the open water. For now, every time they came across a loose boat, Reese lowered the throttle and checked for signs of Riley while calling out his name. She even requested for a member of the team to climb into each boat with a cabin just in case he took shelter there.

Lunchtime came and went, but all anyone ate were snacks and MREs. Thankfully, Reese remembered to restock the boat with water bottles this morning so everyone could stay hydrated. People tended to forget the need to drink fluids if the sun wasn't bearing down on them. However, when doing exasperating work like this, hydration was a necessity. Niles was the one who didn't seem to want to drink as much as needed, but Reese and the others stayed on him about it and told stories of rescuers becoming dehydrated.

With the storm weakening some, more residents opened their front doors and windows as the boat came into view. Every time the team came across people, they asked if they saw Riley. Unfortunately, no one provided good news. They only posed questions because by now pretty much everyone in town had heard about the missing five-year-old boy, and nearly all of them wondered how they could help. Reese explained that the best way to assist was for citizens to remain in their homes but to keep an eye out and call the authorities if they noticed anything that might lead to finding Riley.

Television and radio stations across the country reported the case, sending a shockwave of sadness from the East Coast to the West Coast. Complete strangers alluded to Riley in every conversation. If anything good stemmed from his disappearance, it was the reminder to parents to hug their kids a little tighter. Child therapy experts and leaders from water rescue teams across the country weighed in on the situation. Everyone gave an opinion on the best course of action. Fortunately, Niles wasn't seeing or hearing any of this; he just knew his son was still missing and that the search and rescue teams in New Bern were doing everything imaginable to find his son and so was he.

After dinnertime rolled around and darkness settled across the city, Riley still hadn't been located, and Niles found himself hoping for the best but beginning to expect the worst. He watched the faces of the professional rescuers all day, and even though they were relentless in their pursuit, he could tell hope was fading. They searched late into the night using the spotlights to navigate the water which had been slowly receding throughout the day.

Back at the fire station, Niles ate very little from the buffet table. After showering, he curled into a ball on his cot. Reese wanted to comfort him but realized he hadn't been alone for a single minute throughout the past two days. Hence, she wandered around the building and let him have some time to himself. She could tell he felt responsible even though he audibly blamed Eden and Kirk several times. He kept mentioning how he hadn't listened to his gut guiding him to evacuate Riley.

An hour or so later, after eating a hot meal and talking strategy with the captains and some of the other first responders, Reese nestled near Niles.

"Hey you," she whispered, searching his wide-open aqua green eyes.

"Hey," he uttered, sounding defeated.

"Can't sleep?" she asked.

"I couldn't even if I wanted to."

Reese rubbed his shoulder gently. "We'll get back out there after our team rests up a little."

One team was still on the water dedicated to searching for Riley; that crew rested for a little while earlier in the evening before taking over for Reese's team. Niles wanted to go with them but Reese and both captains strongly advised against the idea.

"Where is he, Reese?" Niles cried.

Reese felt tears bubbling in her own eyes. She wished she knew the answer. She led the search in every direction she could think of and tapped into every bit of training she experienced. They looked high and low and everywhere in between. "He's in God's hands, Niles," she finally breathed.

"You think he's gone?" he asked with tears streaming down his tired face before falling onto the dingy sheet.

Reese shook her head side to side. "I didn't mean it like that," she explained. "You believe in God, right?" she asked.

"Right now I'm not sure," Niles answered honestly.

"A miracle is what I'm expecting," Reese shared. "God knows exactly where Riley is and that's the most important thing."

"God already has one of my sons," Niles reminded her, sobbing harder.

Reese moved in closer and draped her arm around Niles. "I know," was all she knew to say.

37

arly Saturday morning, the hurricane conditions became noticeably better yet still no sign of Riley North. Reese's team climbed into their gear, attended another briefing, and headed to the waterline. Like the day prior, the National Guard had large gas containers on hand to fill the boats. Rescues still took place, but the calls came in at a slower rate. More of the swift water rescue teams now dedicated time to helping find Riley. Each crew searched a specific location in order to cover every possible area in the vicinity of where he went missing.

Reese, Niles, and their two team members explored the downtown business district from Union Point Park to the New Bern Farmers Market. The streets, positioned like a grid, made it easy to navigate, but as much stuff seemed to be floating in the water as in the residential area. The flooding subsided quite a bit leaving just enough river water in the streets to maneuver the boat. Gusts of wind continued slapping the stoplights and road signs along with the faces of those in the boat.

Niles took note of the boarded-up windows with messages written to Hurricane Florence, some of which he and Mickey helped install before evacuating to Hickory. *Pray for New Bern* was how the sign he stared at in this very moment read. Never in his wildest dreams had Niles imagined being back here on a boat searching for his missing son even though he had a premonition of something terrible happening. It was surreal in so many ways. He figured the next time he was downtown, he and Mickey would be ripping sheets of plywood off these boarded-up windows. The extent of the damage everywhere made it difficult to imagine how this quaint town would ever return to the beautiful place it was only days ago. Thinking about that, Niles remembered his dad often saying things could be replaced but people couldn't.

Over seventy professional firefighters from the City of New Bern helped across the town, many walking the areas outside the waterline searching for Riley or anyone else in need of assistance. Firefighters poured in from other areas as well with the large majority eager to help find the missing boy. In full force police officers helped with the search and secured homes and businesses. A curfew was in effect but many citizens still tried to help one another and look for Riley. With hundreds of people dedicated to helping with the mission and focusing on one goal within the community, no one cared who found him, just that he was located.

Calls with clues came in sporadically. A few people stumbled across stuffed animals and blankets they thought could belong to Riley but none did. One man even found a child's camouflage shirt which broke Niles's heart upon hearing the news trickle across the radio. However, once a photo made it to Eden, she confirmed the clothing—a different pattern and a size too small— did not belong to Riley.

All the random objects in the water from homes and businesses added complexity to the search. The authorities couldn't overlook a single thing that might lead to Riley's whereabouts, and Reese's mind continued to work overtime making sure she didn't miss anything. Even though walking through the shallower water became easier, she continued reminding her team about the risks of bacteria, pathogens, snakes, ants, manholes, and other dangers that came to mind whether because of sight or memory.

When the winds settled, a helicopter rescue team deployed to the area and began searching by air. Another flew in later in the day to assist in the mission. Also hundreds of firefighters volunteered from all over the county and beyond going door to door asking if anyone saw Riley.

By day's end, it seemed not a square inch in downtown New Bern hadn't been combed over, but the rescue teams knew if Riley was still alive he could be moving while they searched. It was doubtful he would walk up to a complete stranger even though he was probably cold, tired, and hungry. Any number of people could have been within a few feet of him if he hid which is why the team leaders pressed their staff to look in the same areas over and over. Every new set of eyes offered an opportunity to find something that they possibly overlooked.

Reporters and camera crews from television stations near and far set up throughout the downtown area, most of them finding a spot near the waterline. Some even ventured out in boats trying to get a closer look at the water rescue teams in action as well as footage of the home from which Riley went missing. Both Eden and Niles received calls from local and national news stations even though they had no idea how these people unearthed their numbers. Reese advised Niles not to talk to the media, and so far he'd dodged them. It helped that his voice mailbox was full leaving him barely any time to check the messages let alone respond to friends, family members, or the media.

Near the end of the day, he looked Reese square in the eyes and said, "I don't want to go back to the fire station."

"Why not?" she asked while assuming he wanted to continue the search as he had every other time they headed in for a break.

"They're going to be there waiting for me," he forecasted.

"Who?"

"The media."

Reese nodded. "Probably."

"I can't talk to them, not now," he pleaded. "Plus, I don't think I can sleep on that cot one more night." Sleep wasn't the best word because he barely slept the last two nights. "My body is wearing down," he admitted for the first time.

"Where do you want to go?" Reese asked.

"Home," he answered solemnly. "I want to go home." He hadn't slept in his own bed in days, and he felt it would be the best place to rest during this phase of the storm if the treehouse still stood. The words he chose triggered the memory of how Riley, ever since he began putting sentences together, would say, 'I want to go to bed now' then put himself down. Niles wondered how Riley put himself to bed these past few nights, and the fact his son wasn't used to being rocked or held at bedtime gave him a flicker of hope that his little boy might have gotten more sleep than he had since his disappearance.

As midnight approached, Reese steadied the boat next to another search and rescue vessel then the two local members of the team climbed aboard the other after giving Reese and Niles a hug. Situations like what they dealt with had a way of bonding people. Even though the past several days seemed like a blur in many ways, Reese knew she and Niles would remember many of the people involved for the rest of their lives.

A few moments later, Reese steered the boat toward the Neuse River eventually crossing over the choppy surf heading in the direction of Niles's treehouse. Niles made this trek many times although not very often in the dark and definitely not through such hazardous conditions. However, he managed to navigate Reese to his property with the help of the bright spotlight. As they approached, he shifted the light left to right, soon concluding that either the storm took the dock or water submerged the entire structure. Upon further inspection, Niles realized the floodwaters, still overtaking his low-lying property, enabled Reese to maneuver the boat through clusters of trees all the way to the foot of the treehouse.

Once there, with the light illuminating the structure, Niles hopped into knee-deep water and tied off the line to one of the support trees.

"Looks like the building inspector was wrong," he acknowledged.

"Do what?" Reese inquired with a puzzled face.

"When Mickey and I built this place, the inspector said it probably wouldn't withstand a hurricane."

Every support tree still stood and from the outside it appeared there was very little damage to the treehouse. When building, they carefully selected each tree based on size, age, root structure, and other factors related to healthy trees.

"That's wonderful news," Reese responded.

They spent a few minutes securing the boat to the nearby trees, then Niles guided Reese up the ladder leading to the deck, each holding a flashlight as they climbed.

"This place is so cool," Reese proclaimed, staring upward as she took it all in as best she could given the conditions.

"Thanks," Niles replied, wishing he had the energy to grin.

"You really built this yourself?"

"Mickey and I did," he answered as he stepped off the last rung then offered his free hand to Reese.

"Thank you," she obliged. "You guys did a fantastic job."

The beams from the flashlights revealed a layer of pine straw covering the deck along with random pinecones and sticks. As Niles and Reese made the full circle around the treehouse, they didn't notice any structural damage.

"Crap," Niles growled out of the blue as they stood at the front door.

"What is it?" Reese asked, thinking he must have noticed

hurricane damage she'd yet to spot.

"Mickey has my house key," Niles revealed, sighing into the night's sky.

Reese smiled then pulled out the tool she used at the hotel to help Niles get into his room. "Remember this?" she asked, dangling it in front of him like a piece of candy.

"You're always prepared," Niles remarked.

A few seconds later, the front door swung open and two rays of light illuminated the living area. Niles flipped the switch out of habit forgetting the electricity was still out. He instantly recalled making that mistake dozens of times during power outages.

"I'm sorry it smells a little stale in here," Niles apologized.

"That's what happens when the electricity is out for a couple of days."

"That coupled with the stench of Mickey's socks," he teased but still couldn't muster a laugh.

Reese giggled. "Mickey kind of seems like one of those people who thinks his socks don't stink."

Niles let out the slightest chuckle. "Na, he's not really like that but he is confident."

"I guess all I have to go on is his approach at the bar."

"He was just trying to help me out," Niles reminded her.

"Did he?"

In the flashlight illuminated room, Niles glanced at the glow surrounding Reese. "More than he'll ever know," he announced realizing how fortunate he'd been to have Reese by his side these past few days. If he hadn't met her, he might not have even made it back to New Bern let alone been able to search for his son.

"I guess that makes him a great friend."

"The best," Niles confirmed as he fought the wind to close the door. "I'll give you the tour," he offered, shining his flashlight toward the oven. "That's the kitchen," he announced, turning the beam. "That's the living room." Another turn. "There's my bedroom." Next light shift. "Mickey's bedroom." One last light point. "The bathroom."

"The place looks cozy," Reese acknowledged. "I love all the exposed wood," she pointed out as her head rotated, taking it all in and realizing Niles's description of the place hadn't done it justice.

"It's home," he uttered. "Mickey and I used the wood from trees we cut down on the property," he shared.

"You guys are quite the handymen."

"We both grew up building things, so it comes naturally, I guess."

Reese continued studying the inside of the treehouse: the wood, the photos of Riley and his artwork on the fridge, and the bar overlooking the boarded-up windows which otherwise probably offered a fantastic view of the river they just crossed. "It's one of the neatest places I've ever seen," she spoke honestly.

"Thanks."

Hearing Niles talk made Reese feel good; this was the most she'd heard his voice in the past couple of days. Of course, carrying on conversations with anyone out on the water during the hurricane had been nearly impossible. Each of them simply said what needed to be spoken related to the rescue mission and pretty much nothing else. They had no time to talk about their lives, their fears, their dreams . . . they simply all shared the hope of finding Riley. Now, Reese hoped being at home would help Niles feel a little more comfortable and maybe in some ways keep his mind off things. However, she had a hunch that everything in and around this treehouse reminded him of his little boy.

"Is it okay if I use your restroom?" Reese asked, studying the home for clues as she maneuvered gingerly through unfamiliar territory in the dimly lit surroundings.

"Of course," he agreed, "just make sure to shine your flashlight on the seat before sitting to be certain Mickey didn't pee on it."

Reese laughed. "Blame it on the guy who isn't here," she pointed out.

Niles shrugged his shoulders, and when Reese disappeared into the bathroom he shined the flashlight at the fridge and walked in that direction, not because of hunger but because he wanted to stare at the photos of Riley. Over the past couple of days, scrolling through countless pictures of his son on his phone reminded him that he couldn't look at the images enough. He wanted to pull Riley right out of the photos and hold him as tight as ever. If only it were that easy, he thought to himself.

Reese emerged from the bathroom to find Niles standing in front of the refrigerator. Looking at him from behind, she noticed how his silhouette almost appeared frozen, and she knew exactly what he was doing. Even though she didn't know how gazing at pictures of your child wondering if you would ever see him again felt, she knew the feelings she experienced on countless nights while studying the wrinkles on her dad's face. Hoping not to disturb Niles's thoughts, she stepped gingerly toward a small couch. Still, the presence of her light gave her away and in a startled fashion he turned as if he forgot she was even there.

"I'm sorry for interrupting," Reese offered as she sunk into a soft cushion.

"That's okay, I was just—" Niles paused for a moment searching for the right words. "Just lost in thought, I guess," he finally uttered.

"Do you want to talk about him?"

"Who?" Niles asked even though he knew who she was referencing.

"Riley," she spoke softly. "I can't wait to meet him."

Over the years, Reese learned the art of positive affirmations. At this moment she believed that eventually she would kneel down, look into Riley North's precious eyes, and tell him how amazing his dad was.

"Yes," Niles sniffed.

"What is his favorite color?"

"Green," Niles revealed.

"What cartoon does he watch most often?"

"The Adventures of Paddington Bear."

"That sounds like a cute show. Do you like to watch it with him?"

"Some mornings we lie in bed and watch it over and over."

"It's amazing how kids can watch the same shows and movies hundreds of times and never get bored of them."

"I often think the same thing."

"Do you get tired of watching Paddington Bear?"

Niles settled on the cushion next to Reese. "Never," he admitted, "but I spend more time enjoying Riley's reactions than I do watching the show. I love the way he laughs at the same scenes over and over; even though I know when it's about to happen, I still love witnessing the miracle every time."

Reese asked question after question about Riley, taking in every bit of information as a friend and a detective. She loved hearing Niles talk about the trails he walked with his son, the nights they spent studying the stars, and about all the scars and scrapes they endured together while being boys. In so many ways Niles reminded her of a little boy; it was like he realized that growing up was a trap. The treehouse symbolized his youthful spirit, and something about being in this place gave her energy even under the circumstances.

"We should probably get some shut-eye," Reese mentioned, knowing she wanted to start the search back at daybreak.

As each of their flashlights stood tall on the small coffee table in front of the couch, Niles studied her eyes for a moment. "You're probably right," he finally uttered.

"I'll sleep here on the couch if that's okay."

"You can have my bedroom," he offered.

"I can't do that, I know you are looking forward to sleeping in your own bed and you deserve that."

"I'll stay in Mickey's room. His bed is basically the same as mine; it just smells a little worse," Niles announced with a smirk. "That's why I didn't offer his to you."

"He might say the same about yours," Reese teased thinking about the offer and imagining how pleasant sleeping on a real mattress would be after spending the last couple of nights on a hard cot.

"Probably," he agreed, "but I'm almost positive my sheets are clean."

"Are you sure you're okay with me taking over your room?" she asked, watching for any form of hesitancy.

"I want you to," Niles said then walked her to the bedroom.

Standing at the edge of the bed which took up most of the space in the room, Reese thought about how she and Niles hadn't kissed since arriving at his place. It wasn't the first time this crossed her mind; while talking on the couch, the urge to lean in and touch his lips struck her several times but making the first move in his house, especially under the circumstances, didn't feel right. Even so, she found herself hoping he would kiss her now and maybe they would stumble onto the bed and lose themselves in the moment. She imagined how it would feel to have his body pressed against hers but in a way that seemed like taking advantage of his vulnerabilities. Niles certainly hadn't come across as the type of man who would want to take advantage of her although initially she thought he might be because of the condom incident. She wondered how many times they would laugh about that story. A lot, she hoped. She liked him. She liked his treehouse, his simple yet complex life. She adored his love for his son. It turned her on in a way a man never had before, maybe because she never dated a man with a child or possibly because Niles North was as unique as his living quarters.

Niles allowed himself to become lost in Reese's eyes once again while showing her around his room using the flashlight beam. It simply contained enough space in which to maneuver and store the necessities, and the one and only door gave away the absence of the typical walk-in closet and master bathroom. He simply explained where she could place her bag, told her she was welcome to sleep on either side of the bed, and that there were more blankets if she needed them.

"It's a little warm in here with no air conditioning, so I think I'll be fine," Reese responded.

Niles thought about touching her arm or hugging her neck or kissing her lips or even what it would feel like to make love to Reese Kirby. When he finally looked at his and Riley's bed, he suddenly wanted to ask her not to sleep on Riley's side. Riley was the last person who slept there. At the moment Niles found himself thinking that if he never saw his son again he'd never want to wash the sheets nor allow any other person to sleep in Riley's spot.

Reese sensed the sudden shift in Niles's demeanor as he stared blankly at the pillows on the bed. She wondered what he was thinking and was pretty sure it had something to do with Riley.

"Will you please sleep on that side of the bed?" Niles requested pointing his flashlight to where he slept every night whether Riley was or wasn't with him. Then without another word he walked out of the room, closing the door behind him. However, he didn't make it to Mickey's room before starting to cry uncontrollably although not audibly. With both knees on the floor as if praying, he dug his face into the couch cushions where he sat earlier with Reese. He let his emotions spill all over the fabric as the thought of never lying next to his son in that bed again consumed his thoughts.

After setting the flashlight on the nightstand located beside the bed where Niles asked her to sleep, Reese stripped off her holster then removed her t-shirt and shimmied off her yoga pants. There was no way she could sleep fully clothed tonight unless she had no other option like at the fire department. However, the station's temperature was much cooler, so sleeping with clothes on hadn't been too uncomfortable.

A few minutes after planting his face on the couch, Niles rose to his feet but instead of going to Mickey's room, he tapped on his bedroom door for the first time in his life. Usually, it remained open. The only time it was shut when he wasn't in there was when Riley still slept or changed clothes and even then he just opened the door. Riley was five; he didn't care.

Lying flat on her back atop the sheets wearing only underwear and a bra, Reese flinched at the subtle knock on the dark door. She'd flipped the flashlight button off the moment she removed her clothes. The funny thing is she just reached for it again and about stood up to put on her clothes after remembering something Niles told her the other day. He and Riley slept on this bed together every night they were with one another. Kicking herself, she knew she didn't have to be a detective to figure out that's what he thought when he glared at the bed.

Rather than hopping up and putting her clothes on, Reese slid beneath the thin sheet. "Come in," she called out feeling naked all of a sudden.

The door opened and Niles stepped into the room with his flashlight shining directly at the floor beside his feet. If Reese didn't know who it was, the image would be frightening because she could only see the silhouette of his body. It reminded her of a horror film as he stood there in silence for a moment.

"I'm not sure how to say this," Niles started then stopped, an uneasy lull suddenly filling the air.

Knowing what he most likely thought, Reese decided to speak for him. "You want your bed back," she stated confidently while attempting to express with her tone of voice that she was completely willing to sleep elsewhere.

"Riley sleeps on that side," Niles shared, lifting his flashlight in the direction about which he spoke.

Although the sheet covered her breasts as did her bra, for some reason Reese pulled the sheet a little higher when the light exposed her bare shoulders.

Niles couldn't help but glance at Reese's skin wondering if she was nude. Of all the thoughts he had about her, about the two of them, about a possible future together, he hadn't imagined her naked. He hadn't considered seeing her naked or being in her presence while she was naked. Suddenly, he felt nervous.

"I made sure to stay on the side you asked me to lie on," she announced, showing respect to his wishes as her fingertips touched the edge of the mattress.

"Thank you," he uttered sincerely.

"If you give me a moment to dress, I'll let you have your bed," Reese said. "I'll be happy to sleep on the couch." She was kind of afraid to sleep in Mickey's room after Niles's comment. Even though it was hot and she felt a little sticky, the linens on this bed smelled fresh and felt surprisingly cool against her bare body. Maybe that had more to do with the nervous chill bumps popping up on her skin than anything else, she considered.

"You're welcome to stay put if you want, but I decided I want to sleep where Riley sleeps."

While crying, Niles came to the conclusion that one day someone would lie on Riley's side of the bed; most likely it would be him but it could possibly be Reese if she accidentally rolled over while sleeping. Even though the thought of her being in his bed felt kind of nice, he wanted to be the first person to lie where Riley slept. He wanted to smell the scent of his son on the pillow that held Riley's little head night after night. He wanted to feel the presence his son left there, wanted to soak it all in while it was still fresh. Eventually, he knew the smell would winnow away and he'd have to wash the sheets.

"Are you sure?" Reese asked hesitantly. In a way, she felt like she was invading his privacy although they basically slept together each night in the fire station.

"I like having you near me," Niles affirmed.

A few moments later with Reese still beneath the sheet, he set his flashlight on the opposite nightstand then pulled fresh clothes from a nearby cubby. The mesh shorts and t-shirt currently clinging to his body emitted an odor and he didn't want that to taint the smell Riley left behind. Clicking off his flashlight, Niles decided to climb into the new set of clothes in the dark. He thought about asking Reese if she preferred for him to change in the other room then decided it probably didn't matter since she was either naked or partially undressed beneath the sheets.

Once in the clean clothes which were a little more challenging to put on in the dark than Niles anticipated—he had to catch himself on nearby furniture a couple of times—he respectfully collapsed on top of the sheet under which Reese rested.

"If you change your mind about me being in your bed, please promise me you'll let me know," Reese requested.

As her softly spoken words entered his ears, Niles turned on his side facing Reese with his nose pressed against the pillow beneath his head.

"Okay," he responded.

The air in the room stilled for a few minutes. However, the wind on the other side of the walls continued to swirl, creating all sorts of creaking sounds and causing the treehouse to shuffle a little.

"Are we safe here?" Reese eventually asked hesitantly after feeling the sudden shift. In a way it felt like they were being rocked to sleep, but she wanted to be sure the structure wasn't going to randomly drop out of the trees like a collapsing elevator.

"Yes, there are high-tech springs attached to the trees that allow the house to drift with the wind," Niles explained.

"So it always does this?"

"Usually, you can't feel the movement unless there is a heavy gust of wind which is very rare when there's not a hurricane going on outside."

Reese reached over and touched Niles's arm. "Well, you're welcome to climb under the sheet with me," she announced. "It might make me feel a bit safer."

38

cross the Neuse River, Eden and Kirk finally slept soundly. Once again, alcohol and medication to help dull the pain filled their night. During the hours that mostly crept by like the slow-moving hurricane, Kirk often thought about how he didn't really know Riley or Eden, so the hurt he felt was a contagious type of grieving picked up from Eden, who was noticeably at her wit's end. Nonetheless, he tried to keep an upbeat attitude hoping it would help.

Throughout the night he did everything he could think of to keep Eden's mind occupied. He sang dozens of songs, some originals written by him or his band. Others were familiar lyrics from popular music groups. Every once in a while Eden would doze off to the sound of his voice, but she usually woke within fifteen or so minutes.

Things seemed to crash to a new low an hour ago upon the realization that the cooler at the end of the bed was now only filled with room temperature air. Ironically, Kirk recalled showing up at Eden's house for what he thought would be an amazing hurricane party with enough beer to last two people several days. Looking back, this was the worst party of his life even though the intimate moments he shared with Eden were nice. He often found himself wishing to escape, but at the same time recognized the human soul possessed a desire to mourn for those in its presence who were troubled.

With all the stores closed and the house still surrounded by water, there was no way to get more alcohol. Eden and Kirk noticed the water receding throughout the evening, yet there was still so much filling the yard it was dangerous to walk outside.

One of the things hurricanes do is bring torrential amounts of rain that soak into the ground and loosen the soil. In Grandyma's yard, the floodwaters added to this potentially hazardous equation which for hours on end weakened the root systems grounding the trees which surrounded the house. Many people made the mistake of thinking only the heaviest gusts of wind would knock over trees but that wasn't always the case. As Eden and Kirk lay sprawled out across the dingy sheets beneath their sweat-soaked bodies, a large oak tree outside the window began to lean. A constant wind coming off the river nudged it ever so slightly for the next thirty minutes stretching the roots like rubber bands. One by one the roots snapped starting with the smaller ones causing the tree to inch closer to the roof covering Eden's and Kirk's motionless bodies. Then, it happened—a strong wind didn't blow; lightning didn't strike; absolutely no warning sounded. The oak tree, planted on the property more than one hundred years ago, took its last breath and fell where the steady wind pushed. The outer branches struck the shingles first; many penetrated straight through even before the heart of the massive tree reached the roofline. When it did, there was no mercy. The oak forced its way into the home just as the floodwaters had but not quietly. The loud thump not only woke Eden and Kirk but several of the neighbors.

During a hurricane when a tree falls, everyone within the sound of the thump typically checks every square inch of their home then looks out the windows trying to figure out where it landed. This time, things were different inside Grandyma's house. The ceiling fell through, two-by-fours snapped like twigs, and debris and tiny dust particles took over the room as the branches stabbed like sharp knives into the floor, the mattress, and everything else standing in their way. For Eden and Kirk, there was no chance to run, hide, or move out of harm's way. They didn't even realize what happened and little did they know that their lives were simply at the mercy of a tree which had been climbed and adored for years on top of years.

39

*O*n the wee hours of the morning, when the call came across the radio about a massive tree falling onto the residence where the little boy went missing, neither Reese nor Niles heard the news. Upon settling into bed earlier, Reese asked if it was okay if she turned off the radio hoping the two of them could have their first quiet night in a few days. With random gusts of wind still whipping around outside the treehouse and scattered bands of heavy rain peppering the roof, she knew *quiet* was a relative word. However, the sounds of nature flexing their muscles was much more peaceful than the interruptive roar of the radio or the plethora of surprising noises present throughout each night spent at the fire station.

Initially, Niles hesitated about breaking free from the radio's steady stream of communication. He, understandably, wanted to be the first to know if anyone found Riley or if new information surfaced. Once Reese reminded him they each had a cell phone within reach and could adjust the settings to where emergency calls would ring through, he agreed. Everyone they worked with the past few days collected their numbers, and she felt confident the authorities would call immediately if anything happened.

When Reese's and Niles's conversation ended, his breathing

quickly became heavy, pleasantly surprising her, and for a little while she watched the rise and fall of his chest as he slept. During those quiet moments, reality seemed to settle in like a slow fog finding its way into a sleepy forest. The thought flashed across her mind that she hadn't been in bed with a man in quite some time and she had to admit it felt kind of nice although very different. In a way it was calming that no sexual desires were on display, just two adults lying on a mattress together conversing until Niles fell asleep. She did most of the talking in hopes that would help ease his busy mind. When she closed her own eyes, she figured Niles would probably wake up off and on throughout the night.

Niles slept soundly for a couple of hours before a loud clap of thunder interrupted a dream about searching for Riley in waist-deep water inside an abandoned building. He experienced similar dreams every night since his little guy went missing; some were nightmares, and in others he dreamed of finding Riley only to wake up temporarily excited before succumbing to reality. Ultimately, both types of dreams were nightmares. Once again, Niles found himself silently begging God to let someone, anyone find his son, and he knew that thousands of similar prayers had gone up over the past several days.

While the rain pounded on the treehouse's roof, Niles glanced at Reese after almost forgetting she was in bed with him, yet the moment's realization felt comforting. Something was relieving about having someone with you to walk through the hard times. He always appreciated that when he and Eden were together.

As Niles's eyes adjusted to the dark room and Reese's face became more visible, he considered whispering her name or even touching her arm; however, he knew she needed sleep as much as he did. Instead, his mind drifted to feeling guilty for not being out on the water searching for his son, and he considered turning on the radio to see if anything was happening. That's when he remembered his cell phone and felt dumb for not checking it the moment the thunder woke him. Hurriedly, he snatched the device hoping to find a message, one that read *We've found Riley*, but as he stared at the overwhelmingly bright screen, no new messages presented themselves. In a way, he figured he should probably be relieved because during the daytime hours countless messages from friends and relatives asking questions about the search flooded his inbox. Many of which remained unanswered. Every now and then he sent out a blanket message to everyone by copying and pasting the exact words.

Niles drifted back off to sleep an hour later, or maybe it was three hours; he wasn't really sure. Seconds now felt like minutes and minutes felt like hours. When he woke again, sunshine ever so slightly crept in through the cracks around the plywood-covered windows, and he found himself itching to climb out of bed. He hadn't seen the sun in four days which also reminded him this marked day four since Riley's disappearance. He imagined that many people gave up on ever finding his son, at least alive. Reality hit hard. He wondered at what point the authorities would stop searching, and when he realized Reese's eyes twitched open, that was the first question he asked.

"They will never stop searching," Reese promised in a sleepy tone although she knew the answer was somewhat generic—one given at a podium when the press asked the same question. "I will search with you until we find Riley," Reese guaranteed.

"Thank you," Niles answered, but he saw straight through the first part of her answer. "I realize the search will always be open until he's found, but when will the teams of trained searchers give up?"

"Niles, I can't answer that question and I really don't even want to make an attempt; there are so many variables," she admitted, still half asleep and worrying about saying something she couldn't rescind if this conversation didn't take a positive turn. "The mission is to find Riley and that's where our focus needs to remain."

"I know; however, I can't help but think of children who are kidnapped, and it seems eventually everyone except their parents stop looking for them."

"Those investigations are only closed when the children are found, and we don't think Riley was kidnapped. The only red flag has been lowered." As soon as the words *red flag* slipped out of Reese's mouth, she remembered what Niles didn't know, what he didn't need to know, and now she'd done what she was trying not to do—say something she couldn't take back.

Niles lifted his upper body from the bed as quickly as if it shot out of a cannon. "What red flag?" he demanded to know, sitting up straight and glaring into Reese's eyes.

"Nothing," Reese answered, shaking her head as though she shook away the thought.

"What red flag?" Niles shouted louder, grabbing her arm.

Sensing his sudden surge of anger, Reese flipped her wrist to loosen Niles's grasp—although his hand wasn't squeezing her, it was kind of just there—and immediately hopped out of bed to create distance.

"We had to investigate every possibility, make sure there was no foul play involved," Reese offered, trying to skirt the underlying issue.

"Why haven't you told me about this?" Niles asked, pouncing out of bed then invading Reese's side of the room all the while barely noticing her exposed skin. Any other time if she was standing in front of him wearing only a bra and panties, his eyes would have instantly been drawn to her flat stomach, alluring breasts, and the curves of her hips which he previously noticed through the fitted drysuit.

Reese took a step back realizing she was cornered between Niles and the wall. "I didn't want to scare you."

"You didn't want to scare me?" he screamed. "My son is missing; I am terrified."

Reese felt like crying but she couldn't; defense mode took over and she needed to stay strong and focused. "I want your mind to be only on finding Riley."

"There's nothing capable of changing that," Niles stated. "Whether he was swept away by water, ran out of the house scared looking for safety, or if someone—" Niles didn't want to say the word "—kidnapped him."

"Niles, this is what I do and I know how the human brain works. When a person thinks their child might have been kidnapped, their focus changes. They start wanting to not only find the child but also the person who took their child."

Niles's mind raced a hundred miles per second. "Who?" he pleaded.

"Who what?" Reese asked, stepping back into the corner as Niles came so close she could feel his breath. Close enough that if it was someone she didn't know, she would have already used force to move him away.

"Kirk," Niles hollered. "It's Kirk, isn't it?"

Reese watched a new shade of red boil onto Niles's face, and she could see his jaw tightening along with his fists and every muscle in his body. She didn't think he would be violent toward her, however, she was preparing for the worst. She thought he might grab her, blame her, push her up against the wall, and let out his frustrations on her—but he didn't.

Without thinking twice, Niles skipped across the bed, nearly hitting his head on the ceiling, snatched up his cell phone and shoes, and ran out the bedroom door.

Reese quickly grabbed her own phone and the radio then slipped on yesterday's clothes and her boots, but by the time she made it into the living room, the sound of the front door slamming evaporated. She felt certain Niles ran to the boat and was pretty sure that even though it belonged to her department, she wasn't invited. More specifically, he was heading for Kirk and if she didn't stop him, this probably wouldn't end well. Niles possessed the skills to injure seriously or even kill a person with a few blows. She witnessed his precision when they fought the group of bikers, and she heard his story about the drill instructors. Those guys were as tough as nails. If he took down several of them in a matter of moments, she knew what he was capable of doing to the average man who would have no idea how to defend himself against a trained fighter.

Reese rounded the front corner of the treehouse quickly and sprinted down the side of the structure heading toward the back corner. Niles was nowhere in sight and far enough ahead she couldn't even hear his footsteps. He either made it to the stairs or more likely, she thought, he probably hopped onto the netting and rolled down. He talked about doing that with Riley, and it was perhaps the quickest way to the ground. Regardless, she knew he would make it to the boat a decent distance ahead of her, but he still had to untie or cut the ropes if he happened to have a knife in his pocket.

When Reese circled the back corner of the treehouse with her eyes wide open trying to locate Niles, an unexpected surprise met her. Her head immediately collided with Niles's elbow, and the force of the impact made her think her body might flip over the railing. She never imagined he would be standing in that spot so there had been no time to slow down, brace herself, or even guard her face; she just ran right into him.

Instinctively, Niles lunged for Reese hoping to keep her from stumbling into the railing. He knew she'd be coming after him but hadn't expected her to round the corner at full speed and run into his elbow, which was protruding outward because his hands covered his head as he stood facing a sheet of painted plywood.

Reese felt Niles's arms catch her then he carefully led her to the ground where she sat trying to regain her balance. He let go of her and stood back up, and from her vantage point she could see him sobbing while staring at a picture on the plywood which appeared to have been drawn by a child—Riley.

"What is that?" Reese asked, feeling fuzzy.

"I know where he is," Niles stated.

"Who?" she inquired unsure if the reference implied Riley or Kirk.

"He's on the ark," Niles proclaimed, then ran a few steps and tumbled down the netting as he'd done a hundred times.

Reese didn't feel like getting up and definitely didn't feel comfortable running, but as she stared at the picture Riley drew, she knew even if he was on the ark, Niles would have no idea where to find him. They saw boats all over downtown New Bern. The winds and waves could have taken the vessel anywhere it pleased over the past few days. Ultimately, she knew Niles understood precisely where to find Kirk and that's why she made herself get up off the deck floor and chase after Niles.

Following Niles's example, Reese rolled down the net knowing if she took the ladder, she would be more likely to fall with her equilibrium still off-center from the blow to the head. Upon making it to the bottom of the net, she landed in the water and then heard the boat crank. Niles somehow loosened the rope but now had to drive by her to get to the river, and she knew she had one chance to hop onto the vessel as he drove past. Thankfully, he wouldn't be able to pick up much speed, but as the watercraft moved in her direction, she could tell by the tilt he pushed the throttle to the max.

Niles glanced at Reese as he approached her on the narrow path leading to the Neuse River but had no intention of stopping for her because he felt like she betrayed him. His mind remained confused, though, because inside the house he felt confident Kirk had something to do with the disappearance of his son. Then when he rounded the back corner of the treehouse, the sun filtered through the canopy of trees and a single ray landed straight on the picture Riley drew of the ark which somehow stopped him in his tracks. Now, his gut told him Riley was in the ark. One way or another, he intended to figure this out and find out why Kirk was a red flag then deal with that on his own. He knew if Reese made it to the boat before he could get it moving, she would try to stop him from getting to Kirk and he didn't want to have to fight her verbally or physically.

As the front of the boat reached the spot where Reese waited she lunged from the tree she climbed to get out of the floodwaters allowing her more power to push with her legs as well as some height.

Niles couldn't believe it when he saw Reese jumping from the tree like a monkey. As she soared through the air, she reached for one of the rails protruding from the boat using it to stop her momentum and forcing her body onto the floorboard. Upon landing, she tumbled across the floor before the seating at the back of the boat impeded her movement.

There, Reese let her body lean against the bottom part of the seat. Now that she was in the boat, the sense of urgency diminished. Niles was either searching for the ark or heading to Grandyma's house. If the latter was his intention, she would have some time to regain strength and do what she could to keep him from making a huge mistake.

Guiding the boat carefully, Niles realized the floodwaters receded drastically, and at parts of the narrow channel between the treehouse and the Neuse River, he figured they were in less than a foot of water.

When the boat emerged on the river's side of the tree line, both Niles and Reese noticed at the same time how it seemed as though they entered a new world. The sun shone sharply amidst the backdrop of a Carolina blue sky clustered with grayish clouds causing the water to shimmer. The surface was a little choppy for a typical day but nothing like what they experienced the last few days and no rain. The one thing that immediately caught their attention was the most amazing rainbow either of them had ever seen. Stretching from one side of the Neuse River to the other, every fully visible color appeared as bright as the welcomed sunshine.

Niles dropped the throttle and let the boat settle on the water. He stared at the rainbow then turned to Reese.

"Do you see that?" he asked.

How could she not, she thought? "Of course, I do," she answered even though her head was still pounding and things looked a little fuzzier than usual. "It's beautiful."

"But do you see where the rainbow rises and falls?"

Reese studied the curved lines a little closer. "Yes, I do," she responded, although she wasn't sure which end was the rise and which was the fall.

"The first night while in the shower at the fire station, I had a vision about a rainbow," Niles shared thinking about how at the time it seemed weird.

Reese lifted her aching body from the bottom of the boat and couldn't help but notice how calm Niles seemed in contrast to his temperament just minutes ago. "Really?" she asked inquisitively. "Because I had a dream about a rainbow."

Niles furrowed his brow. "That's interesting," he commented while pointing to the edge of the rainbow across the river. "The rainbow appears to begin at Grandyma's house," he said.

Reese hadn't realized this before when Niles asked if she saw where the rainbow rises and falls. It did though; the left end appeared to be settled near Grandyma's house. Slowly, her eyes followed the natural phenomena across the sky to the edge nestled on the Bridgeton side of the river. "Is there any significance regarding the location where the rainbow falls?" she asked out of curiosity. It didn't fall on Niles's treehouse; she realized that.

"I'm not sure exactly what is at that location but I'm going to find out," Niles declared pushing the throttle full on then positioning the search and rescue boat in that direction.

If God gave signs, this had to be one.

40

The search and rescue boat scooted across the surface of the river like an arrow shot from a bow. Niles knew they traveled at a much higher velocity than any recorded on the speedometer the past few days, yet it still seemed to be taking forever to reach the end of the rainbow. In fact, the thin needle stretched as far right as possible. He found himself praying that the bright colors painted across the sky wouldn't disappear before he and Reese could reach the landing spot, and he silently pleaded with God to find his son there. However, he questioned whether it was even remotely possible.

A voice suddenly crawled out of the radio, but Niles and Reese could barely make out the words against the roar of the motor as the propeller left a noticeable wake in the background. Reese stretched her fingers toward the volume button turning it to max volume while holding onto the metal bar framing the windshield around which the wind whipped. Standing side by side with Niles, they listened intently as the emergency management director gave an update on Hurricane Florence. Quite obviously, the storm moved out of town overnight, but the damage it left behind devastated the community in countless ways. The man mentioned more than twenty thousand residents lost power in the storm. At least twenty-five roads were unusable, and many areas still remained underwater, only accessible by boat. Flooding damaged an estimation of more than four thousand homes and three hundred businesses.

As Niles and Reese absorbed the staggering numbers both seemed somewhat numb to them. The last thing the emergency management director said was the rescue crews saved more than seven hundred people and rescues were still underway. While Niles knew this news should excite him, it didn't. In fact, the realization that his son wasn't one of those hundreds of people saved shot a stream of sadness or maybe even anger throughout his entire body.

Sensing Niles's emotions, Reese slipped her left hand around his right arm as he continued to steady the boat toward the arching rainbow. As they closed in on the spot where it appeared to drop, she realized that she had yet to check her phone in all the commotion this morning. A moment later, while studying the screen, Reese discovered a handful of unread messages. When reading the last one, she felt the boat begin to slow as Niles let off the throttle. Looking up, she immediately covered her mouth. "Oh, no," she called out.

As Niles steered the search and rescue boat into a small opening in what from their vantage point appeared to be a completely wooded area, he felt his guard pop up. "What?" he asked wondering if she saw something he missed.

"A tree fell on Grandyma's house last night and both Eden and Kirk were taken to the hospital," she announced.

Absentmindedly rubbing his ring finger with the thumb on the same hand, Niles instantly felt a flood of mixed emotions while carefully navigating the boat through an opening between two tree lines less than three times the width of the vessel. Directly above, branches dangled loosely creating an arch over the canal, and Niles maneuvered around several fallen trees and large limbs. Up ahead, he could see a clearing where he knew the waterway would open and they would find a somewhat hidden pond-like area where he and Riley caught tons of fish over the years. That's where the rainbow seemed to fall, and Niles wondered what if anything they would discover. He also found himself thinking about Eden. Was she okay?

"Are they alright?" he asked Reese although he couldn't care less what happened to Kirk.

"That's all the information the text from Captain Stark provided," Reese revealed, wishing she knew more as her attention turned to the clearing ahead where the rainbow seemed to land.

As the boat coasted into a circular-shaped body of water that looked like the perfect swimming spot, Niles and Reese surveyed the area. Niles searched the tree line for the ark and Reese looked for anything that might catch her attention. As with most places, the water here was undoubtedly out of its normal bounds seeping in through the dense trees. Plenty of times Niles and Riley tied off the boat here and either swam or wandered through the woods, but it never looked anything like this, he recalled. Usually, a sandy bank on the far side offered a place where they could dig their toes in the sand, search for driftwood, or sit to have a picnic lunch.

After giving the area a couple looks over from the mouth of the pond, Niles guided the boat into the middle for a better view. The colors of the rainbow fell softly into the water like mist spilling from the sky creating one of the most magical views Niles and Reese ever witnessed.

If circumstances were different, Reese could imagine the two of them anchoring the boat, pulling one another close, and taking advantage of this once-in-a-lifetime opportunity. In all her life, she'd never seen the end of a rainbow so clearly. Honestly, she didn't even know if a landing spot existed; the colors always seemed to kind of disappear in the clouds or into the tops of trees. Here, however, the evidence showed that the rainbow plunged directly into the water and the vibrant strands of colors looked and felt like dew falling from the sky.

When Niles drove the boat to the far corner of the pond, he thought he caught a glimpse of something nestled inside a thick area of the forest that looked out of place but then he began to second guess his weary eyes. There was no way this was happening, but as they inched closer he could see the distinctive curves in the wooden frame of a vessel his very hands created.

"It's Riley's ark," Niles shouted into the air as loudly as his exasperated lungs would allow.

Reese's eyebrows instantly rose in amazement. She hoped to find something here but doubted the chances. "Oh, my God," spilled from her mouth.

Niles suddenly felt his heart pounding like an uncontrollable drum as he swiftly drove the boat as far as the waterway would allow.

"Riley," he hollered from the helm into the woods time after time hearing his own echo like a boomerang while hoping to hear the reciprocated voice of his five-year-old son any second now.

When they were less than ten feet from the tree line, Reese's gut told her what was about to happen and then she watched it play out.

Niles dropped the throttle all the way down, let go of the steering wheel, and jumped waist-deep in the murky water before Reese could say another word. Instinctively, she grabbed the wheel and completely steadied the boat then threw out the anchor as Niles made his way toward the ark yelling Riley's name at the top of his lungs as water splashed all around him.

Before the anchor hit bottom, Reese snatched the medical bag containing a complete first aid kit and more. She also grabbed two bottles of water, a granola bar, and an MRE which she tossed into the bag. It was doubtful that Riley would eat the latter, but it would be the best quick nutrition for him if they could talk him into forcing it down. After strapping the bag to her back, Reese leaped out of the boat and began trudging in Niles's same direction. Rushing through the water wearing the life jacket she slipped on as they followed the rainbow, she took in the sight of the ark. It looked exactly like a miniature version of Noah's ark, which Niles described previously. Still, she stood amazed by the sheer sight of the vessel for more than one reason, and she found herself thanking God it weathered the storm.

Niles audibly prayed to find Riley inside the ark, but as he used the trees and low-lying limbs surrounding the vessel to pull himself closer, he began to realize there was a chance his son wasn't even in the boat. It could have drifted here just as easily with no one in it. Also, why hadn't Riley stepped out onto the deck? If he was inside, surely he heard his name being called out.

Niles wasn't sure how much time elapsed from when he spotted the ark but guessed it had been a minute or two. Everything seemed to be moving at a snail's pace. He was very aware of every little detail—the weight of the water on his clothes in comparison to how it felt in the drysuit the past few days, the smell of the sap seeping from the pine trees, the sounds of birds chirping as if life was in perfect harmony, and the sight of the ark rocking ever so slightly against the trees making a somewhat eerie sound as the weather-treated wood scraped against the rough bark. The rare clarity of the moment reminded him of the wreck when he watched his entire family's world change in slow motion but could do very little to alter fate. Even though today's situation differed in that he had full control of where he was heading, as he reached upward for the outer wall of the ark and pulled himself out of the river with greater force than ever before, he knew this moment was in God's hands.

When Niles's bare feet touched the deck making a fresh set of prints, he imagined what he might find inside. Since discovering the ark, multiple scenarios played in his mind, and he found himself hoping for the best yet preparing for the worst. Chances were the result might be somewhere in between. The best would have been his son running onto the deck and jumping into the water minutes ago to meet him with open arms. The worst would be finding Riley inside then realizing his son had joined his brother Cameron in heaven. There was also the chance, maybe the highest of all the possibilities, that Riley wasn't even in the ark; perhaps he'd never been in the ark. He was somewhere else out there in the wild blue yonder, and the search would creep along for days or weeks or the rest of his life. That scared Niles nearly as much as the former, maybe more in some ways.

Waist-deep in river water, Reese watched Niles step through the dim opening that led to the ark's interior where all of Riley's stuffed animals resided. Similar to what Niles was experiencing, Reese's mind imagined and processed more than what seemed capable in such a short amount of time. She remembered Niles talking about the animals Riley placed inside and she envisioned them spread out, each having their own area like on Noah's ark. She hoped Riley was there amongst his stuffies, munching on snacks in the corner, and possibly so scared by all that happened over the course of the last few days that he hadn't emerged at the sounds of their voices. Her mind imagined the possibilities of the state in which they might find Riley if in fact he was on the vessel. She prepared to do whatever it took whether that meant giving CPR or rushing him to the hospital but most of all she prayed she could share a hug with a little boy she never met but learned so much about.

Niles's eyes scanned the interior. Once again, he saw everything vividly even though the light filtering in from behind him was dull. He noticed the grain patterns of the wood, the curved handles on the built-in storage bins, and the scattered snack bags covering the floor. However, his eyes gravitated to the far corner where Riley's stuffed animals sat piled together making what looked like a makeshift bed. Amid all the soft fur and colors beyond the rainbow, Niles locked his eyes on the backside of the curled up body of his son Riley North.

An instant later, Niles wasn't sure how he made it from the opening that led to the interior of the ark to falling into the bed of stuffed animals and wrapping his arms around his child. Still, all of a sudden, he cradled Riley there as memories emerged of hundreds, possibly thousands of times he held his son in his short five years of life. Each moment flashed through his mind like a perfectly crafted slideshow but this time was different. This image was still and real, and he knew he would never let it go.

41

Standing in the doorway of the ark, Reese took in the sight of Niles and Riley amidst the cocoon of stuffed animals. She heard the soft cries erupting from a grown man as he experienced a moment she knew would shape the rest of his life. Unsure of what to do or say, she waited for something to trigger her instincts. Neither Niles nor Riley moved or spoke, and in this instance her gut told her not to act.

Niles North absorbed the warmth of his son's body. Then, just like on so many mornings when the two of them lay in bed together, Riley barrel-rolled inside his dad's arms ever so slowly. Niles watched a beautiful grin stretch across his little boy's face as though he expected to wake and find his dad there. Tears effortlessly dropped from Niles's face like rain dripping from a roof, and he knew without a shadow of a doubt this was the happiest moment of his entire life.

The instant Reese witnessed Riley's little body begin to turn into his dad's, she felt her insides start to unthaw. Before the slow movement she questioned whether he was alive. His body remained so motionless that she feared the worst.

"I love you, Daddy," Riley spoke with ease.

Niles expected he would be the first to speak, but honestly he was at a loss for words. His emotions spilled all over the stuffed animals and until he heard Riley talk, words didn't seem adequate for the moment.

"I love you, too, Riley," Niles cried over and over, realizing those words were the most powerful ones in existence.

"I know that, silly," Riley giggled.

Watching a miracle unfold, Reese felt tears tickling her cheek. They found Riley and he was alive. After spending days out in a hurricane that brought with it the flood of a lifetime, this sweet boy actually lived through it. Although she hoped and felt confident they would find him all along, reality suddenly felt surreal. He shouldn't have made it. A five-year-old was no match for nature's fury, but this little guy beat the odds somehow.

"I love you so much," Niles whispered while stroking his son's matted hair.

Reese somehow began to put her emotions aside in order to assess the situation closer and properly from a first responder's perspective. The weathered camouflaged pajamas still covered Riley's body. His face appeared flushed; his voice sounded weak; and his hands shook a little from the chill in the air. She almost took a step toward him, then he glanced her way and noticed her for the first time.

"Hey," Riley offered.

Following the sound of his son's voice, Niles turned his head and saw Reese standing there with a relieved smile looking as beautiful as she was. Even though he should have known she would have made it to the ark by now, this was the first time he realized she stood there.

"Hey, Riley," Reese replied, grinning as she wiped a line of tears from her cheeks.

"Are you a police officer?" he asked gently.

"Yes, my name is Reese," she responded simply.

Niles lifted his head a bit higher and held it steady with his palm as his elbow dug into the bed of stuffed animals. "That's Detective Reese Kirby," Niles added. "She's my police officer friend," he confirmed.

"Wow," Riley clamored. "Do you have a police car?"

Reese chuckled. "I do, and a police boat," she shared with raised eyebrows.

Riley's pale face lit up a smidge. "I want to see them."

"You certainly can; you can even sit in them if you like," Reese offered, stepping toward Riley and Niles.

"Really?" Riley asked, looking to his dad as if to ask for permission.

"Certainly," Niles agreed.

"May I sit here?" Reese asked, pointing to an empty spot in the stuffed animals near Niles's feet while focusing on Riley's skin and his movements, realizing they weren't out of the water yet. She didn't want to frighten the little guy nor his dad, so she kept her tone even and her movements gentle.

"Of course," Niles agreed.

"How are you feeling?" Reese asked Riley.

"Okay," he responded.

He was dehydrated; she could see it in his eyes. "When is the last time you've eaten or drank?"

Riley shrugged his shoulders.

Like Niles, when entering, Reese noticed the snack bags covering the wooden floor. There were also empty water bottles scattered around but not enough for several days. Who knew how quickly he drank them or possibly how long he waited to start drinking at all. Kids without parental supervision often didn't think about hydration, especially a child battling a massive hurricane in a small boat.

"Do you have any water or juice left?" Reese asked, reaching for the nearby cooler while thinking about how Niles's decision to keep snacks and beverages in the ark probably saved his son's life.

Riley shook his head side to side.

"Are you thirsty?" Niles asked.

"Kind of," Riley answered.

As Reese expected, the cooler was empty. While talking, she studied Riley's body searching for cuts, bites, or anything else that might need attention. She noticed a few scratches on his arms and figured they might find other issues hidden beneath his clothes, but she wouldn't suggest removing those until he became more comfortable. Ultimately, she wanted to transport him to the hospital as quickly as possible. Still, at the moment, she knew the best thing was to hydrate him before having him exert any energy.

Niles, grateful his son now rested in his arms, assumed it had as much to do with Riley being lethargic from days of battling high waves, heavy winds, and torrential downpours as with how much he missed him and the relief of seeing him. He still couldn't believe Riley had been so sound asleep that he hadn't heard him and Reese calling his name or climbing onto the ark. When first laying eyes on his little boy, he thought he was dead. The fact that Riley hadn't heard them nor was he moving scared Niles as much as anything he'd ever seen. The instant he felt his son's heart beating, he promised God he would always remember this miracle. He knew his child shouldn't be alive. Some adults probably wouldn't have survived the elements Riley made it through.

Reese pulled the medical bag off her shoulders and reached inside. "Drink this," she instructed Riley, offering him a water bottle. "I also brought food; I imagine you must be hungry," she added, pulling out the items.

Riley lifted his arm weakly to accept the opened water bottle and a little spilled out the top as he moved it toward his mouth.

"That's okay," Niles commented, making sure his son knew it didn't matter if he made a mess; it never really mattered, and he always cringed when parents freaked out about their kids making mistakes. "Drink as much as you can."

Water dribbled down Riley's chin onto his animals as he took a sip, but Reese also noticed the small amount going into his mouth. "Have some more," she encouraged a moment later. Getting a dehydrated child to drink fluids was much like getting a sick person to hydrate. As badly as the body starves for hydration, the mind often fights against gulping the water. "Here, try some of this," Reese offered, unwrapping the granola bar then handing it to Riley.

Fortunately, Riley took the bar but only bit off a pea-sized chunk.

"Riley, one of my jobs as a police officer is to check out kids who have been caught in storms," Reese revealed, trying to ease into the upcoming request as gently as possible. "Is it okay if I have a look at you kind of like your doctor might?" She prayed he wouldn't relate her choice of words to receiving a shot at the physician's office.

Riley glanced at his dad.

"It's okay," Niles agreed, realizing Reese's motives.

"Thank you," Reese answered. She already felt his skin when giving him the water bottle and she'd been studying his pupils. The visible cuts didn't look too bad, but they were brighter red than she preferred. When Reese held the granola bar toward his mouth, she leaned in and took a good listen to his breathing. "Riley, we're going to make your daddy hold either your water or granola bar, whichever you're not eating or drinking at the moment, okay?" Reese said winking at Riley, trying to make it fun for him but wanting him to have one or the other in his own hands at all times so he might be more likely to drink and eat.

Riley grinned a little then Reese slipped the ear pieces of a stethoscope into her ears and placed the metal end on Riley's chest over his camouflaged shirt. She listened to his heart and to his breathing. She wasn't a medical doctor but she could immediately hear the wheezing she caught a hint of earlier.

"While you get another sip of water, I'm going to lift up your awesome shirt and listen closer," she explained.

Riley gave her a funny look and placed his hand on his shirt near his belly button.

"Want me to listen to Dad's first?" she inquired, smirking as she lifted up Niles's wet shirt without asking permission.

Niles's eyes shifted from Riley to Reese. He thought her plan was cute, and the moment reminded him of when the two of them were in the hotel room together the first night and his shirt came off.

Riley giggled watching Reese listen to his dad's stomach.

"That feels good," Niles offered while playing along.

"My turn," Riley uttered, lifting his own shirt.

This song and dance went on as Reese studied every part of Riley's little body. Eventually, she and Niles removed his clothes and Reese wrapped a dry towel around his trembling body. The pajamas smelled like a mildewed sock, and although not sopping wet at the moment, they didn't do his body any good sticking to him after being saturated with sweat, rain water, and who knows what else. Reese couldn't wait to hear the stories this little boy would be able to tell, but first she knew they needed to get him to the hospital where he could be checked out more thoroughly by a team of physicians whom she would make sure waited on him upon arrival.

Niles took note that his son drank about a quarter of the sixteen-ounce water bottle and maybe ate a third of the granola bar. He wasn't sure if it was good or bad that Riley didn't seem particularly thirsty or hungry, but he was thankful Reese checked him out.

"Let's get you to the police boat," Reese encouraged, hoping the idea would give Riley a little more energy.

He grinned but he hadn't talked as much the last few minutes. Reese knew this was a lot to take in, and she thanked God she and

Niles found him rather than strangers. Although she knew if anyone from the swift water rescue teams found him, they would have taken care of him as if he were their own child.

Reese encouraged Niles to climb into the river first although Riley hadn't let go of his daddy since the two of them embraced. He literally had at least one hand on his father the entire time which made sense because he most likely experienced separation anxiety as well as other underlying issues. She figured it would be easier to get him to let go of his dad on the boat for a moment while he slipped into the water than for Niles to hand him down to her in the water. It took a bit of coaxing, but eventually they convinced Riley to help his dad into the water, giving him a reason to keep a hand wrapped around his father. Once Niles was in, Reese helped Riley onto his chest then hopped in with them.

Reese smiled as they slogged through the water, thinking about how Riley resembled a monkey wrapped around his dad's chest, like Banana, whom Riley carried tightly. He'd demanded his favorite stuffed animal make this journey with them.

"The river is much calmer now," Niles pointed out to Riley, knowing the high waves must have scared him to death.

"That's the same thing Jesus said," Riley mentioned.

Reese heard his cute reply and smiled at him. "In the Bible story?" she asked figuring since he literally owned an ark he heard lots of Bible stories.

Riley shook his head east to west. "When Jesus and Cameron came to see me."

Niles swallowed a lump in his throat which hadn't been there until that very instant.

"Oh," Reese sighed unsure how else to respond.

"They came to see you?" Niles asked with a furrowed brow pulling his head back to look into his son's hazel eyes.

"Yes, right after I got into the ark," Riley explained with confidence and newfound energy.

Niles still tried to walk but his son's story altered his focus. "Jesus and Cameron were in the ark with you?"

"No, they never got into the ark, but I invited them."

"So, where were they?" Reese asked, puzzled.

"Walking on the river," Riley explained nonchalantly.

Reese began to wonder if Riley was delusional. He'd been through a lot. He obviously heard about Jesus walking on water although it had nothing to do with the ark, but a five-year-old combining that tale with the Noah's ark story made sense.

"You saw them walking on water?" Niles quizzed curious about what else his son would say while thinking some of the same things as Reese.

"Yep, and I walked on water with them."

"You did?" Niles questioned.

"I was scared at first, but then Cameron said it was easy."

"Cameron told you walking on water was easy, huh?" Niles probed. It sounded better than schlepping through it like they did now he wanted to say, but he didn't want to make light of a story his son told as though it was the truth. "Was Cameron little like in the pictures at Mommy's house?"

Riley shook his head no.

"What did he look like?" Niles wondered curiously.

"Just like me," Riley confirmed. "He was even wearing camouflage pajamas."

"That's cool," Reese offered, entertaining the story.

"But he looked different, too."

"How so?" Niles asked.

"He had a big scar above his eyebrow."

Niles nearly collapsed face-first into the Neuse River. As far as he knew, no one ever mentioned to Riley the injuries his brother sustained in the car accident. They'd just told him Cameron was in heaven now. "He did," Niles replied as tears began to crawl down his face.

Reese saw Niles's reaction and immediately found herself

listening more intently as she and Niles all but stopped walking.

"I think the Bible says people in heaven will have perfect bodies," Niles reminded Riley then kind of wished he hadn't, afraid it might upset his son or make him think he didn't believe him. "Why did Cameron have a scar?" he asked regardless.

"Jesus said scars are perfect."

Reese suddenly felt a flood of tears exit her swollen eyelids. "That's amazing," she professed. "What else did Jesus say?" she wanted to know regardless of whether this was a real story or one Riley made up to help endure the hurricane.

"When He asked if I wanted to walk on water, He held out His hands and showed me the scars on them; He said everyone has perfect scars just like Him."

For a moment, Niles remained speechless. He glanced at Reese who also seemed to be at a loss for words and then back to Riley. "Was walking on water easy like Jesus and Cameron said?" Niles finally asked.

"Yeah, because Jesus made the water calm even though the hurricane was all around us."

"Wow," Reese chimed.

"When they left, they told me I'd be safe as long as I stayed on the ark until you found me."

"You believed them?" Niles asked.

"Dad, they were walking on the water!"

"Right."

"What else did they tell you?" Reese queried.

"Jesus told me that your daddy is in heaven."

Reese's eyes nearly jumped out of their sockets. She hadn't expected Riley to relate anything about the story to her life. "My daddy?" she investigated

"He told me that my daddy and a policewoman would find me," Riley informed them. "That's when he told me your daddy is in heaven."

How could this kid possibly know her dad was in heaven? She wanted to ask Riley that directly but he was five. "Did you see my daddy?" she asked, wondering whether he would add another person to the story at this juncture. She guessed she was playing detective with a child now but she had to know how he would respond.

"No, he didn't need to come."

"Why not?" Niles asked curiously.

Riley shrugged his shoulders. "I don't know; that's just what Jesus said."

What beautiful words of wisdom from a child, Niles realized regardless of how this story came about.

"Did Jesus tell you anything else about my daddy?" Reese probed.

"Yes."

"What?" she asked sweetly.

"Your daddy has a perfect scar, too."

"He does?" she inquired knowing exactly where her father's scar was after the surgeons worked on the gunshot wound and stitched up the bullet hole.

"It's over his heart," Riley claimed. "But Jesus told me your daddy's heart is made of gold."

Reese's mouth fell open, wide enough to drink the entire Neuse River. Never in her life had she heard truer words and never before had she felt closer to Jesus than at this very moment while in the presence of a five-year-old hurricane survivor who somehow experienced God in a way that people only dream. Maybe it was a dream, but either way his words were as real as the tears falling from both hers and Niles's faces as both realized the truth from their own perspectives.

A minute later, all three of them and Banana sat safely in the search and rescue boat which Riley thought was as amazing as they found his story.

"I'll drive," Reese said although she doubted Niles would put up a fight because just like Riley, he didn't want to let go and she didn't blame either of them.

"Riley, do you want to turn on the blue lights?" Reese checked, and while he was captivated by the experience, she whispered to Niles that they needed to take his son to the hospital to be evaluated.

Niles studied Reese's eyes then looked at his son, still nestled in his arms. He hadn't previously thought about where they would go from here. Honestly, he wanted to take Riley home to relax, but it made sense to have a doctor double-check everything. Plus, Riley's mom was at the hospital—*His mom is at the hospital*, Niles suddenly shouted inside his own head. Amidst all that happened since learning about the tree falling on Grandyma's house, he'd completely forgotten about it.

"Where's Mommy?" Riley suddenly asked as if he knew something was wrong.

42

iles carried Riley to the backseat in the boat and kept him occupied talking about all the cool features of the police watercraft while Reese quietly radioed in the good news and made the request for an ambulance to meet them at the river's edge. She hoped that particular means of transportation wouldn't frighten Riley but figured maybe he would think it was fun like the search and rescue boat. The paramedics would be able to hook him up to an IV immediately which is what he needed because the water bottle in the little guy's hand remained more than half full.

As Reese guided the watercraft through the small opening leading back to the wide-open Neuse River, she noticed the rainbow had vanished. When she turned to look at Niles, she caught him looking into the sky realizing the same thing. With a smirk on her face, she slowly shook her head side to side as she locked eyes with one of the most beautiful people she'd ever met.

Niles found himself wishing he'd taken a picture of the rainbow to print and show the whole world what led him and Reese to his son. However, the image etched in his mind was all the evidence he would ever need. He doubted he would tell anyone besides family and close friends Riley's story about walking on the river with Jesus and Cameron. Most people probably wouldn't believe it, and he didn't want to subject his son to an onslaught of questions from cynics.

Before Reese, Niles, and Riley made it to the waterline where hundreds of people including first responders, friends, and random citizens clapped profusely as the search and rescue boat came to a halt, Niles explained to Riley that he would get to ride in an ambulance. At first, Riley displayed signs of hesitancy, but the more the three of them talked about it the more he became okay with the idea.

It amazed Niles how quickly news spread. The media had cameras set up and a slew of reporters stood near the water's edge holding microphones just hoping for the first interview. As Niles stepped out of the boat wearing the boots he finally found time to put on, he bear-hugged his son and ran right through a hole that a group of first responders made for him leading them directly to the ambulance's opened doors.

Reese watched from the boat and found herself wishing she could head to the hospital with Niles and Riley but knew she had to find a place to park the boat and figured by the time she made it to shore, the ambulance would be long gone. Of course, there was no way she would ask Niles to wait on her. As the thought dribbled across her mind, she spotted Captain Jensen jogging into the water toward her.

"I know you want to go with them," he shouted. "I'll find a place to dock your boat," he offered.

Reese didn't hesitate to accept the offer. Once he took over the reins she sloshed through the water just as Niles had and found Captain Stark waiting at the waterline to direct her to a squad car waiting to take her to the local hospital.

Sitting in the ambulance next to Riley who was now hooked to IV fluids, Niles caught a glimpse of Reese running through the water and climbing into the police car. He hoped she would be joining them at the hospital.

The ambulance rushed Riley to the rear entrance of the emergency room where a team of doctors waited for him as Reese promised. She scurried in right behind the stretcher on which Riley lay and in a matter of moments they were in a private room where a pediatrician led the questions. The woman reminded Niles very much of how Reese interacted with Riley on the ark.

Over the next hour, multiple physicians inspected Riley's body from head to toe, and dozens of tests were run. They checked the little fellow for everything from the common cold to hypothermia. The hardest part was waiting on the results.

In the meantime, Niles sat at his son's bedside, their hands connected the entire time. Early on, Reese came over and whispered into Niles's ear what Captain Stark told her on the ride over.

"The tree that fell on Grandyma's house came right through the bedroom roof where Eden and Kirk were apparently sleeping," she informed Niles, making sure the doctor who was tickling Riley's toes while making funny faces also distracted him. "Kirk is fine but a branch pierced through Eden's stomach requiring emergency surgery—"

Before Reese could finish her sentence, the door burst open and a pleasantly plump lady with curly gray hair rushed in, basically dragging the security guard behind her.

"Honey child, I'm telling you that's my grandbaby right there on that bed," she announced pointing to Riley with her free hand while the security guard stood attached to the other.

Niles stood up. "It's okay," he told the man. "She's with us."

The guard let go of her arm. "She just rushed right past me and said she didn't have time to check-in."

"Baby, I didn't," she noted, making a beeline to Riley's bedside. "Are you okay, sweetie pie?" she inquired with a concerned tone.

Watching the look on the security guard's face, Reese chuckled beneath her breath. This was Grandyma she suddenly realized without needing an introduction.

After Grandyma kissed and hugged Riley a hundred times covering nearly every inch of his body, Niles and Reese spent the next five minutes catching her up on how and where they found Riley, what the doctors had been doing, and inconspicuously mentioning the test results on which they were impatiently waiting.

"Grandyma, I walked on the river with Jesus and Cameron," Riley randomly announced.

"That's wonderful, darling," she replied. It was instantly apparent to Niles and Reese that the comment went straight through one ear and out the other because Grandyma just started kissing and hugging him again and telling him he was a big boy and he'd be out of this hospital in two shakes of a shiver.

"Where's Mommy?" Riley asked in the midst of her pampering.

"Oh, baby," she responded softly then looked at Niles as though asking if he told Riley about what happened, but she didn't know Niles literally found out all he knew the moment before she scurried through the doorway. "I've been upstairs with your mommy, and the doctors are taking excellent care of her just like they are you," Grandyma shared unable to stop a few tears from sliding down a face that felt twice as wrinkled as it had a mere week ago.

Cringing, Niles thought to himself, *always leave it up to Grandyma to tell the truth* as he contemplated a way to change the subject. Reese found herself thinking the same but decided it didn't seem to be her place in this room filled with family.

Surprising all of them, Riley spoke up first. "It's okay, Grandyma," he comforted. "Jesus told me Mommy is going to have a scar on her tummy but that she would be okay because all scars are perfect."

Niles suddenly felt another lump enter his throat. Grandyma hadn't spoken a word about the tree or where it pierced Eden's body.

The whole room seemed to fall silent then a knock came at the door. A moment later, a doctor in a white lab coat walked in with a folder in his hands.

"All of Riley's tests are looking positive," he shared. "We are waiting to hear back from the lab on a couple more, but I'm hopeful we will only need to keep you around for observation moving forward," he mentioned rubbing Riley's hair while speaking.

Everyone in the room breathed a sigh of relief, but the moment was suddenly interrupted by a commotion in the hallway.

"Sir, you can't be back here," a voice called out.

"I'd like to see you try to stop me," a second voice echoed through the hallway, and Niles instantly knew the identity of the person who emerged in the door frame moments later. "I'm his Uncle Mickey."

Mickey charged into the room much like Grandyma, and once again Niles stood up to address the exasperated security guard who was now standing in the door jamb looking as though this had been the most challenging day ever on the job.

"He's with us, too," Niles commented again.

At the same time, Riley called out, "Uncle Mickey!"

The security guard crossed his arms and puffed out his chest in an attempt to show a sign of authority. "You know, there is a limit to how many people can be back here," he warned.

The doctor turned. "These circumstances are a little different," he proclaimed. "Let's show a little grace for our favorite patient," he added, winking at Riley.

"Just don't let the media in, please," Niles requested.

The security guard threw up his hands as if in defeat and walked away without speaking another word. A moment later, the doctor exited as well.

"Riley, you are a superhero," Mickey announced. "How in the world did you survive three days in the worst hurricane that hit New Bern in ages?"

Riley grinned and shrugged his shoulders. Everyone laughed, and then he began telling Mickey about Jesus and Cameron. This time, Grandyma made a big deal out of the story, and Niles figured it no longer mattered if the media found out; she'd tell the whole world by the end of the day.

Obviously the IV fluids replenished Riley's energy, and he also ate a lemon ice pop that one of the nurses brought and now munched on pretzels. He seemed to be relishing all the attention and enjoying telling stories about being on the ark during the flood.

"How did you get on the ark in the first place?" Mickey inquired, and everyone perked up because they'd been wondering the same thing but hadn't asked yet because things had been so hectic.

"I woke up on the couch in Grandyma's house, and there was water all over the floor and it was splashing onto me."

"Oh, Lord," Grandyma proclaimed.

"I called for Mommy but she didn't come."

"She probably couldn't hear you because of the loud hurricane," Reese inserted knowing Eden deserved some grace both now and moving forward.

"Tell Grandyma how high it was, darling."

"It came up to my knees," Riley showed, touching them as he explained.

"What did you do then?" Niles inquired.

"I walked to the back door and that's when I saw the ark."

"Was it tied up in the backyard where your Grandpa had his crew leave it?" Grandyma investigated.

"Nope, it was up against the house, right beside the deck."

"Wow," Reese spouted, knowing the ark had to break free of

the restraints at some point but amazed how it seemed to have floated right to the back door to pick up Riley.

"So you just jumped in?" Mickey asked. "That's superhero stuff right there, my man."

"Daddy always said the best place to be in a flood is the ark."

Grins and giggles filled the small room.

"What happened after you got into the boat?" Niles queried.

"First, I checked on all my animals to make sure they were okay. Then, I decided to come back out and call for Mommy, but I was so far away from the house," he said, tearing up a little and stopping mid-sentence.

"It's okay, darling; you're safe now," Grandyma comforted.

"Before I knew it, I was out in the middle of the river, and that's when Jesus and Cameron showed up." Riley talked through the story once again telling details causing goosebumps to form on every arm in the room.

Both Niles and Reese looked at one another; each suddenly remembering the captain saying a boat without a motor couldn't have made it across the Neuse River from the New Bern side to the Bridgeton side at any point on the front end of the hurricane. However, the ark apparently took Riley out into the middle of the river and who knew where else. What Niles and Reese realized for sure was the ark hadn't been anywhere near Grandyma's neighborhood or in downtown New Bern while they and the other teams searched. Without a shadow of a doubt, they would have found the vessel. The ark would have stuck out like a sore thumb just like every other boat that ended up against a building, a house, or in trees. There were no wooded areas in downtown New Bern, nowhere for a boat to hide.

Riley went on and on about the things he did during his days on the ark. He talked about playing with stuffed animals and taking care of them, crying because he missed his mommy and daddy, eating snacks, sleeping, peeing off the side of the boat, and sitting on the deck of the vessel when the wind and rains calmed.

When his story winded down, a knock came at the door.

"Come in," Niles commented.

When the door opened, the security guard stood on the other side, and everyone in the room waited to hear what he had to say. "Detective Kirby, you have visitors in the hallway and they have authorization to be back here."

Each person in the room tried not to laugh at what sounded like a jab but a few snickers came out.

Reese furrowed her brow. Captain Jensen? Stark? Maybe the team members who worked alongside her and Niles the past few days?

She wandered toward the hallway and as soon as she took a left turn beyond the doorway, a broad grin overcame her face. "Hey, guys," she exclaimed immediately, reaching out for hugs.

Captain Lawson, Dominguez, Johnson, and Brown were all standing there wearing casual clothing and smiles of their own.

"I can't believe you all are here," Reese expressed. "What did you do, close down the station?"

"The Chattanooga Police Department agreed to send over a team to fill in for us so we could assist you in the search," Captain Lawson explained.

"I guess you didn't need us, though," Dominguez teased.

Reese snickered. "I still need you," she promised.

"That's good because we're here for a week," Johnson added.

"I guess now we can help with community clean up," Brown chimed.

"I think there are still evacuations underway for people trapped in homes in low-lying areas, so there might be some excitement left," Reese proclaimed.

"Speaking of excitement, we brought doughnuts," Captain Lawson revealed, pulling a box from behind his back.

The whole team laughed. "It's a good thing none of us are in uniform," Reese pointed out. "I was wondering what you were hiding behind your back," she added.

"I guess detectives can't hide anything from each other," Captain Lawson snickered.

"Speaking of that, how in the world did you know every move I was making between Hickory and New Bern?" Reese finally asked.

"Well, the GPS in the Humvee kind of gave you away," Lawson shared.

"I should have known you had access to the navigation system," Reese sighed. "How did you know to ask me about Niles North?"

"You ran a background check on him when you were in Hickory. So, I figured he was someone you crossed paths with there. Once you headed toward New Bern, which is where the report shows North living, I figured he had something to do with it and was most likely with you."

"I guess I learned from the best," Reese offered.

"Your dad was the best," Captain Lawson argued.

"You're right; I learned from two of the best."

Brown cleared his throat and cocked his head asking for some recognition.

"Brown, we all know Kirby ate your dinner at the shooting competition," Dominguez reminded him.

"Literally," Johnson laughed.

"I want a rematch," Brown requested.

"You just better be glad you didn't bet your badge," Dominguez reminded him.

Johnson immediately elbowed Dominguez and attempted to nod inconspicuously in the captain's direction.

Reese picked up on the interaction and figured the captain probably had, too. "It's okay," she announced, "Captain Lawson knows about both shooting competitions."

"The first one saved me a lot of paperwork," Lawson revealed with a faint grin.

Everyone's eyes bulged a little but knew precisely what he meant.

"Do you think the little guy is feeling up for a doughnut?" Lawson asked, holding up the box.

Reese checked in with Niles, Riley, Grandyma, and Mickey to make sure it was okay if the guys came in to say hello and bring Riley a treat. All of them seemed completely fine with it, especially Riley who was just as excited about meeting four more police officers as he was about the doughnuts.

"I always knew cops loved doughnuts," Mickey teased.

Niles shook his head but knew he shouldn't be surprised at any comment that came out of his best friend's mouth.

"Don't tell our secret," Johnson laughed.

"Let me tell you a story about a time this guy tricked me into asking a police officer directions to the doughnut shop," Mickey said pointing at Niles.

Remembering the story, Reese burst into laughter and Niles's face grew a bright shade of red.

The officers stayed just long enough to hear the story, share doughnuts with Riley, and agree to give the little fellow a ride in the patrol car they drove to New Bern. While Reese walked them out, Niles found himself thinking about Eden again. He still didn't know her current condition, if the surgery had been successful, or any other details regarding the injury. He assumed she was still alive because Grandyma mentioned being with her before coming to find Riley, but he hadn't asked anything further because he didn't want to take the chance of the answers scaring Riley. He thought about texting the question to her but then remembered he forgot to grab his phone in his haste to leave the treehouse this morning. He wondered if messages waited there about the tree falling on Eden and updates about everything else that transpired with her since the accident.

The one person he hadn't seen since arriving at the hospital was Kirk, and he was thankful for that. He hoped the guy didn't

JOEY JONES

show up in Riley's room, and he knew if he did, the security guard wouldn't have to worry about kicking him out. Niles would take care of that himself even though it seemed Kirk didn't have anything to do with Riley's disappearance other than helping distract Eden from her responsibility as a parent.

Niles thought about asking Riley if Mickey could sit with him while he went into the hallway to talk to Grandyma but in all honesty he didn't want to leave his son for a single moment. It was hard to imagine ever letting Riley out of his sight again after what the little guy went through. He tried to let go of the thoughts about Eden, but he was concerned for his son's sake just as much as his own. Even though he enjoyed getting to know Reese, he still loved Eden. Eden was still the mother of his child, and it was hard to think of her being gone.

As Niles's mind churned, he kept coming back to the perfect scars comment Riley made regarding Eden. What did that mean?

43

Later in the evening on the day Niles and Reese rescued Riley, the final lab results came back.

"It's a miracle," the doctor explained. "This little boy is as healthy as a horse."

Riley spent one night in the hospital for observation with his dad at his bedside then released the following day. When the little guy walked out of the facility with his entourage, they found the media, friends and family, and even complete strangers waiting for a glimpse of the boy who beat Hurricane Florence. The story of how he weathered the storm in the ark that his father built circulated the entire globe and become a trending topic across the Internet.

An empty podium awaited them outside the hospital for a press briefing. The emergency management director spoke first while in the background Riley, Niles, Reese, Grandyma, Mickey, and some of the search and rescue team members stared at a sea of reporters and cameras. Niles reluctantly agreed to answer a few questions from the media. As he did, Riley again clinged to him like a monkey while Banana dangled from his fingertips. One of the reporters asked Riley if he was scared, and to his dad's surprise, Riley went on to tell the whole story about walking on water.

So much for keeping the story a family secret, Niles realized, as police officers escorted them from the interview area to Reese's Humvee. Riley flipped the switch to turn on the blue lights then climbed into a child's safety seat Reese grabbed at a local store which just reopened yesterday evening. She also picked out fresh clothes for Riley, Niles, and herself since they all smelled like river water.

In the days that followed, residents of New Bern and those in the surrounding areas affected by Hurricane Florence began to pick up the pieces the storm left behind. Niles spent the entire first day with Riley, Mickey, and Reese. Bringing the ark back to the treehouse dock was a priority because both Niles and Reese feared that with all the buzz about the ark some people might be searching for it in hopes of making a quick buck off its sudden popularity.

While picking up the vessel in which Riley rode out the storm, they happened to stumble across Mickey's small boat and salvaged it in one piece. This allowed Reese to pass off the search and rescue boat to Captain Lawson, Johnson, Dominguez, and Brown so the four of them could aid in evacuations. Once Niles, Riley, Reese, and Mickey secured the ark to the dock, which thankfully the hurricane hadn't ripped away like many others, the four of them lounged at the treehouse for a while. Then they took down the plywood covering the windows and eventually played on the obstacle course before ordering pizza that they drove Mickey's boat to pick up due to the driveway still being flooded. The temporary island the treehouse currently stood on proved to be a blessing in disguise because it kept the media at bay. However, several random boats hung out near the dock where those onboard snapped photos and took videos of the ark.

That night, Reese stayed at the treehouse again with the guys although this time she slept on the couch because she and Niles thought that was best for Riley. Niles snuggled up close to his son, and although he didn't sleep a whole lot that first night at home with his little guy, he felt more comfortable than ever before.

The next day as everyone sat around eating breakfast on the treehouse deck overlooking the Neuse River, they talked about what they wanted to do with their time. Initially, everyone thought they preferred to relax following all the excitement from the days prior, but after talking they decided helping others with hurricane cleanup was the right thing to do. The four of them loaded as much gear as possible into Mickey's boat and trekked across the calm river to Grandyma's.

Niles felt confident the excitement was over now that Riley had been found and the hurricane had vacated the area losing strength as it moved west. He assumed life would get back to normal, or at least a new normal. However, as they docked on the riverside of Grandyma's house thanks to the water receding and began to walk toward the rusting hinges which once held French doors, Reese spotted movement inside the home. She quietly pointed out a person to Niles and Mickey, and as they closed in on the opening, they saw at least three more people wandering around the home carrying an array of items.

"Grandyma must have hired people to clean up her home," Mickey figured.

Reese held up a hand motioning for them to halt and following her lead they all slowly moved behind a large maple tree. "I don't think these people were invited," Reese predicted as she honed in on their body language.

"They're looters," Niles suddenly announced, noticing that the items in their hands didn't appear to be damaged.

"That guy is spray painting the wall," Mickey pointed out.

Riley hid behind his dad's leg.

"We should call the police," Reese suggested.

"You are the police," Mickey cackled a little too loudly, and Niles punched him in the arm telling him to quiet down.

"This isn't my jurisdiction plus there are at least four people in the house and only three of us and a five-year-old who we have to protect," Reese pointed out seriously.

Without further discussion, she reached for her phone, but things began to happen quickly a moment after she made the call.

"Hey!" shouted a man from behind, startling all four of them because his voice came from the opposite direction of the house they were watching like hawks.

Niles, Reese, Mickey, and Riley turned in unison to face the man walking from the nearly destroyed shed toward them. Apparently, he'd been in there pillaging and Reese immediately realized she didn't like the fact that an ax swayed like a pendulum at his side.

"Stop," she yelled, holding out her left hand and reaching for her firearm with the right. All her fingers found though was her own body; she'd left her gear at the treehouse because she decided not to play the role of a police officer today. She wanted to help at Grandyma's, be with Niles and Riley, and not risk the temptation of being pulled away with the search and rescue team. She never imagined they could run into trouble here.

The man didn't listen very well, and as the four of them stepped back all of a sudden there was an array of voices coming from the direction of the house. When Niles turned, he saw four additional men and one burly woman heading their way.

"You guys need to leave," Niles demanded.

"Yeah, you're not welcome here," Mickey added.

"Triangle," Reese called out talking to Niles and Mickey as she realized they were outnumbered six to three.

Immediately, Niles, Reese, and Mickey formed a triangle where they could see every possible angle, and Niles kept Riley on the back of his leg inside the wall of protection.

"What do we have here?" the guy leading the pack from inside the house shouted as the others began circling around like a swarm of bees.

"We don't want any trouble," Reese stressed facing the tall and slender, rough-looking figure.

"We do," a scraggly-faced man said with a sly grin.

Mickey eyed the man with the ax who slowed his steps but stood only about ten feet away.

"We claimed this house," another homely-looking guy spouted. "Go find your own house to rob," he cackled.

This crew reminded Niles of pirates, and he got the feeling they weren't typical looters.

"We'll do that," Niles responded, playing their game but only because his five-year-old son gripped his leg as tightly as a baseball bat. "Just let us leave and we won't bother you."

"Too late for that," the leader of the pack announced. "We're going to have to hold you here until we finish claiming our goods."

"We have a child with us," Reese pointed out, hoping for mercy.

"Good, he can help spray paint this beautiful house while the three of you are tied up in the corner watching," the most muscular-looking person in the bunch suggested with a laugh. "Or would you rather be in the closet?" he asked. "Or we could tie you up to this tree."

"This is Grandyma's house," Riley bravely announced.

The eyes of the guy holding the ax lit up. "This is your Granny's house, huh? That means you can show us where all the good stuff is hidden."

"Yeah, we like jewelry and money," the burly woman added.

Reese's, Niles's, and Mickey's eyes darted among each of the characters trying to get a feel for who was who if things got uglier.

In one swift motion, Niles snatched Riley's arms away from his legs, turned, grabbed his son beneath the armpits, said, "Grab the branch," and flung him to the lowest hanging limb about eight feet high. Thankfully, it wasn't the first time Niles tossed Riley into this tree although on this occasion dire circumstances prevailed and Niles prayed Riley didn't understand the severity of the situation.

Instinctively, Riley grasped the branch flawlessly and pulled himself up to safety.

"Climb as high as you can," Niles instructed, "and don't come down until I tell you it's safe."

"My friend," the leader proclaimed, "I can promise you no one here is safe."

"You guys are in for a rude awakening," Mickey declared, staring into the hungry eyes of the ax guy.

"I'll chop that tree down," the man threatened, tapping his palm with the ax handle.

"You'll have to chop me down first," Mickey dared.

The man flashed an eerie grin then reared back and swung the ax violently in Mickey's direction which was precisely what Mickey hoped he'd try. The blade missed Mickey's face by a foot and its weight carried the man's entire body with it making him completely off balance. An instant later, Mickey's left foot drove deeply into the man's rib cage, collapsing his body to the wet ground as he lost hold of the tool.

Reese saw the action out of the corner of her eye, and with the sudden surge of adrenaline she also felt relief realizing Mickey could fight like Niles.

"The pretty girl is mine," the bulky woman declared, heading straight for Reese.

"Good, because I didn't want to hit a woman," Niles disclosed, lunging toward the head honcho then swiftly sweep-kicking the man's legs out from under him.

The woman swung full force at Reese who stepped back to dodge her punch. Reese watched in surprise at how her assailant kept throwing blows like a boxer trying to back an opponent into a corner. Reese maneuvered quickly while trying to keep the integrity of the triangle intact.

Mickey dropped onto the axman, straddled his torso, gave him one elbow to the head, then watched his eyes roll back. Hurriedly, Mickey reached for the ax to fling it further away, but someone tackled him from the side before he could secure it in his hands.

Above, Riley climbed from branch to branch like a monkey while glancing over his shoulder watching the scene play out below. He wanted to come down and help his dad, Uncle Mickey, and the policewoman, but the sound of his dad's voice when tossing him into the tree left an impression.

Niles stood to his feet. "Who's next?" he asked.

Amidst the swarm of punches, Reese took one to the cheek but kept her balance enough to latch on to the woman's arm twisting her elbow violently as they fell to the ground. Although Reese had a good hold on her and knew the pressure was hurting the woman, she didn't like the idea of wrestling with someone who probably outweighed her by seventy-five pounds. The beastly woman clawed and grabbed with her free hand while they rolled in the mud. Reese tried to finagle her legs around the woman's waist hoping to take control of the match but her opponent's strength proved to be a deterrent.

Nearby, Mickey found himself in a similar situation on the ground with the most muscular guy out of the whole bunch. He dodged a few punches but also took one to the ear and was currently on the bottom of the stack when the fellow made the mistake of lifting his torso and rearing back for a haymaker punch. Seizing the opportunity, Mickey dug his fist into the man's stomach. As the force caused his adversary to crumble over, he shoved his hand into his chin. Two seconds later, Mickey landed on top having his way.

The scraggly-faced guy who commented about having dibs on the house stepped up at Niles's request still wearing the same wry grin. He began dancing around like a chicken doing all kinds of weird moves in what Niles felt was an attempt to intimidate him, but he could tell the guy was merely putting on a show. Nonetheless, Niles didn't let his guard down because he knew the fellow had some crazy in him. He also appeared to be giving his buddy who had his feet swept out from under him time to gather himself. A moment later, the two of them attacked Niles simultaneously.

Once Reese freed her off-hand, she dug two fingers into the dark eyes of the woman atop her. As her foe let out a scream, Reese shifted her entire body weight in one direction and rolled, breaking the woman's arm audibly and eliminating another looter from the fight.

Mickey stood on the ground in time to watch Reese join him upright, and after hearing the sound of the cracking bone, her tactics quite impressed him. Just when he was about to go after the one person unaccounted for—the homely looking spectator—he realized Reese had already committed. Mickey then turned his attention to the two assailants coming at Niles, one resembling an entire swarm of bees himself, but by the time he made it to Niles's side, he watched his buddy perform his signature roundhouse kick. The force of the motion penetrated straight through the scraggly guy's busy arms landing a defeating blow on the right side of his head. Niles then spun around only to take a jab to the face by the leader who apparently wasn't intimidated by the fact that most of his friends lay on the ground bruised, bloody, or unconscious.

Up in the tree, Riley was the first to hear the sounds of police sirens in the distance, and eventually he spotted the blue lights coming down the street, one patrol car after another like his toy car convoys. He watched his daddy and Uncle Mickey fight in the octagon many times, but this seemed so much different. He never saw anyone swing an ax at another person. It scared him when that happened and he silently prayed ever since.

Reese stepped toward the man in front of her somewhat like a boxer, and he lifted his hands just the same.

"I don't really want to hit a woman," he divulged.

"You probably won't," Mickey laughed, encouraging her.

"Then drop down to your knees and put your hands behind your head," Reese suggested seeing the police cars coming to a screeching halt on the street and knowing law enforcement would cuff him in a matter of moments.

When the homely-looking man turned and saw the officers approaching, he ran toward the other side of the house, but Reese saw it coming and sprinted after him. Thankfully, the first officer hustling in their direction was Captain Stark. As Reese ran she yelled out to him, "Arrest everyone except Niles and Mickey," making sure he would know the good apples from the bad. However, she assumed he probably remembered Mickey from the briefing outside the hospital yesterday. The guy stood out with his puffy hair and tall, scrawny build not to mention his goofy personality.

Niles exchanged blows with the leader of the pack as two of the officers approached the altercation. Three others joined the chase with Reese while the rest subdued and handcuffed everyone except Mickey. Niles figured he had time for a couple more shots at taking this guy out before the officers interfered. He swung his left fist, but the man blocked it. When he began to swing his right, the guy grabbed his arm. He was strong and mean, and as the two of them struggled against each other, Niles could see evil staring into his eyes. Seemingly all tied up, Niles knew better than to think the struggle couldn't end in a moment with a knockout blow. According to his martial arts background, he had nine limbs, now he just needed to decide which one to use. His legs were in an awkward position holding ground, so he chose the only option left. When Niles's forehead connected with the leader's nose, blood spewed like a water sprinkler resulting in the man falling as slowly as a freshly cut tree.

Niles didn't stand around to soak in the victory but instead ran to the tree where he sent his son to safety.

"Riley, we're all safe now; you can come down."

Riley dropped from one branch to the next like a skilled monkey and flew into his father's arms without notice.

"Where did you come from?" Captain Stark said grinning through a furrowed brow.

Before Riley could answer, the distinctive sound of a bullet charging out of the barrel of a pistol silenced the scene in the backyard. Reese and the officers chasing the assailant were out of sight on the other side of the house, and no one on the river's side knew who fired the gun or if anyone had been struck. All Niles could think about was Reese. She didn't have a firearm; he knew that. At his house, he had a conversation with her about where she should put her weapon so it would be secure. He also saw her reach for it earlier before the fight broke out.

With Riley in his arms, Niles ran along with Mickey, Captain Stark, and every other officer without a handcuffed person. When they rounded the corner of Grandyma's house, they saw a motionless body lying on the ground near the road. At first, they could only see legs because of those standing around, then they watched two officers drop to the ground to administer help to the person who'd been shot.

Moments later, they found out when Reese tackled the man, a struggle began on the ground, and at some point, he reached into his pocket and pulled out a pistol. The officers standing by pulled their handguns but were unable to get a clear shot because of Reese's body hovering over the man holding the gun.

When Reese first practiced close combat handgun training with her father years ago, he taught her multiple ways to disarm a person, but this time the man beneath her had been able to get one shot off before Reese ever realized he had a gun. Once the bullet penetrated skin, blood stained their clothes as well as the wet grass around their bodies. Lying atop the man, Reese forced her left hand between his torso and her own and felt the gun's handle with her fingers. She didn't have room to fully grab the pistol without lifting her body, and she was afraid if she raised her torso, he'd fire off another shot before she could grab the weapon. The only opportunity she saw was to slide her pointer finger into the space behind the trigger. She did just that, feeling the man squeeze the trigger repeatedly. The thickness of her finger stopped the gun from firing. Not sure where he shot her, Reese lifted her body and grabbed the pistol barrel with her right hand. Seconds later, she yanked the gun from the man's hand as the officers pounced on him, handcuffed him, and held him on the ground just as Niles and everyone else made it around the house.

Standing with blood dripping from her clothes, Reese examined her body from head to toes. She couldn't feel where the bullet entered, but she heard that such was often the case. She wondered if this is how her dad felt when he'd been shot. The entire scene from her father's murder flashed in front of her eyes and she imagined meeting him in heaven with a scar of her own.

Seeing the blood on Reese's clothes, Niles tried to hide his son's view while still running toward Reese as he watched her drop to her knees. He met her there and wrapped his free arm around her, catching her as she fell effortlessly into his embrace.

The moment before is when she realized what one of the officers on the ground said next: "He shot himself in the stomach."

44

Grandyma's house didn't get cleaned at all that day, but the authorities cleared the yard of all the troublemakers. It turned out the guy who shot himself in the stomach only nicked the skin enough to send blood spewing everywhere. Ultimately, he'd be okay but would spend time in prison for attempted murder. That night as Riley played nearby, Niles, Reese, and Mickey sat on the deck at the treehouse beneath a blanket of stars and talked about how fortunate they were that the shooter hadn't pulled the gun earlier during all the fighting.

The next day, they almost stayed at the treehouse to avoid any chances of more drama. However, Grandyma's home still needed work, and the longer the place remained open to the elements, the more damage would occur. They met Grandyma and Riley's grandfather at the house where his construction crew also showed up to assist. They all spent the day removing ruined furniture, cutting up the tree that landed on the residence, patching the roof, ripping out sheetrock, sweeping, and completing dozens of other tasks to clean the home as much as possible. Even Riley pitched in while Niles kept him close by his side. At the end of the day, the three heaps of trash by the road were taller than Mickey. Riley said they looked like piles of sand. He wanted to climb on them, but everyone warned, "No," in unison knowing they wanted to steer clear of any chance of an injury.

The following day they spent at Grandyma's again doing much of the same. It was unfathomable how much damage a flood and a fallen tree could do to one house. Reese really liked being around Grandyma, and the better acquainted they became the more she realized why Niles maintained a good relationship with the woman. Grandyma pretty much called Reese every term of endearment in the book from sweetie pie to sugar, and the lady was as sweet as every one of those words.

The rest of the week, Niles, Riley, Reese, and Mickey ventured into downtown New Bern each day where they removed plywood from boarded-up windows, discarded damaged furniture, tossed ruined sheetrock, and trashed piles of other items from stores and homes. After safely rescuing every resident in the low-lying areas, Captain Lawson, Johnson, Dominguez, and Brown joined Reese, Niles, Riley, and Mickey to assist with cleanup.

The next week, the judge awarded Niles temporary full custody of Riley due to Eden being in the hospital and because of the trauma caused to the boy due to his mother not evacuating him as promised. The judge said when Eden's condition improved, he would hear both sides and consider the best long-term custody situation at that point. For Niles, the decision almost seemed bittersweet. He wanted evenly split custody with Eden, but for the time being he felt bad that Riley couldn't spend time with his mother at home. The surgery had been rather extensive and the medical team working on her case wasn't sure how long she'd remain in the hospital recovering. Even though Niles was still furious with Eden for not evacuating Riley, he took his son to the hospital every day to visit his mom. One good thing Niles decided about her being there was that she couldn't drink alcohol or abuse prescription drugs, and he hoped the break from both would help her quit.

A week after arriving in New Bern, Captain Lawson, Johnson, Dominguez, and Brown headed back to Tennessee with the patrol car they drove as well as the Humvee pulling the search and rescue boat. However, they left Reese behind, at least temporarily. She and Niles grew closer, and she decided after all that happened in such a short period, from the altercation with the man who murdered her dad to the intense search for Riley to nearly being shot herself, she needed time to figure out where her life was heading from here. Nonetheless, she couldn't seem to keep her nose out of police work. Captain Stark invited her to the station to examine the child abduction case in which Kirk's band was in question. The two of them happened to discover evidence leading to the arrest of a person who attended both the festival and Benny's solo gig from where the kids went missing but under two different names. In the end, the authorities cleared Kirk and his band.

Niles was glad that in the time since finding Riley, Reese convinced him to let justice play out in Kirk's case. All along her gut told her Kirk wasn't involved. In the end Niles was happy he hadn't punched the guy in the face because he certainly wanted to every time he saw him. They were in the same hospital room a handful of times when Niles took Riley to see Eden, but thankfully Reese had been there with him to help keep the peace. It turned out that maybe Kirk was a good guy after all. He spent nearly every day with Eden as she recovered from the surgery. Although Niles knew it would take some time before he'd be okay with his son being around the man without his presence, letting go made sense. Reese regularly reminded Niles of how Kirk helped search for Riley when he went missing. Everyone who searched for Riley risked life and limb and that included Kirk.

Two weeks after Hurricane Florence devastated New Bern, Eden rolled out of the hospital in a wheelchair. It would still take time and physical therapy before she would be back to normal, but the surgeon assured everyone she would be herself again. Niles felt bad for Eden when Kirk wheeled her into the courtroom, but when the judge granted him fifty percent custody of his son and on the way out Eden said, "Niles, you deserve equal custody," Niles felt much better about how things would turn out. The agreement allowed Niles to have Riley one week then his mom to have him the next, and the schedule would flip flop like that every week.

The judge ordered Eden to attend an active local Alcoholics Anonymous group to have support from people who battled similar addictions. Soon after the day in court, Reese, who earned Eden's and Grandyma's respect, shared how a lady in her hometown came to the jail every week to meet with women who found themselves in custody whether for drug charges or incarcerated for a separate issue. She explained how much it seemed to help many of those people, and she prayed the twelve-step program would prove beneficial for Eden as well because it really did seem like the woman had a good heart and loved her son immensely. Niles and Grandyma also talked Eden into seeking the counsel of a professional therapist who could help her walk through the loss of Cameron and the guilt she bore from losing Riley in the flood even though the separation turned out to be temporary.

Eden moved in with her parents so that Grandyma could help take care of her while healing from the wound to her stomach and the ensuing surgery. A by-product of the temporary living situation was that her mother could secure and personally dispense the prescribed medications as well as make sure no alcohol entered the house. Kirk also agreed to stop drinking and promised to be an accountability partner for Eden. In the best interest of both parties, Eden's boss gave the approval for her to work from home until she fully recovered.

The local business community came together to show support and appreciation for Niles, Riley, and Mickey who along with

Reese volunteered their time to help with hurricane cleanup. A car dealer donated a brand new truck to the landscaping business. A sign company wrapped the entire vehicle in graphics that featured cartoon grasshoppers riding and pushing lawn mowers and the newly official name *Three Little Grasshopper's Landscaping* inside a custom logo. The hardware store where the guys often bought equipment and supplies gave them a new trailer, zero-turn mower, and every other piece of equipment needed to run a professional lawn service. Of course, Riley made sure to tell everyone that the grasshopper's name and cartoon characters were his ideas.

In the months that followed, the guys received more work than they could handle; Niles's and Reese's relationship flourished; Riley was as happy and healthy as ever; and Eden's conditions improved drastically. The wound to her stomach healed; she hadn't swallowed a single drop of alcohol nor abused prescription drugs since going into the hospital for emergency surgery; and she and Kirk continued to spend time together regularly. Reese talked Niles into joining Eden at some of the counseling sessions. They both forgave one another for Cameron's death even after the truth came out that Eden didn't buckle Cameron that day. Niles swore to take the secret to the grave, but apparently Eden knew all along that she made the mistake; she just hadn't admitted it to herself or anyone else. Niles felt pleasantly surprised by the weight lifted off his shoulders after carrying the burden of the secret, yet he promised not to tell anyone who didn't already know. Similarly, it became evident that most of Eden's physical agony since the car accident came from unresolved repressed emotional pain which now subsided by leaps and bounds with regular therapy.

At times, Reese found herself hoping Niles and Eden would get back together so that the two of them with Riley could continue the happy family they once knew. However, realistically and maybe somewhat selfishly, she wanted Niles all to herself. Even though he was younger than her, in many ways he was the most mature man she ever dated, and she couldn't help but notice how he no longer felt for the ring that once occupied his finger. He was an amazing dad, too, and on the days when he and Riley enjoyed father and son time alone, Reese used the opportunity to read the books she picked out before leaving Chattanooga to assist with Hurricane Florence. Although she didn't technically have a job, she also never seemed to have much free time while in New Bern. She stayed busy as a consultant with the police department and helped with things on the business side of the landscaping company so that the guys could spend most of their time at the job sites, at least after they all enjoyed breakfast at The Country Biscuit nearly every morning.

At Christmastime, Niles took Reese to Mickey's family's old tree farm in Hickory where they first met. Instead of staying at the motel where they once occupied separate rooms, they rented a log cabin on the mountainside overlooking the tree farm. They spent the days hiking trails and the evenings in the hot tub on the back porch. Although Niles missed Riley like crazy, Reese's company proved to be the best medicine. They snuggled close at night and even brought along Banana because Riley insisted. Riley and Reese bonded in their time together. She loved playing with him on the treehouse obstacle course and navigating the local rivers and creeks in the ark with him and Niles.

On Niles's and Reese's last day in the mountains, they wandered into the tree farm one last time, and as if fate intervened in their lives once again, light snow began to fall. Holding one another close, they watched rows of green Christmas trees start to turn white. Although it would have been the perfect time for an engagement proposal, both Niles and Reese knew they weren't ready for that yet. However, from his pocket he gently slid an elegant silver necklace with a rainbow pendant, and with a smile on his face and snowflakes dancing in the air around them, he asked Reese if she would move to New Bern permanently.

"Yes," she answered. "I certainly will."

Photo Credit: Amy Smith

A Note from the Author

Thank you for reading WHERE THE RAINBOW FALLS! I am honored that you chose to invest your time in this book. If you haven't yet read my other novels, A BRIDGE APART, LOSING LONDON, A FIELD OF FIREFLIES, THE DATE NIGHT JAR, and WHEN THE RIVERS RISE, I hope you will very soon. If you enjoyed the story you just experienced, please consider helping spread the novel to others in the following ways:

- REVIEW the novel online at Amazon.com, goodreads.com, bn.com, bamm.com, etc.
- RECOMMEND this book to friends (social groups, workplace, book club, church, school, etc.).
- VISIT my website: www.Joey-Jones.com

- SUBSCRIBE to my Email Newsletter for insider information on upcoming novels, behind-the-scenes looks, promotions, charities, and other exciting news.
- CONNECT with me on Social Media: "Like" Facebook.com/JoeyJonesWriter (post a comment about the novel). "Follow" me at Instagram.com/JoeyJonesWriter and Twitter.com/JoeyJonesWriter (#WhenTheRiversRise). "Pin" on Pinterest. Write a blog post about the novel.
- GIVE a copy of the novel to someone you know who you think would enjoy the story. Books make great presents (Birthday, Christmas, Teacher's Gifts, etc.).

Sincerely,
Joey Jones

About the Author

Joey Jones' writing style has been described as a mixture of Nicholas Sparks, Richard Paul Evans, and James Patterson. The ratings and reviews of his novels A BRIDGE APART (2015), LOSING LONDON (2016), A FIELD OF FIREFLIES (2018), THE DATE NIGHT JAR (2019), and WHEN THE RIVERS RISE (2020) reflect the comparison to *New York Times* bestselling authors. Prior to becoming a full-time novelist, Joey worked in the marketing field. He holds a Bachelor of Arts in Business Communications from the University of Maryland University College, where he earned a 3.8 GPA.

Jones lives in North Carolina with his family. Fun facts: He is not a fan of cold weather yet ironically enjoys frozen grapes and an iced cold glass of chocolate milk.

Joey Jones is currently writing his seventh novel and working on various projects pertaining to his published novels.

Book Club/Group Discussion Questions

1. Were you immediately engaged in the novel?

2. What emotions did you experience as you read the book?

3. Which character is your favorite? Why?

4. What do you like most about the story as a whole?

5. What is your favorite part/scene in the novel?

6. Are there any particular passages from the book that stand out to you?

7. As you read, what are some of the things that you thought might happen but didn't?

8. Is there anything you would have liked to see turn out differently?

9. Is the ending satisfying? If so, why? If not, why not, and how would you change it?

10. Why might the author have chosen to tell the story the way he did?

11. If you could ask the author a question, what would you ask?

12. Have you ever read or heard a story anything like this one?

13. In what ways does this novel relate to your own life?

14. Would you reread this novel?

Also by Joey Jones

A BRIDGE APART

A Bridge Apart, the debut novel by Joey Jones, is a remarkable love story that tests the limits of trust and forgiveness . . .

In the quaint river town of New Bern, North Carolina, at 28 years of age, the pieces of Andrew Callaway's life are all falling into place. His real estate firm is flourishing, and he's engaged to be married in less than two weeks to a beautiful banker named Meredith Hastings. But, when Meredith heads to Tampa, Florida—the wedding location—with her mother, fate, or maybe some human intervention, has it that Andrew happens upon Cooper McKay, the only other woman he's ever loved.

A string of shocking emails lead Andrew to question whether he can trust his fiancée, and in the midst of trying to unravel the mystery, he finds himself spending time with Cooper. When Meredith catches wind of what's going on back at home, she's forced to consider calling off the wedding, which ultimately draws Andrew closer to Cooper. Andrew soon discovers he's making choices he might not be able, or even want, to untangle. As the story unfolds, the decisions that are made will drastically change the lives of everyone involved and bind them closer together than they could have ever imagined.

Also by Joey Jones

LOSING LONDON

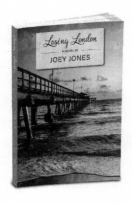

Losing London is an epic love story filled with nail-biting suspense, forbidden passion, and unexpected heartbreak.

When cancer took the life of Mitch Quinn's soulmate, London Adams, he never imagined that one year later her sister, Harper, whom he had never met before, would show up in Emerald Isle, NC. Until this point, his only reason to live, a five-year-old cancer survivor named Hannah, was his closest tie to London.

Harper, recently divorced, never imagined that work—a research project on recent shark attacks—and an unexpected package from London would take her back to the island town where her family had vacationed in her youth. Upon her arrival, she meets and is instantly swept off her feet by a local with a hidden connection that eventually causes her to question the boundaries of love.

As Mitch's and Harper's lives intertwine, they discover secrets that should have never happened. If either had known that losing London would have connected their lives in the way that it did, they might have chosen different paths.

Also by Joey Jones

A FIELD OF FIREFLIES

Growing up, Nolan Lynch's family was unconventional by society's standards, but it was filled with love, and his parents taught him everything he needed to know about life, equality, and family. A baseball player with a bright future, Nolan is on his way to the major leagues when tragedy occurs. Six years later, he's starting over as the newest instructor at the community college in Washington, North Carolina, where he meets Emma Pate, who seems to be everything he's ever dreamed of—beautiful, assertive, and a baseball fan to boot.

Emma Pate's dreams are put on hold after her father dies, leaving her struggling to keep her family's farm. When a chance encounter with a cute new guy in town turns into an impromptu date, Emma finds herself falling for him. But, she soon realizes Nolan Lynch isn't who she thinks he is.

Drawn together by a visceral connection that defies their common sense, Emma's and Nolan's blossoming love is as romantic as it is forbidden, until secrets—both past and present—threaten to tear them apart. Now, Nolan must confront his past and make peace with his demons or risk losing everything he loves . . . again.

Emotionally complex and charged with suspense, *A Field of Fireflies* is the unforgettable story of family, love, loss, and an old baseball field where magic occurs, including the grace of forgiveness and second chances.

Also by Joey Jones

THE DATE NIGHT JAR

An unlikely friendship. An unforgettable love story.

When workaholic physician Ansley Stone writes a letter to the estranged son of a patient asking him to send the family's heirloom date night jar, she only intended to bring a little happiness to a lonely old man during his final days. Before long, she finds herself increasingly drawn to Cleve Fields' bedside, eager to hear the stories of his courtship with his beloved late wife, Violet, that were inspired by the yellowed slivers of paper in the old jar. When Cleve asks her to return the jar to his son, Ansley spontaneously decides to deliver it in person, if only to find out why no one, including his own son, visits the patient she's grown inexplicably fond of.

Mason Fields is happily single, content to spend his days running the family strawberry farm and his evenings in the company of his best friend, a seventeen-year-old collie named Callie. Then Ansley shows up at his door with the date night jar and nowhere to stay. Suddenly, she's turning his carefully ordered world upside down, upsetting his routine, and forcing him to remember things best left in the past. When she suggests *they* pull a slip of paper from the jar, their own love story begins to develop. But before long, their newfound love will be tested in ways they never imagined, as the startling truth about Mason's past is revealed...and Ansley's future is threatened.

Also by Joey Jones

WHEN THE RIVERS RISE

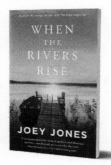

Three hearts, pushed to the limit. Can they weather another storm?

High school sweethearts Niles and Eden shared a once-in-a-lifetime kind of love until an accident—and Eden's subsequent addiction to pain medication—tore them apart. Now divorced, their son Riley is Niles's whole world, and he'll do anything to keep him safe.

In constant pain, chronically tired, and resentful of Riley's relationship with his dad, Eden is a shadow of the woman she once was. When she meets Kirk, a charismatic drummer who makes her feel alive again, she's torn between evacuating with Riley before a hurricane hits and the exciting new life that beckons.

Reese has never quite gotten over the death of her father, a cop who was shot in the line of duty. Now a detective herself and the only special operations officer on the East Ridge, Tennessee, police force without children, she volunteers to go help as a potential category five hurricane spins straight toward the North Carolina coast.

As Hurricane Florence closes in, their lives begin to intersect in ways they never imagined as each is forced to confront issues from the past that will decide the future...their own, each other's, and Riley's.

Emotions swell like the rivers in the approaching storm in this poignant story of guilt, second chances, and the lengths we'll go to protect the ones we love.

Made in the USA
Middletown, DE
10 June 2023

32342685R00168